An Unkosher Death

ALSO BY JUDITH GROUDINE FINKEL

Texas Justice
Where Danger Lurks
The Stooge Gene

An Unkosher Death

Judith Groudine Finkel

Book Daze Publishing
Houston, Texas

Book Daze Publishing
Houston, Texas

Printed in the United States of America

Author photo by Katherine Poeppel
Cover and book design by M. A. Demers

ISBN: 978-0-9899619-3-6 Paperback
         978-0-9899619-4-3 Kindle Format
         978-0-9899619-5-0 ePub Format

DEDICATION

This book is dedicated to Howard, my bashert.

ACKNOWLEDGEMENTS

I am indebted to Eric Finkel, Howard Finkel, Robert Hargrove, Linda Jacobs, Riki Weinstein, Madeline Westbrook and Mario Zamora for their editing skills, suggestions and support.

Houston, Texas

The doctor put on her plastic raincoat and secured the hood over her head. She stepped outside, determined to find her cat.

Instead, through the heavy downpour, she saw a woman lying in front of a black SUV.

She rushed to her, turned her over and checked her wrist for a pulse. Finding none, she pressed her fingers to the victim's neck, hoping to get one there. Being unsuccessful, she began cardiac resuscitation. With the woman's crushed ribs, the sternum was right against the heart, making the attempt easier.

"Let me help." The woman's husband, also a physician, had run out of the house and was now beside her.

She looked up at the driver who was standing outside her vehicle shouting, "I can't believe this is happening to me. I can't believe this is happening to me."

"Get your phone out and dial 911," the doctor ordered.

She was so involved in trying to save the victim that she barely registered a tall thin figure hurrying from the scene.

Chapter One

This was the worst part of being a rabbi.

Everyone thought it was presiding at funerals. But Rabbi Deborah Stein found one saving grace in preparing for a funeral. The family, desiring a eulogy befitting their loved one, filled her with stories of how wonderful the deceased was. At that time the bereaved remembered only what was best and most loving about the departed, and Rabbi Stein enjoyed hearing each and every one of those reminiscences.

There was no silver lining in what Deborah was about to listen to. It was gossip, disguised as a need to let her know that some terrible thing was happening at the synagogue, so she could put a stop to it.

Last fall she'd chosen the Day of Atonement to deliver a sermon about how Judaism prohibits *lashon hara,* derogatory speech about another person, giving examples of how difficult it is to make amends once the harmful words have left our mouths. She admitted she was still working on abiding by the teaching herself and committed to trying to break the habit by refraining from gossip for one hour each day. She'd chosen two to three every afternoon and had challenged those in the congregation to each pick a time to do the same. That was four months ago, and since then no one had told her they'd tried.

Certainly not Leigh Goldsmith, who burst into the rabbi's office and commandeered a chair. A desk filled with open books, attesting to Deborah's research for the coming Sabbath's sermon, separated the two women. Leigh, close to sixty, had a face which showed the remnants of having once been pretty but now suffered from hanging folds of skin, the sort common when someone has lost too much weight too quickly. Deborah worried her congregant might have a digestive disease like Crohn's or an eating disorder. Either could explain her almost skeletal appearance. Neither Leigh's dyed blond hair nor her overly applied makeup erased any of her years.

Deborah, with her petite frame and short curly brown hair, looked younger than her forty-five years.

"You won't believe what Roberta Krause said to me," Leigh began.

The rabbi considered the connection between the two women. Roberta was president of the synagogue and Leigh was president of the Sisterhood. As such, they were working on the committee, chaired by Roberta, to commemorate the synagogue's sixtieth anniversary.

Leigh tapped her blue polished fingernails on the rabbi's desk. "Roberta set the next committee meeting for a week from Thursday, and when I said I couldn't make it, she asked for a volunteer to give me a report. Isn't that the most obnoxious reply you've ever heard?"

"I'm sure Roberta realizes what an asset you are, and how much you'll be missed next week. It would have been nice if she'd mentioned that. But remember she retired from a company where she was an efficiency expert for thirty years, so she tends to be efficient with her words as well."

"And this happened in the Goldsmith conference room."

Deborah recognized the comment as a reminder of how much money the Goldsmith family contributed to the synagogue.

"I'm sorry your feelings were hurt."

"You should be. I'm most responsible for your being here in Houston. When they made me head of the selection committee, I was determined to find a female rabbi."

Deborah knew that if someone as thorough as Roberta Krause had chaired that committee, she likely wouldn't have gotten the position. Instead of asking all the necessary questions about why Deborah was leaving her California synagogue, Leigh had jumped to the conclusion it was because of sexism.

Leigh pouted. "Roberta doesn't like me."

"I suspect she does. But would it matter if she didn't? We want to live our lives so we like ourselves. That's what counts."

"You sound just like a rabbi." Leigh stormed out of the office.

Deborah followed her and looked down the hall, wanting to make sure she was all right.

Roberta Krause walked by. She was so preoccupied that the rabbi had to move directly in front of the statuesque white haired woman to get her attention.

"How are things going with the anniversary committee?" Deborah asked.

"My time table is right on schedule." Roberta looked at Leigh's disappearing figure, shook her head and added, "Though we could be ahead of schedule."

Deborah decided that two grown women should be able to settle matters without outside help.

Later she would regret her decision.

Chapter Two

"I'm home," Deborah called.

No answer.

She closed the door, walked through the hall of her modest three bedroom Houston house and peeked into her living room. No sign of Isaac there or in the dining room. She spotted him in the kitchen – eyes closed, ear buds likely transmitting pounding music which he was gyrating to as he stuffed peanut butter covered graham crackers into his mouth. Deborah couldn't help but smile. Her son had the same lack of rhythm she did but with his father's height and long legs, it was exaggerated to the point of the comical.

She put her hand on his arm.

He opened his eyes, giving him a startled expression which he quickly erased with a ferocious grimace.

"If I was in the Israeli Defense Forces and you surprised me like that, you could be dead."

"You're not in the IDF so I guess I'm safe."

"Just four more years."

Isaac was fourteen and constantly threatened to return to Israel where he'd been born and where his father had died. He wanted to enter the IDF at the age of eighteen like most Israelis did.

Deborah tried to tousle his dark brown hair which was even curlier than hers but he took a step backward to prevent her touch.

"How was school?"

"Secular subjects were bearable, but you wouldn't believe the time we wasted on studying this week's Torah portion, like I'm even going to shul to hear it."

Deborah bit her lip. What better way to rebel against a mother who's a rabbi than to threaten to stay home from the synagogue on the Sabbath. Isaac's was more than the typical adolescent rebellion. He'd been angry with her from the time they'd left Israel when he was eight. His father, her beloved Dov, had been killed in the 2006 war in Gaza so when another Gaza war began in 2008, the memories were too terrible. That coupled with her fear that if she stayed, someday her son would wind up fighting, and perhaps dying, propelled her to leave. Besides, she'd been homesick for the States. When she'd gone to Israel after her rabbinical ordination, she'd only planned to stay for a year of additional study, but there she'd met Dov.

Dov was Hebrew for bear, and he was a bear of a man – tall, wide shouldered, barrel chested. He had to be careful not to crush Deborah when he embraced her. She thought of him as such a tower of strength that she hadn't focused on the possibility he might be killed when his Reserve Unit was called up. Her shock had been enormous. She'd blamed that shock on her not being emotionally capable of comforting Isaac the way she should have. Two years later when she decided to escape the place that had left such a void in her life, she hadn't realized what a void that escape would cause in Isaac's life. To try to compensate, every summer Deborah took Isaac to Israel so he could spend time with his paternal grandparents and childhood friends.

Dov had been amused by Deborah's reasons for naming their son Isaac. Of the three patriarchs, Abraham, Isaac and Jacob, Isaac had been her favorite – the only one who had just one wife. And even when Rebecca tricked her husband into giving his blessing to her favorite son Jacob, instead of Esau, he'd shown no malice towards her. Deborah pictured him as a loving and forgiving man.

Maybe someday her son would live up to his name.

Isaac took the buds out of his ears. "Your mother called."

"What did she say?"

"She talked about all the snow in Pittsburgh and then grandma stuff – questions about school, my friends, blah, blah, blah. Then I told her how the Sisterhood presented you with a new tallit and yarmulke."

"You love to start trouble, don't you?"

Isaac grinned. As Orthodox Jews, his maternal grandmother and grandfather were opposed not only to the ordination of women as rabbis but also to any woman wearing a prayer shawl or skull cap. They pretended their daughter wasn't a rabbi but instead a glorified religious school teacher.

Leigh Goldsmith had made a point of telling Deborah how it had been her idea to give the rabbi those gifts as a thank you for her support of the Sisterhood.

Deborah understood that Leigh was relaying this information so that when the time came, she would expect the rabbi's support.

Chapter Three

"Who is that handsome man waiting to see you?"

Deborah looked up from the sermon she was writing to see her assistant Margo who wore a black jersey sheath set off by a colorful scarf and stiletto heels. Her hair had been straightened into a page boy with bangs. It cupped her light brown skin. Deborah, in her navy blue slacks and white blouse, felt dowdy in comparison. Margo had offered to give her a makeover. Deborah was considering it.

"What's he look like?"

"Blond hair, hazel eyes, a physique too good for a middle aged man. And he is so polite."

"I have an appointment with Tom Johnson. Must be him."

"Did I mention he was not wearing a wedding ring?"

"Margo, please."

"Someday I'm going to convince you that you can date without upsetting Isaac or becoming fodder for gossip."

Deborah laughed. "I know you'll never give up. Send him in please."

Deborah came from behind her desk to shake Tom Johnson's hand. His smile revealed a slight gap between his front teeth. Margo had forgotten to mention he was tall; Deborah just reached his chest. He wore a light blue long sleeve shirt, perfectly pressed tan slacks and mud splattered brown loafers.

They sat down next to each other on the two chairs in front of the rabbi's desk.

"I appreciate your letting me take your time. I'm not a member of your congregation. I'm not even Jewish. And I don't plan to convert."

"That's good news."

"It is?"

"We Jews have a duty to discourage converts, so you've saved me that chore."

"Why?'

"If you're already living your life according to Jewish principles – the most important being 'to love your neighbor as yourself' – you're doing what the study of Judaism would hopefully accomplish."

"Any other reasons?"

"Keeping peace in the family is one of our highest aspirations. Someone's deciding to leave his family's faith can result in estrangement. And frankly, it's one thing to grow up with anti-Semitism, but it can be quite difficult to suddenly have to deal with it."

Considering how Tom gave her his full attention when she answered him, Deborah felt sure his questions were the result of intellectual curiosity rather than an effort to make polite conversation.

"What I want is some guidance on how to study Judaism. Having never had religion in my own life, I've always wanted to learn about the world's religions, and now that I'm retired I have the time."

Deborah almost commented that he looked too young to be retired, but stopped herself. She'd guessed he was in his late forties, but he could be in his mid fifties.

Deborah stood and walked to the shelves behind her desk. When she found what she wanted, she sat down and showed it to Tom.

"This is the first volume of Rabbi Telushkin's books on Jewish Ethics. I have two copies so I can loan you one."

"You think I should start my studies with Jewish ethics?"

"Ours is a religion which emphasizes behavior. We assume if you're Jewish, you have the kind of faith that brings you to services to praise God. What we have to learn is how to behave according to God's teachings."

Tom opened the book and read from the Table of Contents. "Developing Goodness, Judging Others Fairly, Gratitude." He rested the volume on his lap. "There's a lot to learn."

"And if you get tired of reading it, all I ask is that you return it."

"I'm a retired attorney so I'm used to legal ethics. It'll be interesting to see how, and if, Jewish ethics differ."

"What kind of law did you practice?"

"I defended white collar criminals. That's how you got referred to me."

Deborah must have looked surprised because Tom quickly added, "One of your congregants was a witness, not a criminal."

"Who was that?"

"Roberta Krause. She's the reason my client went to jail. She figured out he'd embezzled from the company where they worked, understood how he'd done it, and had the numbers and charts to prove it. She was unflappable during my cross examination."

"How long will he be in jail?"

"There was jury misconduct so the appeals court overturned the verdict and ordered a new trial. Poor Jerry Evans. He'll only be out of jail until that new trial when Roberta testifies again."

"If you were on opposite sides…"

"About a year and a half after my client's conviction Roberta saw me at a restaurant and told me she thought I'd done a good and fair job cross examining her, and that it wasn't my fault my client was guilty."

Deborah laughed. "That sounds like Roberta."

"I asked her to join me for lunch, and when I mentioned my interest in learning about Judaism, she suggested I see you."

Tom gazed at Deborah's desk. "Is that a Three Stooges mouse pad?"

"I'm impressed. Not many people notice it."

"I've been a fan since I was a young boy."

"I've been a fan since I took a college course entitled, 'Comedy and Society.'"

"How did they fit in?"

"Name one of your favorite Stooge flicks."

"Easy. *G.I. Wanna Home.*"

Deborah smiled. "The one where the Stooges are discharged soldiers. They find out that their fiancées have been thrown out of their apartments so they furnish a vacant lot. When it's destroyed by a farmer on a tractor, they build a two room cottage."

Tom finished the story. "It ends when Curly climbs on stacked chairs to reach the top bunk of a triple bunk bed, and it collapses, dropping him onto Moe and Larry."

"The movie came out in 1946 after discharged soldiers had come home to a housing shortage. My own grandparents had to live with my grandmother's parents for three years as a result. The movie allowed people to laugh at this societal problem."

"I get it. Then there were that series of movies making fun of the Nazis."

"While Charlie Chaplin was the first actor to play Hitler, in 1940 Moe was the first American to," Deborah said.

"*You Nazty Spy.*"

"Which ends with Moe, and Larry and Curly as his two henchmen, running away from a rebellious crowd and into a lion's den."

"I remember the sequel *I'll Never Heil Again.*" Tom smiled. "That one ends with a shot of the stuffed heads of Moe, Larry and Curly mounted on a wall."

"The Stooges were taking on the Nazis before almost anyone else in America did."

"You've given me a whole new perspective of my heroes."

"When my son Isaac and I lived in California, we made an annual pilgrimage to the Stooge Film Festival. Fans came from around the world."

Tom held up the book Deborah had given him. "So when you're not reading Rabbi Telushkin's book, you're watching Three Stooges flicks?"

Deborah laughed. "Something like that. Feel free to make another appointment if you want to discuss anything you read in the book." She grinned. "Or anything about the Stooges."

Shortly after Tom left, Margo returned. "That well-mannered, handsome hunk told me he wanted to make a contribution to the synagogue, so I showed him the list of funds to choose from. Guess which one he picked?"

"They're all worthwhile."

"Rabbi Stein's Discretionary Fund. He's also generous." She waved a check in front of Deborah. "Five hundred dollars."

"He didn't have to do that."

"He wanted to show you how much he appreciates you." Margo kissed the check and left.

The rabbi returned to working on her sermon which was entitled,

"Why You Should Tell Your Children to Have Friends of All Faiths but Marry Within the Jewish Faith."

***

An hour later, Deborah heard two quick loud knocks on her door. Before she could say, "Come in," Mel Freed strode into her office.

Mel's white hair and the laugh lines around his mouth and eyes gave the incorrect impression he was kindly. Now in his late seventies, he had a few years before sold his plumbing business to a national chain and had needed something else to be in charge of. He was president-elect of the synagogue, so in a few months he'd have his chance.

"I don't like what I'm hearing about the committee that's planning the shul's sixtieth birthday celebration."

"Roberta told me they're right on schedule."

"That's not going to last if she and Leigh keep having cat fights."

The rabbi took a deep breath. "Two women having disagreements over important issues is no more a cat fight than two men doing the same."

"Just so you know. If the event doesn't come off the way it should, I'm holding you personally responsible."

Mel left as quickly as he'd come in.

Deborah wondered why she had to challenge the person who would have the most influence on whether her contract with the synagogue was renewed.

She spoke to the empty room. "Because that's who I am."

Chapter Four

Deborah left her office and walked to the synagogue's rose garden where she often took congregants in need of comforting. Its small size and the three brick walls surrounding it produced a sense of intimacy. She enjoyed sitting on the swing, large enough for three people, which hung from the roof of the wood gazebo. From there she had a perfect view of the short bushes which produced the rich red Home Run Roses she admired.

She took her lunch out of a paper bag and unwrapped her lox, bagel and cream cheese sandwich. The cream cheese was the one third less fat kind, and her can of soft drink was diet. She had to watch what she ate since her only chance to exercise came from the treadmill she had at home.

The January mid-sixties temperature led Deborah to wear the purple cardigan with green flame stitching a synagogue member had knitted for her.

She'd been savoring her solitude for a few minutes when she heard, "We have the same hideout."

"Hello, Roberta," the rabbi said as the older woman joined her on the swing. "I'm happy to share my lunch with you."

"No thanks." Roberta pointed to the garden shears she'd placed at her feet. "I'm here because our friends need a little pruning."

"Thank you for taking care of them."

"One of my satisfying jobs in retirement."

"I met a retired friend of yours today – one you sent to me, Tom Johnson."

"Tom's a good guy, even if he was an attorney. First he worked in the District Attorney's office, and then he went to the dark side and became a criminal defense attorney."

"He seemed a bit young to be retired."

"He's mid-fifties. Since he could afford to retire when his wife was diagnosed with breast cancer, he left his practice so they could enjoy their time together."

"How kind and loving."

"Actually, it was a disastrous three months. She had a virulent form of breast cancer, and all he did was watch her suffer."

Deborah was surprised at the anger with which Roberta spoke. Her congregant's hands turned into fists which she rested in her lap, one on top of the other.

"She should have thought of dying the moment she started suffering, then she could have spared the person she loved from having to go through that."

For a fleeting moment Deborah wondered if Roberta was suggesting suicide as the solution, but decided she must have misunderstood.

"Tom may have wanted those months with his wife no matter what the circumstances."

"Well, anyway, he was a good attorney. Jerry Evans doesn't stand a chance with anyone else representing him."

Roberta picked up her shears and went over to the nearest bush.

Deborah watched her as she examined each rose before she began to prune. Even as she engaged in what might be considered menial labor, Roberta remained dignified. She kept her back ramrod straight when she dropped to her knees to work. The rabbi could always count on her to do whatever she said she would. Deborah suspected Roberta performed many extra jobs without anyone knowing about them.

Roberta completed her work and sat down next to Deborah with a tired sigh.

"Is all going well with the anniversary celebration planning?" the rabbi asked.

"Except for the fact I'm dealing with someone with narcissistic personality disorder, all is well."

"I don't understand."

"I told my husband who's a psychologist about Leigh's behavior and forwarded the emails Leigh has sent me. So many of them show her exaggerated feelings of self-importance. He's using them, without mentioning her name, in an article he's writing about that mental disability. He said she's a classic case."

"I'm sorry if things are unpleasant. Perhaps I can help."

"Don't worry about it. Sometimes the illogic in her emails is amusing. First she writes that I'm to stay away from her, to not even sit near her, and in the next email she blasts me for ignoring her at our most recent meeting."

"Perhaps the three of us can talk."

"No need. What counts is that the anniversary celebration planning is right on schedule."

Roberta got up slowly, waved and left.

Deborah moved to the middle of the swing and considered what Roberta had said about how Tom had watched his wife suffer for three months. Her loss of Dov had come so quickly. Tom had had time to prepare, but his final memories must have been excruciating. Her shock at Dov's death had unmoored her, but at least she had happy memories of their last few hours together.

***

The door to their apartment opened before Deborah put the key in the lock. Dov lifted her off the ground as he hugged her.

She had only a few seconds to enjoy being engulfed by his muscular arms and chest. Then the realization hit her.

"You're home early because your Reserve Unit was called up."

"We've got to stop the bad guys from firing rockets into Israel. It won't take long."

His confidence convinced her.

Deborah kissed the back of Dov's deeply tanned hand.

He bent down, lifted her up and carried her into the bedroom.

"Do we have time before Isaac comes home?"

Dov's resonant laugh rang out. "We'll break the speed limit if we have to."

Dov kissed the crevices of her body so quickly that she felt like she was being tickled, which only heightened her desire.

That was her Dov – no matter how limited their time, he made sure she was satisfied.

As he was about to get up from the bed, Deborah said, "Wait, one more kiss to keep me going until you come back."

Dov smiled and obliged.

"How can I love one man so much?" she asked.

Before Dov could answer, they heard their six-year-old son closing the apartment door.

"We'll be right there," Deborah said as she and Dov dressed in record time.

When Dov explained to Isaac that he'd be gone for a little while, Deborah turned her face so neither of them could see her eyes fill with tears.

"Can you finish the big puzzle before you go?" Isaac asked. "I'll help you."

Dov slung Isaac over his shoulder and carried him to the card table where the recently started puzzle waited. "It has 500 pieces so we'll do as much as we can and finish when I come back."

When Dov didn't come back, Isaac shook the table until all the puzzle pieces fell to the floor.

Deborah was too dazed to notice.

***

Deborah was startled when her mobile started playing *Hatikvah*, the Israeli national anthem which Isaac had made her ring tone. She pulled it out of her pocket and recognized the caller's number. It was her son's school.

What had Isaac done now?

Chapter Five

Instead of being behind her desk listening to someone who needed help, Deborah was in front of the desk of Alison Eisen, the principal of Isaac's Jewish day school.

"Forget I'm a rabbi. Treat me like any other mother whose child has caused a problem."

"I understand how a child can glorify a parent who's a hero, especially one who gave up his life for the State of Israel." Alison, though barely over forty, spoke with the gravitas of a much older person.

"And he didn't want to leave Israel, and then we moved again from California to Texas. But I'm sure none of that excuses whatever you're about to tell me."

"Here's the short version. Isaac overheard Levi, one of his classmates, say that Israeli soldiers treated Palestinians at checkpoints in disgusting ways. Isaac told him that his father had always treated them politely. He added that if Levi ever said something like that again, he'd punch him out."

"I'm sorry. I'll talk to him and I'll support whatever punishment you deem fair."

Alison buzzed her secretary and told her to send Isaac in.

Isaac entered looking defiant rather than apologetic. He stood, glaring down at his mother and principal, until the latter told him to sit.

When he was seated next to her, Deborah said, "You're right to be proud of the way your father always treated people respectfully when he was at the checkpoints. But he sometimes complained about how he had to train some of the soldiers under him to act the same."

Isaac grimaced and took deep breaths.

"However, even if Levi was wrong, that would be no excuse for talking to him as you did. You showed the kind of disrespect Levi was referring to."

Isaac stared at his mother.

The principal spoke. "In two days I want a five page double spaced report from you about what our sages said about respecting others."

Isaac nodded and left.

"Thank you. That was a good choice," Deborah said.

"I'm going to do as you recommended and advise you as I would any parent."

"Please do."

"Isaac can be remarkably kind. If he sees an unpopular student sitting alone at a lunch table, he'll leave his friends and join that child. But Isaac also has a tremendous amount of anger. He may have good reasons for it, but he needs professional help learning how to deal with it, or he's going to continue to have difficulties."

"Roberta Krause's husband is a psychologist. I'll ask him for a recommendation for someone who deals with adolescents."

"Good plan."

***

Back in her office, Deborah left a message with Dr. Krause's answering service. Calling him made Deborah think about how Roberta had claimed Leigh Goldstein was suffering from narcissistic personality disorder, so she Googled it.

Those suffering from the disorder thought they were special or unique, required excessive admiration, had a strong sense of entitlement, were exploitive of others, regularly showed arrogant or haughty behaviors, lacked empathy…

Deborah was concentrating on what she was reading to the point that she didn't hear Margo come into the room. She only realized her assistant was looking over her shoulder when she heard her say, "I don't know why they need those fancy words when you can just call someone a 'bitch.'"

"Margo!"

"Oh, admit it. You'd love to talk like that. And if you weren't a rabbi, you would."

Deborah laughed.

"Who comes to mind when you read this?" Margo asked.

"Unfortunately this could fit a lot of people."

"Come on. It's like whoever wrote this was forced to spend time with Leigh Goldsmith."

"I wouldn't say that."

"You would, if you could."

"But I can't."

***

Deborah gathered some articles she planned to read at home and was about to leave her office when the phone rang.

"Rabbi Stein, it's Douglas Krause. You called earlier."

"Thanks for calling back. I was hoping you could recommend a psychologist who specializes in adolescents. Isaac, my fourteen year old, is always angry, and that's causing him problems at school."

"A difficult age. I know an excellent specialist in the area – Donald Wright. I'll email you his information."

"Thank you." Deborah added, "I enjoyed spending time with Roberta today when she was pruning the synagogue's rose bushes."

"That must have been before we went to her doctor's appointment."

Worried, but not wanting to pry, Deborah said, "Roberta didn't mention being ill. Can I help?"

Douglas's sigh conveyed his sadness. "She won't let anyone help. She can't bear the thought of being a burden."

"I'm sorry. If there's anything I can do, please let me know."

"After thirty-five years of marriage, I've learned that when Roberta has a problem, she finds her own solution."

Chapter Six

Deborah was sitting on the swing in the synagogue's rose garden enjoying her lunch when she heard footsteps. She turned to see the tall, blue jeans clad figure of Tom Johnson.

"I'm sorry to bother you. I came to return your book, and your secretary suggested I give it to you in person."

Deborah suppressed a smile. Margo and her matchmaking schemes.

"Rabbi Telushkin's first volume on Jewish Ethics is over four hundred pages. Surely you didn't finish it in a week," Deborah said.

"I did, and then I bought his second volume. Sometime I'd like to discuss a chapter in it that challenged me as an attorney. It's an issue of witnesses."

"I hope you never had any like Moe, Larry and Curly in *Disorder in the Courtroom.*"

Tom chuckled. "My favorite scene is when Larry is playing the violin and his bow latches onto the bailiff's toupee."

Deborah continued the story. "When it falls to the ground, Larry thinks it's a tarantula and tries to stomp it to death."

Tom smiled. "And Moe shoots it."

"I used that scene in a sermon I gave on the need to have stronger gun control laws."

"The Three Stooges in a sermon. That's a novel idea."

"I've learned humor can be effective in getting and keeping people's attention."

"Someday I'd like to hear one of those sermons."

"Everyone's welcome. Let's eat and then I'd like to hear about what your serious witness concern is. Do you like chicken? I have two sandwiches. In a fit of pique this morning, my teenage son Isaac deposited his into my lunch bag."

Tom sat down and accepted the proffered sandwich and a napkin. "I remember those days with my daughter. Now that she teaches English in Japan, I even miss her earlier rebelliousness."

"Isaac keeps threatening to move to Israel. I'm sure I'll feel the same way if he does. Even now I miss the way we used to watch Three Stooges films together. Lately he only has time for video games."

Tom finished his sandwich and looked at the garden. "Home Run Roses. I have some in my yard."

Deborah noticed sun spots on the back of Tom's hands, evidence he did his own gardening.

"Roberta Krause keeps ours looking good. Have you seen her lately?" Deborah hoped her question would lead Tom to tell her anything he might know about Roberta's health issues.

"Last time I invited her to lunch, she couldn't make it." Tom flicked a crumb off his jeans. "Maybe some time the three of us will go."

"That would be nice." Perhaps in that sort of environment, Roberta would let Deborah know about any medical problem and what she could do to help. If the lunch happened, she'd have to keep it from Margo who'd proclaim such a meeting a date.

"What did you find troubling in Telushkin's book?" Deborah asked.

"As a criminal trial attorney, my job on cross-examination is to make the jury question the truthfulness of a witness whose testimony has been detrimental to my client. Telushkin quotes a Jewish scholar who says the commandment in Exodus 'to stay away from falsehood,' means that if I believe that witness is telling the truth, I'm forbidden from making the testimony appear false."

Tom's intense gaze convinced Deborah he was serious about learning.

"As I recall, he also quotes an expert on our adversary system who says that according to their Professional Rules of Conduct, attorneys have to represent their clients zealously within the bounds of the law. According to Jewish law, we have to follow the law of the country we live in."

"So, if I consider those Professional Rules a form of the law of the United States, I can follow them, even if they arguably are in conflict with Jewish ethics?"

"My answer would be within limits. For example, destroying the reputation of a rape victim you knew to be telling the truth would be problematic."

Deborah hesitated before sharing a personal story with Tom. "As an attorney, my own father was so concerned about 'staying away from falsehood,' that he's limited his practice to writing wills and setting up trusts."

"He must be proud of you for becoming a rabbi."

Despite her usual reticence to discuss personal matters, Deborah said, "He and my mother are Orthodox Jews who don't believe women should be rabbis."

"That must be rough."

"A little, but in my business I know most people have things much rougher."

Deborah restrained herself from telling Tom how she struggled to subdue her sadness and anger so she could maintain a loving relationship with her parents.

"Thanks for your help with my studies."

"It's a pleasure to have discussions with someone so thoughtful," Deborah said.

"I enjoyed the sandwich. Remember, I owe you lunch."

"With Roberta."

Tom smiled, revealing the gap between his front teeth. "Of course."

***

Tom walked to the synagogue parking lot and got into his car. He should have asked Deborah about the case that really bothered him – the one that led him to limit his practice to defending non-violent white collar criminals.

***

"I'm an attorney, not a miracle worker," Tom told his client.

Ralph Bender paced back and forth in front of Tom's desk. Though he was just of medium height and weight, his fierceness made him seem larger. "There has to be a way."

"There's her 911 call where your voice is clear and her screams telling you to stop hitting her are pitiful. The police arriving just in time to stop you from slamming her against the wall certainly doesn't help. All of her injuries were photographed in the emergency room."

"There must be something."

"She would have to drop the charges."

"How can I get her to do that?"

"You'd have to convince her you'll never hurt her again. And you could talk about how hard it would be on her and your children – financially, emotionally, reputation-wise – if you were in jail."

Bender stopped pacing. "I can do that."

Two days later he called Tom. "She took me back. Dropped the charges. Everything you told me worked."

Three days after that call Bender went into a sporting goods store, bought a gun and chased his wife from their house into their garage where he shot her before killing himself. Both died at the scene.

***

It's just as well he didn't tell Deborah. She couldn't have assuaged his guilt. She would have just thought less of him.

***

Deborah returned to her office to find Jessica Snyder holding her sleeping baby Samantha and visiting with Margo.

Deborah lightly kissed the child's forehead.

"Rabbi Stein, can we visit for a few minutes?"

Deborah glanced at Margo.

"You're free. Let me hold Samantha while you two talk."

Jessica put her baby into Margo's arms. "We won't be long."

As soon as the women entered Deborah's office, Jessica closed the door and sat down in a chair in front of the rabbi's desk. "Every day

I think about how you comforted me when Samantha's brother was stillborn, and how you even spent the night with me when I thought I would never stop crying."

"Thank God you've since been blessed with Samantha, though you'll never forget your first child."

"I'm so grateful you're our rabbi that I joined the committee to decide about renewing your contract. I can't understand Mel Freed's opposition."

"Leigh Goldsmith has mentioned that Mel battled for his preferred rabbinical candidate three years ago, but that she convinced the previous committee to choose me."

"Maybe Mel hasn't gotten over that. He's complained that Leigh never looked into whether your former synagogue was planning to renew your contract, and that he was going to find out if there was a reason they wouldn't have."

Deborah tried to keep her face expressionless. "Your support means a lot to me."

"I'll fight to my last breath to keep you."

"Thank you," Deborah said. But she knew if she had to make a choice, she'd give up the fight herself before she'd let Mel Freed drag her son through the mud.

Chapter Seven

Deborah couldn't believe how she'd let time get away from her. As she rushed into Macy's, she worried whether the gift she was about to choose would arrive in time for her mother's birthday.

She rummaged through her purse for the fifteen percent off coupon, found two and headed for the counter whose case displayed silver bracelets.

Intent on her mission, she didn't notice the man she was standing next to until she heard his soothing voice. "My dear Rabbi Stein, you seem unusually hassled."

Deborah gazed up at a tall thin man with graying hair who would have looked distinguished were it not for the impish grin he was known for. He was also known for being the pastor of Houston's largest African-American Baptist church.

"Reverend Williams, I'm sorry. I was so engrossed in choosing a gift for my mother that I wasn't aware you were here."

"I'm choosing a gift for my wife, so I can use advice."

"Did she give you any hints?"

"She gave me the same words of warning she always does. 'Don't pick anything expensive or our members will think you have your hand in the collection plate.'"

Deborah laughed. "I have two fifteen percent off coupons. We can both be a little extravagant today."

After they made their selections, Deborah said, "My congregation enjoyed our pulpit exchanges. You really wowed them at Friday night services last year. It would be great if we could do it again."

"Sorry, Deborah, but I don't know if I can have you back at my church."

"I…I thought things had gone well."

Reverend Williams' impish grin was even larger than usual. "Too well. For weeks after, the women at my church kept asking, 'Now why is it that we don't have a female pastor?'"

Deborah laughed.

Their purchases made and their good-byes said, Rabbi Stein and Reverend Williams parted company. That's when Deborah heard a familiar voice.

"You're asking me if I have a coupon? Are you such a peon that you don't recognize I'm wearing designer clothes and real jewelry? You actually think I need a coupon?"

Deborah bolted to the gold jewelry counter. A young sales woman, her face pale, was staring at Leigh Goldsmith who, when she saw the rabbi, said, "You won't believe the incompetence."

"Let's finish the sale," Deborah replied, taking the credit card Leigh was holding and giving it to the sales woman.

Deborah felt ashamed that a member of her congregation would treat another person like this.

She spoke softly. "I'm very sorry my friend got upset. You've done nothing wrong. Please accept my apology."

The young woman nodded and with a shaking hand finished the sale and gave Leigh a small package.

"Let's go into the mall and get some coffee." Deborah put her arm on Leigh's and guided her to a small café.

When they were seated and their orders taken, Deborah said, "You must be upset about a lot of things. Do you want to tell me about them?"

The words spilled out of Leigh. "I wouldn't even be in Macy's if it weren't for my daughter Jenny. She refuses to accept any gifts if they come from Saks or Neimans or somewhere decent. She has some crazy political views. She wants me to feel guilty for having money."

"You also must be proud of her. She lives her Jewish values – working on food and clothing drives, tutoring underprivileged children. But mother/daughter relationships can be difficult. Perhaps being angry with Jenny led to your outburst at the sales associate."

"You always take the other person's side. If you'd been at today's planning meeting for the synagogue's anniversary party, you would have taken Roberta's side."

The waitress put their cups of coffee on the table. Leigh pushed hers aside with such force that some of her coffee splattered into her saucer and then onto the table.

"I want to hire the sixteen piece Ricky Gomez Band. Roberta wants some Klezmer music group. I offered to pay for the band, but the committee went with Roberta's plan. She set the whole thing up to embarrass me."

"Isn't it possible that…"

"Then she had the nerve to offer me a ride home. We live on the same block. She used to show off by jogging every day. Now she just walks."

"Maybe there's another way to look at her offer."

"See, you always take the other person's side. Remember, you need me if you want to have your contract renewed."

"If you don't think I'm worthy of leading the congregation, you should vote with your conscience."

Leigh threw down a ten dollar bill and got up so quickly that her purse banged against the table spilling the rest of her coffee.

***

"How was your trip to the mall?" Margo asked.

Deborah took a seat behind her desk and motioned Margo to one in front of it.

"The good news is I picked a gift for my mom and got to visit with Reverend Williams."

"And the bad news?"

"I heard Leigh Goldsmith mistreat a sales person. I apologized for her and failed to maneuver Leigh into doing the same."

"I know you dislike gossip but you need to know lots of folks are talking about today's meeting where Leigh decided Roberta had once again disrespected her."

"Leigh told me about it."

Margo got up to leave but stopped at the door. "If Leigh went after some sales person who only offended her once, I hate to imagine what she'd like to do to Roberta."

Chapter Eight

Deborah refused Tom's offer to pick her up at the synagogue for their lunch with Roberta. If that happened, Margo would call their get-together a date. All she told her secretary was that she'd be gone for lunch and that she'd have her phone with her in case of an emergency.

Having learned enough about Judaism to realize a Conservative rabbi wouldn't want to eat non-kosher meat, Tom had suggested a restaurant that had a nice selection of salads. Though Deborah was on time, Tom was waiting inside the door.

"I suspect Roberta will be here any minute. She's always prompt," Deborah said.

"I was going to pick her up but she called to say she wasn't feeling well and had to cancel."

Deborah and Tom followed the hostess to a booth near the front of the restaurant.

When they were seated Deborah said, "I'm worried about Roberta's health."

"I am, too. The last couple of times I've spoken to her she's sounded tired, not her usual self."

"Her husband made a comment that made me think she might have a debilitating medical problem."

"That's the worst thing that could happen to Roberta. She's the most self-sufficient person I know. I can't imagine how she'd handle it."

When the server came to take their orders, Deborah requested a spinach salad and Tom selected a steak sandwich.

"If Roberta's not well, do you think her being a witness at the trial of your former client will be too stressful for her?"

"There's no choice. She's the star witness against Jerry Evans."

Deborah considered all the stress Roberta must be having at the planning meetings as she tried to deal with Leigh Goldsmith. Deborah decided she'd attend to take some of the burden off her.

Turning her attention back to Tom, Deborah said, "Tell me about your daughter. How did she wind up teaching English in Japan?"

"Courtney was an exchange student there in high school and was determined to go back. The problem was the timing."

"What do you mean?"

"We had gotten Denise's, my late wife's, cancer diagnosis a week before Courtney was scheduled to leave. Denise insisted Courtney go and then begged me not to let her know how bad things became so Courtney didn't make it home until after her mom died." Tom hesitated. "She still hasn't forgiven me."

"All we can do is our best for those we love and then hope in time we'll be forgiven if we've made a mistake."

"That's a comforting philosophy."

"It helps me deal with my son's anger at our having left Israel after his father was killed."

"Roberta told me you're a widow and a single mom." A faint blush crept up Tom's cheeks, telling Deborah he wished he hadn't let her know he'd been asking about her.

When the waitress brought their orders, Tom insisted Deborah share the potato chips which accompanied his sandwich. As they were finishing their meals, they heard a voice that held a challenge. "Who's your friend?"

Deborah tried to hide her discomfort upon seeing Mel Freed who was looking from her to Tom and back again.

Tom stood, introduced himself and held out his hand to the white haired man who studied him, appearing to take in Tom's good looks and his jeans and corduroy jacket.

"You're not a member of our congregation."

"I'm a friend of Roberta Krause who had to cancel last minute on the lunch the three of us had planned."

Deborah admired Tom's finding a way to make his relationship with Deborah clear to a man who was anxious to see it as something it wasn't. When Mel walked away, Deborah said, "You handled that well. Thanks."

"I didn't want Mr. Freed to scandalize your congregation by spreading a rumor you're dating a non-Jewish man. I assume you wouldn't do that, would you?"

"I…I don't plan to date any man until my son's in college. He needs all the attention I'm not already giving the synagogue."

Trying to get over the awkward moment, Deborah commented, "We got here just in time. Everyone walking in since we arrived has a wet umbrella."

Before Deborah could think of anything else to say, her phone rang. "I'm sorry. It could be a synagogue emergency, so I have to take the call."

Margo's voice. "I have terrible news. Roberta Krause was hit by a car and killed."

"Oh, no. How could that have happened? I can't believe it."

"She was walking in her neighborhood when it suddenly started raining really hard, so the driver didn't see her."

"I feel awful. I need to get with the family."

"The news is even worse."

"What do you mean?"

"The driver was Leigh Goldstein."

When the call ended, Tom said, "You look pale. Can I get you anything?"

Deborah took a deep breath. "It's such a shock. Roberta was hit by a car and killed when she was taking a walk. I've got to call her husband and see what I can do for the family."

"How dreadful. Please let me know if I can do something. I really admired her," Tom said.

"I know."

"Was it a hit and run?"

"No, the driver was another of my congregants. I'll need to go to her as well."

"Leigh Goldsmith?" Tom asked.

"How did you know?"

"Roberta told me about her. She saw Leigh as a textbook case of some sort of personality disorder, and I wondered if the woman could be dangerous."

"You certainly don't think she *intentionally* hit Roberta, do you?" Deborah asked.

"The best advice you can give Leigh Goldsmith is to get an attorney."

Chapter Nine

Isaac wished he could have a do-over for today.

He took off his wet clothes and put them in the dryer, cleaned his mud caked shoes as best he could and went into the shower.

He should never have snuck out of school, but he hadn't been able to resist his chance. The substitute teacher in his advanced Hebrew class had failed to mention his name when taking role. Figuring he wouldn't be missed, Isaac had slipped out of the classroom when the sub was facing the blackboard.

At the time it had seemed like a good idea. He knew more Hebrew than any of his classmates and at least as much as his regular teacher. Someone brought in to teach for a day probably knew even less.

He didn't expect he'd be caught. None of the other kids would rat on him. And if he were caught, all that would happen is he'd have some silly punishment like writing a paper about respecting teachers.

But if his mother knew…He was already having a hard time putting her off about seeing some psychologist about his anger. And she'd be so disappointed in him.

He'd have to make sure his mother never found out he'd skipped school, even if it meant not telling her what had happened.

***

Deborah got Dr. Krause's cell number from Margo and reached him at the hospital.

"They called and told me to come to the hospital, that my wife had been injured in an auto pedestrian accident. When they refused to tell me her condition, I knew she was dead." Dr. Krause's voice cracked.

"I'm so sorry. I had such affection and respect for Roberta."

"I know, and she felt the same way about you."

Deborah had dealt with the deaths of other congregants, but Roberta's loss felt especially painful.

"Would you like me to call the funeral home?" Deborah asked.

"I've already contacted Levy's. They're on their way."

"If you're going home, perhaps I could visit with you there now."

"Yes, please."

Thirty minutes later the rabbi pulled in front of the Krause's home to find Dr. Krause parking his Toyota Camry in his driveway. She got out of her Honda Accord moments after he exited his car and caught up with him as he was about to enter his two-story house. He was only slightly taller than the rabbi which meant he'd been almost a head shorter than his late wife. He ushered the rabbi in and directed her to the living room which was as notable for its functional, dark colored furniture as for its lack of decorative pieces. Deborah again expressed her condolences and gave the bereaved husband a hug before she sat down.

"My dear efficient Roberta left instructions about her funeral. Let me get them and read them to you."

But when he returned to the living room, Douglas only got through the first three words before his tears and grief stopped him. He handed the letter to the rabbi and asked her to read it out loud.

My dearest Douglas,

In deciding which Jewish mourning customs I want observed, I've considered which would be of most help to you and which would be difficult for you and our friends to follow. I know Rabbi Stein will help you go along with my wishes.

I do want to be buried within twenty-four hours, with no embalming, and in a closed plain pine box as is our custom. The only eulogy I want at the funeral is the one Rabbi Stein should deliver. You and the boys can let her know if you have anything special you want her to mention, but don't take up your or their emotional energy, or the attendees' time by talking about me yourselves.

In a perfect world you and our sons would stay home for the seven day mourning period following the funeral with people coming to the house to conduct morning and evening prayers there. However, as a practical matter, it's unlikely ten of our relatives and friends, the minimum you need to conduct services, would make it in the early morning. Since people have to get to work, just plan on the evening services. If there aren't enough people for that, then go to the regularly scheduled synagogue services and say the mourner's prayer there.

Make everything as easy on yourself as possible. You've been a most wonderful, loving husband and deserve only the best. What I mind most about dying is leaving you.

With all my love,
Roberta

Deborah put the letter in her lap, took a tissue from her skirt pocket and wiped her eyes. "It seems as though Roberta expected to die in the near future. How sick was she?"

"Pancreatic cancer. Her life expectancy with her type was three to six months. I wasn't prepared for her to go that soon, let alone suddenly."

"I'd planned to be with her today. She was going to have lunch with Tom Johnson and me but didn't feel well enough to join us."

"She had pretty much lost her appetite, but still had enough energy to take short walks in the neighborhood. The police said there was a downpour which is why the driver didn't see her."

With Dr. Krause referring to "the driver," Deborah realized he didn't know Leigh Goldsmith had been behind the wheel of the car that killed his wife.

Chapter Ten

Before Deborah could tell Dr. Krause that Leigh Goldsmith was responsible for his wife's death, they heard, "Dad, we came as quickly as we could."

Two men in their early thirties burst into the house and then into the living room. The identical twins were a mixture of their parents – taller than their father while shorter than their mother. Both had inherited their mother's aquiline nose and high cheekbones and their father's brown eyes and square jaw. What stood out was their difference from either of their parents – blazing red hair.

"Sorry, rabbi, we didn't know you were here."

Deborah had difficulty distinguishing Ross from Sam so she wasn't sure who had spoken.

The twins made a beeline for their dad. As the three bereaved men wrapped their arms around each other, Deborah felt a combination of sadness for their loss and relief for the way the sons supported their father.

When the three separated, they sat down on the couch with Dr. Krause between the twins and Deborah in a chair across from them. "Rabbi, you know Ross," Dr. Krause said, pointing to the son on his left, and "Sam," he said, pointing to his right.

With the former in a blue shirt and the latter in a white one, Deborah could now tell them apart.

"The rabbi was reading your mother's instructions for her funeral and our sitting *shiva*," Dr. Krause said, referring to the traditional seven day mourning period.

"Of course, we'll do whatever she wanted," Ross said.

"I'm sure it's efficient," Sam added with a smile.

The family did what Deborah had learned to expect from mourners – they told stories about their loved one.

"We're examples of her efficiency – having the two kids she wanted with one pregnancy," Sam said.

"Even my brother's name is efficient. Mom didn't want him to waste time writing Samuel so his legal name is Sam."

"As much as we teased Mom about her efficiency," Sam added, "we appreciated that, because of it, she managed to be at every one of our school programs and teachers' meetings while holding down an important job."

"Through it all, she always made me feel like the most important person in the world," Dr. Krause said.

"And she managed to have the most beautiful garden. Would you like to see it?" Ross asked.

"Yes, please," Deborah said.

Outside, Deborah was greeted by a swirl of reds and pinks and purples, some from Home Run Roses, but most from impatiens.

"We claimed Mom should call her favorite flowers 'impatients' rather than 'impatiens' since she was so impatient," Sam said.

Dr. Krause spoke slowly. "She was impatient about dying, not wanting us to see her suffer."

"She was a very special person. Did you know Roberta was also taking care of the synagogue's garden?" Deborah asked.

"It doesn't surprise me. It probably relaxed her after having to deal with Leigh Goldsmith at those meetings about the shul's anniversary gala," Dr. Krause said.

The rabbi took a deep breath. "The tragic irony is that Leigh was driving the car that hit Roberta."

For a couple of moments all three men stared at Deborah. Then the twins spoke simultaneously. "You're sure it was an accident?"

"That's what the police told me." Dr. Krause's tone indicated he was no longer certain that was correct.

The twins exchanged a glance before Ross said, "We'll look into it further after the funeral."

***

Deborah tried to absorb what had happened at the Krause home as she drove to her own.

Could Dr. Krause and his sons actually believe Leigh Goldsmith had intentionally killed their wife and mother? Leigh could only have planned Roberta's death if she'd known when Roberta would be out walking. More likely they were thinking it was a crime of opportunity. Perhaps they pictured Leigh seeing Roberta and, in a fit of fury, intentionally mowing her down.

Leigh tended to create melodramas in which she was the star and victim, but the rabbi couldn't or wouldn't allow herself to picture Leigh as a killer.

And yet, Deborah remembered how Tom Johnson had told her the best advice she could give Leigh was to get an attorney. Would anyone who knew of the friction between the two women be thinking as Roberta's family was?

Deborah's thoughts continued to flow to her lunch with Tom. Had his comment about his assuming she wouldn't date a non-Jewish man really been his way of finding out if he could ask her out? She'd told him the truth when she said she wouldn't date anyone until her son was in college. She admired Tom's intelligence, kindness and the interest in ethical issues he'd displayed in their few meetings. She smiled, thinking of how Margo would add, "And he's damn good looking."

Mired in a myriad of thoughts as she exited her car and walked towards her front door, the rabbi was taken aback to find a slumped figure sitting on the wooden bench on her narrow porch.

"Leigh?"

"I've been leaving messages on your answering machine for hours. I had to talk to you as soon as possible."

The rabbi sat down on the bench. "I was with Roberta's family."

"Do you know what Roberta did to me?"

"What Roberta did to you?"

"She jumped in front of my car so when she died, everyone would blame me and hate me."

The rabbi took a deep breath. "Leigh, this is not about you. It's about Roberta's death and her mourning family."

"She either jumped or someone pushed her. I'm almost sure she jumped."

"If you think you're going to be blamed for Roberta's death, you should be speaking to an attorney, not a rabbi."

***

After Leigh fled the porch, the rabbi entered her home feeling guilty. She should have treated her congregant as though she were in shock over having caused Roberta's death. Once they got through the funeral, the rabbi would do what she could for Leigh.

Deborah called her son's name, and getting no response, went to his room where she found him sleeping. He must have had a rough day at school.

Deborah called Margo, who after asking about Roberta's family, gave the rabbi an update, which was worse than she'd feared.

"Your phone hasn't stopped ringing. Word is out that Leigh was driving the car that killed Roberta. Some people have asked if it was an accident."

Deborah sighed. "Please send an email to all our synagogue members telling them the funeral is tomorrow at 2:30 in the main sanctuary."

"Considering that Roberta was president of the congregation, that she had loads of friends and the circumstances of her death, expect a huge crowd."

"I'm about to work on her eulogy."

Deborah was in the middle of preparing that eulogy when Isaac came out of his room. "What can I get you to eat?" she asked her son.

"I'm not hungry."

A bad sign, but Deborah didn't have time to find out what the problem was.

Chapter Eleven

Rabbi Stein looked from her chair on the pulpit to the sanctuary filled to its three hundred person capacity. The ark, behind whose doors stood five Torahs with velvet covers, was to her right. Saturday one of those scrolls would be ceremoniously carried throughout the sanctuary before being unwound in preparation for being read. To have Roberta's funeral in such a holy place rather than at the grave site or in a funeral home confirmed what everyone knew; she was an exceptional person deserving of such an honor.

Deborah listened as Cantor Stanton Roth chanted psalms in Hebrew in his beautiful baritone voice. As expected, one was the twenty-third. The other was the thirty-fourth in which God who redeems the souls of His servants is praised. The cantor, attired in a white robe, as was the rabbi, then chanted the *El Male Rachamim* prayer which spoke of God's protecting the soul of the departed forever and merging her soul with eternal life.

The rabbi took a deep breath before she stood, walked to the podium and adjusted the microphone to her height. She began her eulogy with the words, "Beloved wife and mother, friend to many, tireless worker for the synagogue and highly respected professional are just a few of the many praises that come to mind when we think of Roberta."

Deborah shared the stories she'd heard from Roberta's husband and sons which demonstrated the loving and caring wife and mother she'd been, and how her family had found her efficiency both helpful and at times humorous. The audience laughed when the rabbi mentioned that Roberta's twins had praised their mother's efficiency in producing the two of them with just one pregnancy.

The rabbi noticed a figure in large sunglasses, wearing a multi-colored scarf covering her hair and part of her face, enter the sanctuary and take one of the few empty seats in the back row.

Leigh Goldsmith.

Deborah continued, now talking about how Roberta's friendships had enriched so many lives at the synagogue, including her own. "And numerous people from her former work place called me last night to tell me what her friendship had meant to them. One after another told me how her high ethical standards had influenced them. Her capacity to make friends knew no bounds, even encompassing an attorney who admitted he lost a case because she was an adverse witness."

The rabbi looked up from her prepared remarks and saw Tom Johnson smiling at her from the fourth row.

"I thought I knew all the work Roberta performed as president of our synagogue, but she surprised me by the extras she did such as keeping the garden just outside my office looking beautiful."

The rabbi concluded with, "Mine will be the only eulogy as Roberta's family is honoring the instructions she left in a letter about how she'd like her funeral conducted."

Leigh Goldsmith stood and left the sanctuary.

The service ended with Dr. Krause and his sons saying the Mourner's Kaddish, a prayer praising God.

***

At the graveside ceremony, as Roberta's coffin was being lowered into the ground, Deborah spotted a black clad figure at the periphery of the crowd, standing behind a tree. Leigh Goldsmith trying not to be noticed? Deborah couldn't even tell if she was glimpsing a man or a woman.

The coffin reached its destination and the ropes and pulleys were removed. Deborah invited the mourners to shovel dirt on top of the plain pine box.

She looked in the direction of the tree.

The figure was gone.

***

Deborah arrived home with barely enough time to get to Dr. Krause's house to conduct evening services. She spotted Isaac sitting at the kitchen table, his head resting on his arms.

Deborah tousled his hair. "You've sure been tired lately."

Isaac raised his head, grunted and put it back down.

"It would be nice for you to come with me to Dr. Krause's for services."

"I don't want to."

"Comforting mourners is one of the most important deeds of loving kindness we can perform."

Isaac sat up straight. "You just want me to eat there so you won't have to make me dinner."

Deborah took a deep breath. "Tell me what you'd like to eat."

"Don't bother. I'm taking a pizza out of the freezer."

"As you wish." Deborah freshened her lipstick and left the house.

Twenty minutes later she arrived at Dr. Krause's home but had to park part way down the street. She figured all the people who were bringing food to be eaten after services had come early.

When she entered the house, she saw she was correct. Trays of lox and white fish, bowls of tuna fish salad and fresh fruit, and plates filled with bagels and cookies were being crowded onto Dr. Krause's dining room table with plastic plates and cutlery and napkins being squeezed in. A bevy of women was accomplishing this, their high heels clicking on the tile kitchen floor.

All stopped to greet her, some with smudged mascara testifying to their tears.

Their words flew at Deborah. "Too terrible to comprehend." "Unbelievable." "A loss to her family and to the synagogue."

The rabbi murmured responses and then went to find the Krause family.

Dr. Krause greeted her with words she was grateful to hear. "You captured Roberta perfectly in your eulogy."

His sons, who were on either side of him, added their agreement, one noting, "Your affection for Mom was evident."

A slightly hunchbacked man in a blue blazer, who appeared to be about ten years older than Dr. Krause, joined them and expressed his condolences.

"Rabbi, this is Donald Wright," Dr. Krause said.

Guilt infused every inch of Deborah's body. She was meeting the psychologist she'd not yet made an appointment for Isaac to see. How had she let her son bamboozle her into delaying his being with someone who could help him? As soon as Dr. Krause recommended Dr. Wright, she should have called him. Was she too involved with her rabbinical duties to pay proper attention to her son's needs? He thought she didn't even want to bother to feed him. Maybe the synagogue would do her a favor if they didn't renew her contract.

But she loved being a rabbi. Somehow she would rebalance her life so that Isaac knew he came first.

Her thoughts continued as she saw Tom Johnson enter the Krause home. She meant it when she told him she wouldn't date anyone until Isaac was out of the house. She couldn't add one more competing interest to her relationship with her son.

Tom greeted her with the words, "I've never been to a Jewish funeral."

Deborah smiled. "Either you've had no Jewish friends or, at least, no dead Jewish friends."

Tom grinned. "Fortunately it's the latter. I appreciated the funeral's simplicity, and your eulogy which hit all the right notes."

"Thank you."

"Could you explain the significance of the prayer Roberta's family said at the end of the service?"

"It's called the Mourner's Kaddish because various mourners will say it for specific times and on the anniversary of the loved one's death. For example, for a parent it's said for eleven months and for a spouse for thirty days. Despite their loss, the mourners still praise God."

Before Tom could respond, Mel Freed accosted the rabbi. "It's time for you to start services."

"Perhaps you could pass out the prayer books. They're in the large valises Margo delivered this afternoon."

"I'll get some of the women to do it. They're busy chattering about how Leigh Goldsmith didn't dare show up."

When Mel stomped off, Tom said, "I suspect he's not your best friend."

"No, and with Roberta's death, he'll become president of the synagogue."

As much as the rabbi dreaded that, it paled in comparison with her concern about how to handle Leigh's role in Roberta's death.

Chapter Twelve

Mel Freed watched Rabbi Stein as she conducted the evening service at the Krause home. He'd been foolish to think his synagogue would remain a male bastion. Women had taken over everywhere. It was because of them that he was too soon retired.

When he'd sold his plumbing business to a national corporation, they told him they'd like him to stay for a transition period. Though they hadn't mentioned a length of time, he'd assumed it would be for as long as he wanted. Instead, women had pushed him out.

First there were complaints about how he called them "girls." His own wife Florence referred to herself and her friends as "girls," so how was he to know this term was an insult to women? Then came more complaints after he asked these "not to be called girls" to get him coffee. Hell, if they were headed to get some for themselves, they should be offering to bring him some and not waiting to be asked.

His biggest sin was commenting that he couldn't imagine Gloria would come back to work after having her first baby at age forty. She came back as manager of the store he'd turned into a success and told him the company that had bought him out no longer needed him.

After his forced retirement he concentrated his efforts on the synagogue. He was elected to the board of directors and everything was going well until the congregation began its search for a new rabbi almost three years ago. That damn Leigh Goldsmith got herself made head of the search committee, and it was clear she would only settle for a female rabbi. He fought it, bringing to the committee's attention a scholarly male rabbi from Philadelphia. After he spent a weekend in Houston, conducting Sabbath services and meeting synagogue members, Leigh convinced the search committee that he didn't have the people skills a rabbi needed. It was all part of her plan to leave them with her choice, Rabbi Stein, as their only viable candidate.

Something was fishy about Deborah Stein. His Philadelphia rabbi wanted to get out of the cold. Why would Stein want to leave a pulpit in a suburb of Los Angeles and move to Houston? The only logical explanation was that her synagogue didn't want her anymore. He hadn't had a chance to explore that possibility because Leigh had gotten Deborah's appointment approved while he and his wife were on a Mediterranean cruise.

He didn't trust what the rabbi said about her time in Israel either. Was she really married to a war hero or had she even been married at all? Her story gave her an excuse to explain why her son had problems adjusting – poor kid had to leave Israel. Something was definitely wrong with that boy. But when he'd mentioned that to his wife, she'd said he should pay attention to his own children and grandchildren before concerning himself with someone else's.

Why in the almost two and a half years the rabbi had been in Houston had her parents never come to visit? Shouldn't they be proud of her? Or did they know something that made them ashamed?

Then there was that Tom Johnson who obviously wasn't Jewish and who just as obviously was interested in the rabbi. He'd probably come to Roberta's funeral and now to the Krause home to see Deborah, not because he was some great friend of Roberta. Imagine how the congregation would react if their rabbi, who talked about the importance of creating a Jewish home, were to become romantically involved with a guy who wasn't Jewish.

He'd keep an eye on those two.

Tom Johnson watched Mel watching Deborah. From his scowl it was clear the older man did not have warm thoughts about her. It made no sense for Tom to feel protective. If Deborah could handle raising a son single handedly while being a rabbi, then she could handle Mel Freed. And yet, Tom didn't want to add to her potential problems. As much as he enjoyed her company, he'd have to limit the time he spent with her. Otherwise Mel would create a narrative that would harm Deborah's career.

Dr. Krause stopped thinking about how much he already missed

Roberta long enough to watch Tom watching Mel who was watching the rabbi. Tom's look of concern made Dr. Krause think about how Roberta was responsible for bringing Deborah and Tom together. She'd said, "They both deserve to be happy, and they're kindred spirits."

"Roberta," he'd teased his wife, "it's inefficient to match a rabbi with a man who isn't Jewish."

"Love isn't always efficient," she'd replied.

Rabbi Stein was unaware of who was watching whom. She was engrossed with leading the prayers and explaining some, like the Mourner's *Kaddish*, to the non-Jews who were present.

When services ended, and she'd said her goodbyes to Dr. Krause and his sons, she walked to her car.

She had just opened the door, when she was startled by someone tapping her on the shoulder. The light from the car revealed Leigh Goldsmith, in the same printed scarf she'd worn to Roberta's funeral.

"Why didn't you tell me Roberta left a suicide note?" she demanded.

Chapter Thirteen

"Leigh, what are you talking about?" the rabbi asked.

"You said Roberta left a letter of instruction about her funeral. She did that because she knew she was going to kill herself at my expense."

"Someone who's ill and efficient would leave instructions."

Leigh opened the passenger door and plopped into the seat. Deborah joined her in the car, sitting behind the steering wheel.

Leigh tapped her long red fingernails on the dashboard. "If Roberta was ill, it would be all the more likely she'd want to die without suffering and with her mortal enemy being blamed."

"Roberta never considered you her mortal enemy." Even as Deborah spoke, she knew Leigh would never understand she hadn't made the dramatic impression on Roberta she'd sought to.

"I'm going to the police. You need to get me a copy of that letter."

"Is your husband home?" Deborah asked.

"He's on a buying trip for our store. He's cutting it short and should be here tomorrow."

"What about your daughter?"

"She's in Austin with one of her 'help the poor' groups."

"Why don't you wait and discuss this with them?"

"My house is down the block. Let's go there, and we can talk some more."

"I have to get home to Isaac. I've hardly seen him at all today."

"Sure. But you had all that time to spend with Roberta's family."

"They are her mourners. Today was her funeral."

Leigh left the car, slamming the door.

As she drove to her house, Deborah hoped that Leigh's husband Stan and their daughter Jenny would help Leigh put logic above emotion. They should understand that if Leigh claimed Roberta had jumped in front of her car, Dr. Krause and his sons would insist Leigh had intentionally struck their wife and mother. They might do so even if Leigh kept her suicide theory to herself.

Deborah envisioned the disaster that could lead to. As everyone at the synagogue took sides, the congregation would be torn apart. Somehow she'd have to prevent that catastrophe.

She wished she could call her parents for advice, but they'd see her need for help as evidence she couldn't handle her job. Deborah did her best to honor her father and mother, remembering them on every birthday, anniversary and Jewish and secular holidays. She took Isaac at least once a year to see them. They wouldn't come to Houston where they'd have to acknowledge her position.

Perhaps Tom Johnson could help. He'd worked for the District Attorney's office and had also been a criminal defense attorney. He could tell her how to handle the situation before it exploded, or, at least, what to expect if it did. He'd left the Krause home without saying good-bye. She must have been hallucinating when she thought he'd shown even a flicker of romantic interest in her. Just as well he hadn't. She could contact him without concern about how he'd interpret her motives.

Deborah arrived home and called out to her son. Hearing no response, she worried he might have gone out without telling her. Instead she found him in bed asleep.

Was sleep his escape from being with her?

She'd get in touch with Dr. Wright first thing in the morning.

Chapter Fourteen

"There's an attorney here to see you. Leigh Goldsmith's attorney," Margo said.

She closed the rabbi's office door. "He should have made an appointment. I can tell him to make one and come back, maybe in a year."

"I'll see him now. I'd advised Leigh to get an attorney. I should have expected he or she would want to interview me."

"It's a he. Charles Harland from the firm of Harland and Dushane."

"She's going with our city's foremost defense firm."

"If he's not out of here in fifteen minutes, I'll buzz you and say you have another appointment."

"I don't, do I?"

"I've calendared an appointment for me to meet with you then."

Deborah smiled. "Don't know what I'd do without you."

"Don't try to imagine."

A few minutes after Margo exited the rabbi's office, Charles Harland entered. He closed the door, shook Deborah's hand and tried to make his six foot five inch frame look comfortable in a chair in front of her desk.

He looked younger than when Deborah had seen him on television, after he'd successfully defended an accused wife killer. She guessed he was in his mid fifties and that his perfectly coiffed silver hair was either dyed or a wig.

"Thank you for seeing me."

"I don't have another appointment for fifteen minutes."

"My client Leigh Goldsmith said you advised her to get an

attorney. I thank you for the business, but I'm wondering why you thought she needed one."

"Tom Johnson suggested I mention it to her."

"Tom was one of the finest defense attorneys around. Never could figure out why he retired. Is he a friend of Leigh?"

"He was a friend of Roberta Krause."

Charles pulled his chair closer to Deborah's desk and rested his hands on it. "He must have heard rumors that Leigh and Roberta didn't always see eye to eye and figured someone could turn that against Leigh."

"Perhaps."

"It's because of those unfortunate rumors that I'm here. I belong to a church, but I'm sure the same things go on in a synagogue. A little misunderstanding between members can turn into something so big that it tears a church or a synagogue apart."

"You mean something like people believing Leigh's killing Roberta was a crime of opportunity."

"Rabbi, certainly you don't believe that."

"No, but according to some of the calls my assistant received on the day of the accident, quite a few people think it's possible."

"That's why we have to be prepared if anyone acts on those ridiculous suspicions, and why I need your help."

"My help?"

"I need a copy of Roberta's suicide note."

"As far as I know, there is none."

"Don't be coy, rabbi. Leigh said you mentioned in your eulogy that Roberta left a letter of instruction about her death. That's what suicides do."

Deborah looked at her watch. She had six minutes before she had an excuse to kick Leigh's attorney out of her office. "That's what someone who'd been given a short time to live does."

"Roberta's quick death saved her a lot of suffering."

"I will assume it's ignorance rather than malice that leads you to make such a charge. According to Judaism, suicide is a grave sin both because it's a denial that human life is a divine gift and because it constitutes defiance of God's will for an individual to live the lifespan allotted to her."

"You won't help one of your most supportive congregants?"

"I will do everything I can to scotch rumors that Leigh intentionally hit Roberta, but I will not besmirch Roberta's blessed memory in the process."

"Rabbi…"

Deborah stood. "In the future make an appointment if you want to see me."

"Very well. I know how disappointed Leigh will be."

Moments after Charles left, Margo returned to Deborah's office.

"That was one unhappy dude. What'd you do to him?"

"Refused to sacrifice Roberta's memory to support Leigh."

"You know you're going to wind up with a divided synagogue."

"Any ideas on how to prevent it?"

"You'll find a way. You always do."

Deborah hoped Margo was right.

But far more urgent than dealing with irritating criminal attorneys and divided synagogue members was taking care of Isaac, so when her assistant left, Deborah called Dr. Wright's office. She explained to the receptionist that Dr. Krause had recommended Dr. Wright as an adolescent specialist who could help her fourteen-year-old son with his anger issues.

The receptionist must have repeated the same thing so many times that she sounded like a recording. "You'll have to arrive thirty minutes early for the first meeting to fill out various forms, including insurance information. Be sure to bring your insurance cards."

"When is the first available appointment?"

"Next Tuesday at two. You'll need to be here at one thirty."

That would mean Isaac would miss his Hebrew class, but since that was his first language, it shouldn't be a problem.

"Thank you. We'll see you then."

***

Deborah arrived home to find Isaac playing a video game.

"Good news. Dr. Wright, the psychologist I told you about, can see you Tuesday. We need to be at his office at one thirty. I'll pick you up at school at one."

Without stopping his activity, Isaac said, "I don't need to go, and anyway I'd be missing my Hebrew class."

"Since that's your best subject, I'm sure you can get permission to miss it. And, yes, you do need to go."

"One time. I'll go one time."

"We'll see what Dr. Wright says."

Relieved that a visit with the psychologist was close at hand, Deborah went into the kitchen to start dinner. Her thoughts returned to her meeting with Leigh's attorney and distracted her to the point that when she finished making the salad, she put the lettuce in the freezer instead of the refrigerator.

Realizing her mistake and correcting it, Deborah said, "That does it," and went to the phone.

She looked up Tom Johnson's number and dialed.

When he answered, she said, "Hi, it's Deborah Stein."

"So nice to hear from you," he said in what seemed to be a genuinely happy tone.

"I'd appreciate some advice. I'll treat you to lunch this time."

"Somewhere where Mel Freed won't see us, I hope."

Deborah laughed. "Good point."

"Is this about Roberta's accident?"

"Yes, her attorney Charles Harland came to see me. It wasn't pleasant."

"He's quite aggressive. I'll help anyway I can."

Relief permeated Deborah. "What day works for you?"

"How about Tuesday?"

Deborah could have lunch with Tom and then take Isaac to Dr. Wright's. Somehow the synagogue would manage without her for a few hours.

"Fine. I'll pick a place and call you back."

"I'm looking forward to it."

"So am I."

Deborah felt uneasy knowing how much she meant that.

***

At dinner Isaac brought his Biology textbook to the table and insisted he couldn't talk to his mother as he had to study for his test even while eating.

Feeling discouraged about problems with Isaac and at the synagogue, Deborah needed to get in touch with the one person who always came through for her – her dearest friend Miriam in Israel.

Miriam had made sure life went on for Deborah and Isaac after Dov died. Every night she was at their apartment insisting they eat the meals that friends and other soldiers' wives brought. She sat next to Deborah during morning and evening services at the Conservative Yeshiva where they both taught. If she suspected that for the first few weeks Deborah didn't mean the words of the Mourner's Kaddish praising God, Miriam kept such thoughts to herself, intuiting that by the end of the first thirty days of mourning Deborah would recite them sincerely.

Deborah sat down at the small built-in desk in the corner of her kitchen and began an email to Miriam.

What's been going on with you and Avram and the boys? Isaac's already looking forward to spending time with them during our summer visit to Israel.

Lately I've been wondering if moving back to Israel would solve Isaac's problems. He's still so angry about leaving that I'm going to take him to a psychologist who specializes in teens. He'd rather sleep or study than spend time with me, the little we have with my being a rabbi.

I'm still so down about Roberta's death. Besides missing her, I keep wishing she'd confided in me about her cancer diagnosis. I may have been able to help. I'm trying to be sympathetic towards Leigh, but I'm so angry about the way she treated Roberta and the way she views her death merely as an inconvenience that I'm finding that almost impossible.

I hate the legal side of it. Leigh's attorney has already visited me with his theory that Roberta's death was a disguised suicide. Tom Johnson, a retired lawyer friend of Roberta, is going to help me get through that part of it.

Sorry to be hitting you with my problems. You've always been so good at giving me advice that you're the one I turn to.

It must be about three in the morning in Israel so I hope you're in the midst of happy dreams.

When you wake up, please fill me in on all the latest in your life.

Love, Deborah

The next morning when Deborah awoke she found a return email from Miriam.

Dearest Deborah,

I will tell you from personal experience that teenage boys can barely tolerate their non-rabbi mothers. None the less, you're seeking help for Isaac, so stop beating up on yourself.

Roberta may have coped with her cancer diagnosis by NOT talking about it. Sounds like Leigh deserves your suspicion rather than your sympathy.

I hope Tom Johnson, whose name tells me he's likely not Jewish, is at least 80. You don't need any more complications in your life.

Much love, Miriam

Chapter Fifteen

"You've got big troubles."

Deborah looked up from her desk to see Mel Freed looming over it. As a rabbi, she shouldn't feel such dislike for anyone, especially a congregant and more especially the congregant who would have the most influence in deciding her future at the synagogue. But she couldn't bring herself to smile at him because she knew it would be false.

"With Roberta dead, we've lost the chair of the committee planning the synagogue's anniversary celebration," he said.

"I'm sure that since you're president-elect, the board of directors will make you president at their next meeting. You can start now being in charge of that committee."

"No way I'm taking over that hen house."

"We're fortunate so many of our female members are ready to do the work that keeps the synagogue functioning."

Mel's face reddened. "Well, your buddy Leigh Goldsmith, as president of the Sisterhood, should take over the job, but she called saying she wasn't up to coming to the meeting."

"I can't begin to imagine how upset she must be."

"Oh, come on, rabbi, we both know she's not here because she can't face all the people who think she either killed Roberta on purpose or who think, even if it was an accident, she's not sorry."

Before Deborah could respond, he rushed to say, "It's your job to fill in until she's back."

Deborah stood. "It's not my job, but I'm happy to help until a new chairperson is in place."

"Their next meeting's after lunch. Handle it." As he stomped though the door, he almost collided with Margo who was walking in.

"What an arrogant SOB."

Deborah tried to look stern but instead had to suppress a laugh. "I assume SOB stands for 'synagogue office boy.'"

"Right. When I heard his booming voice going on about the anniversary celebration, I pulled the schedule Roberta had given me." She handed the document to Deborah. "It looks like everything is on track."

"Thanks. I'll take this into the meeting."

A few hours later the rabbi walked into the board room with Roberta's plans in her hand. She found twelve women who stopped talking as soon as they saw her, a sure sign they'd been gossiping about Roberta's death. Age wise they were a mixture. Some were old enough to be retired, others were middle aged and had never worked outside the home and some were taking a hiatus from their careers while their children were young. Yet, their attire was similar – slacks with either blouses or pullover tops.

The group divided itself into two, half taking seats on one side of the long mahogany table and half on the other. Above them were pictures of past presidents with only four being women. Roberta's portrait would be joining them.

Deborah sat at the head of the table.

"What a relief to see you. I feared Mel would try to take over," one committee member said.

"Nah, he's afraid of women. That's why he stayed away," said another whose remark was followed by laughter.

"If the synagogue board had more women on it, he wouldn't be our next president," said a third.

Though relieved to know Mel would have no allies in this group if he tried to get rid of her, Deborah didn't want this to turn into an anti-Mel gathering, so she began the meeting. She relied on Roberta's notes to talk about where they were and what they needed to do next.

When they were about to finish, one member said, "Rabbi, there's an elephant in the room we need to stop ignoring. We know you're disappointed in us for gossiping about what happened to Roberta."

"Sometimes when I'm struggling not to gossip, I think of the story of the rabbi and the feather pillow," Deborah said.

She had their attention. "A man, who felt guilty about the damage he'd done to another through his gossip, asked his rabbi what he should do. The rabbi told him to take a feather pillow, cut it open and let the feathers fly in the wind. After doing so, the man returned to the rabbi and asked what he should do next. The rabbi told him to gather up all the feathers. When the man said that was impossible, the rabbi reminded him that the same was true of the words he'd spoken and now had been repeated by so many people."

Deborah stood to leave. One woman after another hugged her.

On her way back to her office Deborah thought she might have tamped down the hurtful accusations. Once there her phone rang, and Sam Krause identified himself.

"Rabbi, when you come to our home at the end of our sitting *shiva*, could you please plan to stay a while."

"Of course."

"Good. We want to tell you our plans for bringing justice to our mother."

Chapter Sixteen

Deborah had been determined to get commitments from six more people. She could count on herself and the three Krause men. But if morning services were to be conducted at the Krause home on the last day of their sitting *shiva*, she needed ten people, the minimum required for a public Jewish religious service. Unlike in her parents' Orthodox Jewish world, all ten would not have to be male.

Having succeeded, she entered the Krause home Tuesday morning a little before seven in preparation for the services to start on the hour.

Activity drew her to the kitchen where the Krause men were making coffee and bringing paper plates and plastic silverware from the pantry. They stopped long enough to give her a group hug.

"We've begged people to not bring any more food," Dr. Krause said. "If you open the refrigerator, it's so stuffed, it's almost impossible to close."

No sooner had he spoken than Jessica Snyder, with Samantha in a baby carrier on her back, walked into the kitchen with a box of Danish from Three Brothers Bakery. "I thought it would be nice to have a little something after services."

Deborah kissed mother and child and put the pastries on a tray Dr. Krause handed her. Jessica was one of the reasons she loved being a rabbi. She often had the opportunity to observe people showing loving kindness towards each other. Jessica must have been at the bakery when it opened at six thirty, having gotten herself and her baby out of the house while it was still dark.

When services ended at seven forty-five, Deborah was grateful for those pastries which kept people at the Krause home a little longer.

She dreaded hearing about Roberta's family's plans to bring her justice. Nothing good could come of it.

When everyone left, Deborah led the widower and his sons on the traditional walk around the block. It signified the family's rejoining society after their most intense period of mourning.

Deborah returned with them to their home where they ushered her into the living room. She sat in a chair across from the couch where they seated themselves.

Dr. Krause spoke first. "We want to explain what we're doing and why."

"Even if we did nothing," Ross said, "the vehicular crime division of the police department would interview us as the family of the deceased in a fatal car incident. After all their interviews and follow-up, they could decide to bring in the homicide division."

Ross must have heard the rabbi's sharp intake of breath because he quickly added, "We're not saying our mother's death was definitely a homicide, but if the homicide division gets involved and thinks that's a possibility, they take their information to the district attorney who decides whether to bring charges."

Deborah bit her lower lip. The research Roberta's family had done indicated they were highly unlikely to turn back no matter what she said. But she tried anyway.

"Dr. Krause, Roberta mentioned that, as an expert on narcissistic personality disorder, you believed Leigh Goldsmith suffered from that malady. But she also said your opinion was that such people are rarely violent."

"I never thought Leigh would plan an attack against Roberta. What I didn't fully consider is that, if she had the opportunity, she might strike."

"I'm sorry. I meant no criticism of you. None of us had reason to believe Leigh was a danger to Roberta, and likely the investigation will determine a tragic accident."

Sam put his arm around his father's shoulder. "We're not going to wait for the vehicular crime division to get in touch with us. We're going to contact them and let them know about Leigh's ill feelings towards Mom."

Deborah had to tell them truth. "You need to know that Leigh will go on the offensive. She'll claim your mother, of blessed memory, committed suicide."

"What?" the twins said simultaneously.

"When I mentioned at the funeral that Roberta had left a letter of instructions about her death, Leigh turned that into a suicide note. Both she and her attorney have asked me to provide it."

"She has an attorney? Guess who's feeling guilty." Ross smirked.

"That was to be expected. Her car hit someone who died," Dr. Krause said.

Relief coursed through Deborah. Now she didn't have to take the blame for Leigh's hiring a lawyer.

"My concern," the rabbi said, "is, as phony as the suicide note claim is, it could lead to awareness of Roberta's underlying, soon to be fatal, cancer. Roberta was such a private person that I hate the thought of her private life becoming public."

The twins looked at each other before Ross spoke. "As bad as we'd feel about that, assuming Dad agrees, we'd take that risk to make sure our mother receives justice."

Dr. Krause nodded. "I'll go along with it."

Something Leigh had said surged from the back of Deborah's mind. "This sounds even crazier, but Leigh told me that Roberta either jumped in front of her car or was pushed. The latter is what you might want to explore with the police."

Dr. Krause looked from one son to the other. "Jerry Evans. Without Roberta as the star witness at his second trial, it's unlikely he'll be convicted again."

"I'm having lunch today with Tom Johnson. I'll mention Jerry to him," Deborah said.

***

Deborah felt frumpy when she saw Tom. He wore a tan leather jacket over a white pullover. Brown boots covered the bottom of his jeans. She was in a long flowered skirt that she'd bought while she still lived in Israel over six years ago. Maybe she should take Margo up on her offer of a makeover, or at least ask her to go clothes shopping with her.

If Tom noticed Deborah's lack of fashion, he hid it. He smiled broadly when he greeted her at the entrance of the restaurant. After they'd settled into a corner booth and ordered, Deborah asked, "What do you hear from your daughter in Japan?"

"She invited me to visit her, though she hasn't set a date. She's not ready to come back to Houston with her mother gone. They were very close. Courtney's an only child."

"I desperately wanted to be an only child," Deborah said.

"Really?"

"So much so that when I was in middle school I remember my mother telling me that she hadn't been able to get pregnant after I was born and the doctor told her she'd never have another child. She went home and cried and was pregnant the next month with my brother. I remember thinking, 'I wish that story had had a happy ending.'"

When Tom stopped laughing, he said, "That's shocking. I pictured you as a…"

"Sweet little thing?"

Tom nodded.

"Hardly. Any time I thought my parents were favoring my brother I'd torment him – teasing him and, until he was bigger than I was, threatening him physically. My parents considered me a slightly less murderous version of Cain."

Tom chuckled. "I've misjudged you."

"You, on the other hand, were probably Mr. Popularity."

Tom looked down at the table and then back at Deborah. "I was an outcast."

"I can't imagine that."

"You have to understand that in small Texas towns two things are sacred – Friday night football and church. I couldn't play football or even try out for the team because back then I had asthma. We lived in north Texas so as the weather got colder I had to miss the games entirely. If that wasn't enough to make me a pariah, conversations about church were. Here's a condensed version. 'What church does your family go to? None. Come with me to mine. No thank you.' End of possible friendships."

"Teenage boys can sure have things tough."

"How's your son doing?"

"This afternoon I'm taking him for his first visit with an adolescent psychologist Dr. Krause recommended. I dealt with his anger when it was directed at me, but now that he'd acting out at school, I understand we're at a tipping point."

Deborah felt unburdened sharing the news which she hadn't even discussed with Margo.

"Sounds like a good move."

After thanking the server when she brought their food, Tom said, "I'm sorry Charles Harland gave you a hard time."

"The only good thing that came out of our conversation is that he praised you as one of the city's best defense attorneys." She hesitated. "Do you miss practicing law?"

"More 'no' than 'yes.' I don't have the stress of having people's futures, even their lives, in my hands. The worse cases were those when I was sure my client was innocent. I knew that if I didn't uncover every scrap of exculpatory evidence and present it so the jury believed me, he'd suffer for the rest of his life."

"That would be quite a burden."

"On the other hand, I'm still so interested in the law that the first thing I turn to in any newspaper are stories about trials and how they turned out."

"And you're enjoying all you're doing in retirement?"

"I'm studying subjects I always wanted to, like the world's religions. I'm thinking of writing a book, perhaps about some of my cases with the most intriguing legal issues. I think I'm okay with retirement because I know if I want to go back to practice law, I can."

"You're an attorney I trust. Charles Harland is another matter."

"Was there something specific he said that upset you?"

Deborah put her fork down, picked up her napkin and wiped her mouth. "Do you remember how at the synagogue I mentioned Roberta had left instructions about how her funeral should be handled?"

"Yes, that sounded just like Roberta."

"Leigh and her attorney have turned that into a suicide note."

"They would only use it that way if the Krauses accuse her of intentionally hitting Roberta."

"That's exactly what they plan to do. Then all the information

Roberta wanted to keep private about her illness will go public. She never even told me she was ill."

Tom moved his arm across the table and was about to put his hand over Deborah's, but pulled back before he did. "She didn't tell me either."

"You were her friend. I was her friend and her rabbi."

"I certainly wasn't her rabbi." Tom's tone was so mischievous that Deborah laughed and Tom joined in.

"There's another possibility. Leigh said Roberta either jumped in front of her or was pushed, so Jerry Evans came to mind."

"I'm on shaky grounds. He was my client."

"Can you just confirm if I remembered something correctly? I believe you told me he was out of prison while awaiting his second trial."

"True."

"Thanks. That's what Dr. Krause and his sons need to know."

***

Deborah had been enjoying her lunch with Tom to the point that she was a few minutes late picking Isaac up at school.

"I thought you'd smartened up and decided I didn't need to see a shrink," Isaac said as he entered the car.

"I'm sorry I'm late. I was having lunch with a friend of Roberta Krause and let the time get away from me."

"Is that the guy you have the hots for?"

"What?" Deborah pulled into the parking lot of a shopping center and turned off the car.

"That's what Ian Freed told me. He's in my Hebrew class. Maybe his grandpa said it the other way around – that the guy had the hots for you. And he's not even Jewish."

"As disappointed as I am in Mel Freed and his grandson, I'm more disappointed in you for listening to such garbage."

"I would have threatened to punch him out, but that's why you're taking me for 'help' in the first place."

Deborah started the car and pulled out of the lot. "I give up. That's why we're going to see Dr. Wright."

On their way they passed the Astrodome. When built in 1964, the first multi-purpose stadium, it was called the "Eighth Wonder of the World." Now the almost circular building sat empty and unused, ignored except for debates about whether it would be demolished or renovated. Deborah considered how we frequently treat the old and infirm the same way. Her Saturday sermon would be about our obligation to take care of them.

They arrived at the psychologist's waiting room in time for Deborah to fill out all the consent and insurance forms and to confirm the medical information sheet on which Isaac had attested to his good health and lack of medications.

Dr. Wright came out of his office and ushered them in. He wore a short sleeve shirt with a collar rather than the jacket and tie Deborah had expected, but this was Houston where more formal dress was almost frowned on. She speculated about whether his slightly hunched back had been with him since birth or was a sign of aging in a man who was likely in his late sixties. He ushered mother and son to a dark brown leather couch where Isaac slouched down next to Deborah. Dr. Wright sat across from them in a chair with flame stitching.

After introducing himself, the psychologist addressed Isaac. "I've asked your mother to be with us for the first few minutes of our visit because I want both of you to understand important legal and privacy issues before you and I start meeting."

He switched his attention to Deborah. "As the parent of a minor you've consented to Isaac's treatment and have the right to know its content."

Isaac muttered, "Shit."

"Exactly," Dr. Wright responded.

Isaac smiled.

"That's why your mother needs to understand that I believe in a 'zone of privacy.' If there's something you want kept private, I will try to honor that unless I believe keeping it private will harm you or another. Should that situation arise, I will tell you I cannot keep it private."

Isaac nodded.

"If your mother insists that I give her information I agreed to keep private, I will ask her to find another psychologist."

Deborah felt uncomfortable about trusting what this stranger decided she had the right to know about her son, but Dr. Krause had recommended him, and she trusted Dr. Krause.

"One more thing. I'm permitted to disclose information you give me to law enforcement officers for certain purposes."

Isaac sat up straighter. "If I told you something the cops could come after me for, they could make you tell them."

"That's correct."

Isaac tapped his foot. "Okay, I get it."

Deborah's heart rate quickened. How much did she not know about her son?

***

With thoughts of the day's events assailing her, Deborah emailed Miriam.

Dear Miriam,

At lunch with a friend I told a story about what a spunky – actually aggressive - child I was and he was shocked. Those who knew me before Dov died and those after see me completely differently. I didn't lose my faith in God when Dov was killed but I did lose so much in myself. I learned how badly I could mess up on my own, especially with Isaac.

He had his first visit with the psychologist today. I had mixed emotions. I'm happy for the help and yet disappointed in myself for his needing it, and almost jealous that someone else will be hearing Isaac's confidences.

As always, much love to you and your family,
Deborah

Miriam's reply was waiting for Deborah when she woke up.

Dearest Deborah,

Of course, Dov's death took a toll on you. Leaving a position in Israel where you taught rabbinical students and becoming a synagogue rabbi didn't help. You understood that a "spunky" rabbi is often dubbed a "controversial" one so you've let the conciliatory side of you predominate. The spunkiness is still there and will show itself when needed.

As to Isaac, trust me, teenage boys, even under the best of circumstances, do not confide in their mothers. What's important is for Isaac to confide in the psychologist.

Love, Miriam

P.S. Maybe someday you'll tell me who your carefully unidentified lunch companion is.

Chapter Seventeen

Deborah lost count of all the people who passed her on the three mile trail at Memorial Park. Most were running, some jogging, and, as much as she wanted to categorize her activity as power walking, that would be an exaggeration. She almost convinced herself that if she took the time to do this more often, she'd soon be faster.

When she'd first moved to Houston, Deborah had been amazed there existed over 1500 acres of park land in an area which was otherwise experiencing a residential building boom. She thought developers would be all over it. She'd learned that the Hogg family had "sold" the land to the city at a ridiculously low price in return for an agreement that the land could only be used as a park.

Texans delighted in telling tales about the Hogg family, starting with Texas Governor "Big Jim" Hogg. Though his daughter Ima had brothers, she became the best known of his children in large part because of her philanthropy and patronage of the arts, and in part because her maternal grandfather's horse didn't move fast enough. When Grandpa learned her parents planned to name her after the heroine in an epic poem written by her uncle, he tried to get to her Christening in time to stop it. But he arrived too late, and thus his granddaughter became Ima Hogg.

Stopping at a water fountain under a blanket of trees, Deborah heard a voice coming from behind her. "Rabbi, how are you enjoying the great outdoors?"

Deborah recognized Jenny Goldsmith, Leigh and Stan's daughter, her blond hair tucked behind her ears, making her bangs more prominent. She wore faded shorts and a tee shirt that had a hole in one sleeve, a contrast to her mother who was only seen in public in fashionable clothes that likely had been made to order.

"How did your trip to Austin go?" the rabbi asked.

"Great. I've been offered a job working for a hunger organization. It makes sure kids who get meals at school also get them in the summer."

Deborah hugged Jenny. "I love the way you live your values."

"My mother thinks I live my life in ways to piss her off."

"Your mother supports good works in a manner different from you. Part of her generosity towards the synagogue goes to our Hunger and Homeless Fund."

"I can't wait to tell her you defended her. Not that she'll believe me. You have to be with her all the way or else…"

"Or else what?"

"Or else you're the enemy."

***

Jenny's remark about how easy it was to become her mother's enemy stayed with Deborah as she drove home. In doing more research into narcissistic personality disorder, she'd learned that if a narcissist felt humiliated, she often lashed out aggressively, occasionally violently. Deborah now understood that every time the synagogue anniversary committee agreed with Roberta's recommendations rather than Leigh's, Leigh felt humiliated. Could the opportunity to hurt her adversary have been too much for Leigh to resist?

As much as Deborah didn't want to believe that, she also couldn't bear to think Roberta had committed suicide. Yet, thoughts of the conversation she and Roberta had in the garden at the synagogue kept creeping into the rabbi's mind. When Roberta talked about how Tom had watched his wife's suffering for three months, she'd added that if only his wife had thought of dying when she'd started suffering, she could have saved her husband from what he went through. At the time, the idea Roberta was condoning suicide had briefly entered and just as quickly left Deborah's consciousness. Now she wondered if Roberta had been giving her a warning of what she planned to do.

Even if that possibility existed, it seemed unlikely she would have chosen to jump in front of a car as a means of ending her life. That method was too inefficient, possibly ending in terrible injuries rather than death. Had Roberta been so desperate that she took the gamble?

The rabbi's thoughts turned to Jerry Evans and then came to a standstill, just like the traffic. She was driving near the Galleria on the Loop 610 West between Interstate 10 and U.S. 59, which was the most congested area of freeway in the state, and an accident had made matters worse. She stopped to let an ambulance, with sirens blaring, pass her and slowly weave its way among the other immobile cars. Once she finally made her way into the one lane that was moving, she saw a car against a guard rail with a pick-up truck crashed into its passenger side door. She said a prayer for those who might be hurt.

Deborah again considered Jerry Evans. He had a motive for pushing Roberta in front of Leigh's vehicle. Roberta's absence at the second trial would make his conviction much less likely. Shame made Deborah dispense with the thought. How could she pin the horrific title of murderer on another human being with no evidence?

By the time she arrived home, Deborah had persuaded herself that Roberta's death was an accident. A few minutes later, as she was about to shower, her phone rang.

Alison Eisen, principal of Isaac's school, greeted Deborah. "When I couldn't reach you at the synagogue, Margo said to try you at home."

"I'm afraid to ask what Isaac has done."

"It's what he did over a week ago, the same day Roberta died. I didn't want to bother you until after the funeral and *shiva*. It's not that terrible, but I thought you should know that he skipped out of Hebrew class."

"He's had his first meeting with a psychologist, so I'm hoping his behavior will improve."

"Let's give him a chance. I won't say anything to him about it, but if there's another infraction…"

"I understand. Thank you."

When the call ended, Deborah felt gratitude for another reason. Roberta and Leigh's neighborhood was on Isaac's route home from school. Thinking that his proximity to the tragic scene could have made him the victim, the rabbi recited a prayer of thanksgiving that he'd been spared.

Chapter Eighteen

"Two police officers are waiting to see you." The warning came from Margo via a call to the rabbi's cell phone as she pulled into the synagogue parking lot.

Deborah took a deep breath. She assured herself that since she'd been thinking about all the possibilities surrounding Roberta's death, her conversation with the police could help them decide they were dealing with an accident.

They rose from their seats as she entered the waiting area. "Rabbi Stein?" the female of the pair asked. Her partner and she were both a head taller than Deborah. The officer's ebony skin and coal black hair were in contrast to her companion's pale face and light blond hair. The song "Ebony and Ivory" came to Deborah's mind.

"Yes, I'm she," Deborah said as she noticed them scrutinizing her black skirt and white blouse. Perhaps they'd been trying to guess how a female rabbi dressed.

"I'm Officer Lana McKee." She held out her hand which Deborah shook.

"I'm Officer George Stanford." Another handshake followed, after which he handed her cards which Deborah glanced at, noting they confirmed her visitors' names.

"I assume you've already met Margo," the rabbi said.

When the officers nodded, Deborah said, "Let's go into my office."

Officer Stanford, the last to enter, shut the door and joined his partner in a seat in front of the rabbi's desk.

"Officer Stanford and I are sorry for your loss of Ms. Krause," Officer McKee said. "We're from the vehicular accident division of the police department, and we're here because both the family of the deceased and the driver of the vehicle think you can be helpful."

"Each to its own cause," Officer Stanford added.

"We'd like your insight into the relationship between the driver and the victim."

Deborah sat up straighter. "As president of our synagogue, Roberta was chair of the committee planning our anniversary celebration. Leigh was second in charge. I wasn't at their meetings."

"You must have heard reports," Officer McKee said.

"Yes, but only second hand information." Deborah regretted the words as soon as she spoke them, realizing they could spur the officers to interview all the committee members.

"Go on," Officer Stanford said.

"Leigh complained to me any time she and Roberta disagreed and the committee went along with Roberta's suggestions. Leigh's feelings get hurt easily."

"We realize you don't want one member accused of intentionally running over another, but you need to be more forthcoming about any bad blood between these women," Officer McKee said.

"You have to understand that Roberta was a retired efficiency expert who wanted to get things done quickly. She didn't take time to worry about Leigh's ego."

The officers exchanged a look, making Deborah suspect they'd already seen Leigh's ego in action.

"Ms. Goldsmith claims Ms. Krause either jumped in front of her vehicle or was pushed. She said she left a suicide note that you mentioned at the funeral," Officer Stanford said.

"Roberta left instructions about her funeral. She wanted to make sure traditional Jewish practices about death and mourning would be followed."

Officer Stanford leaned over Deborah's desk. She recoiled slightly from his nicotine breath. "Ms. Goldsmith said jumping in front of her car would save Ms. Krause from a slow painful cancer death."

"Being hit by a car could have led to a slow painful death due to serious injuries. Roberta couldn't count on dying."

Officer Stanford smiled triumphantly. "Ms. Goldsmith was driving a Range Rover and likely at a speed too fast for conditions.

Good chance that would kill."

Officer McKee, noticing Deborah's look of distress, intervened. "We've read the note. It's someone who figures she's going to die soon – maybe by a cancer death, maybe by a quicker death."

Deborah chewed her lower lip. "Leigh mentioned someone might have pushed Roberta in front of her vehicle."

"The Krause family specifically named Jerry Evans," Officer Stanford said. "Ms. Krause won't be around to testify at his second trial."

"We reminded them they can use Ms. Krause's testimony from the first trial," Officer McKee said.

"I…I didn't know that."

"We're going to check it out," Officer McKee assured her. "A neighbor saw someone hurrying from the scene. Thought it was a tall guy, on the thin side."

The officers rose to leave. After each shook her hand, Officer Stanford said, "We might need to talk to you again."

Before closing the door, Officer McKee added, "As a courtesy, we want you to know we're going to speak to your members who were at those anniversary party committee meetings."

Deborah slumped back into her chair. This tragic situation was about to split her congregation.

Chapter Nineteen

When the doorbell rang after nine o'clock, both Deborah and her son assumed one of his friends had come by. But no sooner had Isaac answered the door than Deborah heard, "I'll get my mom."

Deborah arrived in the entry hall as Leigh Goldsmith stepped into the house. The rabbi took a deep breath and invited Leigh into the living room where her guest looked around until she chose a blue and maroon striped arm chair, which at two years old was the newest piece of furniture in the house. Deborah sat across from her on a much older beige couch.

"I came to see you in person because this is so important to me and to you as a rabbi."

Deborah nodded.

"These two sleazy cops came to interview me. I had my attorney with me. Not that he was much help. When the incompetents' stupidity was more than I could take, I asked for the name of their superior, but my attorney interrupted me before they could answer."

Deborah fought the urge to tell Leigh she was her own worst enemy. Now the police officers would continue their investigation even if they thought they were likely dealing with a tragic accident. They would show Leigh she couldn't push them around.

"They also visited me," Deborah said.

"Did they tell you they planned to talk to everyone on the synagogue anniversary committee?"

"They mentioned it."

"You can stop that."

"I don't understand."

"You're always reminding us how terrible Judaism says gossip is. So you have a duty to tell those women to keep their damn mouths shut."

"Judaism also tells us that we have to follow the laws of the country we live in. As bad as I feel that the police interviews will involve gossip, I can't encourage those women to disregard a request from the authorities."

Leigh stood. "You always liked Roberta more than you liked me."

Before Deborah could respond, Leigh was out the door, slamming it behind her.

Deborah sank into the couch. She needed to talk to someone about the police investigation and what part she and her congregants would play. Tom Johnson could help, but she hesitated to call him. He might misconstrue her motives. While she was debating whether to try to reach him, the phone rang.

"Deborah, it's Tom Johnson. I'm sorry to be calling this late, but my mental telepathy told me you needed to speak to me about the accident investigation."

Deborah was too stunned to respond.

"Just kidding. I saw Margo a little while ago as we were both coming out of a movie, and she told me you seemed shook up about your meeting with the police."

"They want to interview everyone on the synagogue anniversary committee. Leigh was here telling me I should discourage them."

"You're not going to interfere with a police investigation."

"Of course not. But I agree with her that the officers will be inviting gossip, and I fear they'll be exacerbating divisions within the synagogue as well."

"I'm sorry. Did anything else come out of your interview with them?"

"They said Roberta's testimony at the first trial could be read at the second. I guess that gets rid of any motive Jerry Evans would have had to push Roberta in front of Leigh's car."

"I wish I could agree with you, but here's how it will work. The prosecutor will have an attorney read her testimony and will be lucky if the jurors don't fall asleep."

"I don't understand."

"Roberta's testimony was basically about dry numbers, but it was the way she testified. She spoke directly to the jurors, and, if any looked like they didn't comprehend something, she explained it in a different way. Her belief that Jerry was guilty came through in her demeanor as well as her words. Once she won the respect of the jury, her conviction about his guilt swayed them."

"So when someone else reads her words, they lose their effectiveness."

"Exactly."

"If Jerry still has a motive, this next piece of information will interest you. The police said a neighbor thought she saw a tall thin guy hurrying from the scene."

Tom didn't respond for a few seconds. Then he said, "Jerry is short and stocky."

"I'm...I'm confused. If we have another suspect, who could it be?"

"Could be a witness rather than a suspect. Sometimes someone sees something and doesn't want to get involved, so they take off."

Chapter Twenty

When he called to say he wanted to meet with her, Deborah suggested the small rose garden outside her office. Now they sat together on the swing in the gazebo.

"I feel close to Roberta here," Deborah said. "It's the last place I saw her. She was lovingly taking care of the flowers."

"As quickly as Mom wanted everything done, she put up with the slower pace of nature. She was devoted to her garden at home, too."

"You must miss her so much. How are you doing?"

Sam sighed. "It's our dad Ross and I are concerned about. I wish we'd followed your advice and not encouraged him to get involved in the investigation of her death. It's consuming him."

"It's part of his grieving process."

"What's funny is that as a psychologist he understands that. He's even commented on the anger people feel when a loved one dies."

"He could see a colleague for help," Deborah said.

Sam shook his head. "We've suggested that, but he's convinced he can take care of himself."

"I've seen him after evening services and have tried to engage him, but he always claims he's fine and rushes off. Perhaps if you tell me more of what's going on, I can help."

Sam ran his fingers through his hair. "He's distraught that anyone would think Mom had committed suicide, so he's determined to prove either Leigh hit her intentionally or that Jerry Evans pushed her."

"But if Leigh hit her accidentally, it still wouldn't be suicide."

"Dad's not being rational, which Ross and I told him Mom would hate. That remark made us personas non grata for a couple of days.

He's so angry that Leigh even suggested suicide that he's not thinking straight. He even…"

"Yes?"

Sam looked down, grimaced, raised his head and met the rabbi's gaze. "He even called the women on the anniversary committee to question them about how much Leigh disliked Mom. Most of them said they didn't think they should talk to him since the police were planning to. But a few told him about the derogatory remarks Leigh had made and how she'd gone out of her way to cause Mom problems. That infuriated Dad."

Deborah nodded. At least the police's plans to interview the committee members had stopped many of them from feeding Dr. Krause's grief. But getting a preview of what a couple of them were going to say told Deborah how harmful their words would be to Leigh.

"There's another matter I wanted to talk to you about, but Dad's welfare is what's important."

Deborah moved a little closer to Sam and reached up to put her arm around his shoulder. "Your welfare's important, too."

Sam hesitated. "Mindy Kaplan and I are about to get engaged. Mom really liked her. We plan to wait until the first thirty days of mourning are over and then not get married for a year. Mindy didn't make it to the funeral because she was in Africa with a group that delivers medicine there."

The rabbi smiled. "I'm proud of members like Mindy and Jenny Goldsmith who act on the concept of *tikkun olan*, healing the world."

Sam rubbed his hands together. "That's just it. Mindy and Jenny are best friends. Mindy always planned to ask Jenny to be her maid of honor and to invite her parents to the wedding."

"Your father would never hold any of what happened against Jenny, and in a year everything could be fine between him and Jenny's parents."

Noting Sam's look of skepticism, the rabbi added, "At least not bad enough that having them at the wedding would spoil things for your dad."

"Dad is also pursuing the idea that Jerry Evans pushed Mom in front of the car. He found a letter Mom never told him about."

Sam's eyes filled with tears. Deborah squeezed his shoulder.

"From Jerry Evans?"

"No, his wife. She wrote Mom she hoped someday our family would experience the pain of having a loved one torn away."

Jerry's wife. She would suffer as much, perhaps more than her husband, if he were in prison. And she would know that Roberta could put him there again.

Chapter Twenty-One

She was in over her head.

Without expert advice on how police investigations were conducted and what to expect in a courtroom, if it came to that, Deborah had no hope of navigating her congregation through the unpleasant times ahead.

Tom Johnson could provide the help she needed, yet she hesitated to contact him. She hadn't been able to dismiss the thought of Ian Freed telling her son that she and Tom had the "hots" for each other. That was an expression from another era that a man in his seventies would use, so Deborah felt confident Ian had heard it from his grandfather Mel. That man had put her in a position she'd struggled to avoid – being fodder for gossip.

After morning services Monday, Deborah left the sanctuary and caught up with Mel at the water fountain.

"Would you have a few minutes to visit with me?"

He stopped drinking, looked up and said, "Okay," in a quizzical tone, and then followed her to her office where he closed the door and sat next to her in a chair in front of her desk.

Deborah spoke in a firm voice. "One of the joys of being the rabbi of this congregation has been appreciating the interconnections among the members. They care about each other, socialize outside the synagogue and typically treat each other like extended family."

"True."

"We both know the circumstances of Roberta's death have put that in jeopardy."

Mel opened his mouth but before he could speak, Deborah

continued. "If I'm to get the congregation through the investigation and possible court case in such a way that we can keep our cohesiveness, I need your help."

"I don't know anything about that sort of thing."

"Tom Johnson does. He's been both a prosecutor and a defense attorney. But I can't go to him for advice if my efforts to keep the congregation together are described as my having the 'hots' for him."

Deep red coloring went from Mel's forehead to his chin.

"I know you hope to find a rabbi to replace me when my contract's up. If the congregation's in turmoil, you'll have a difficult time convincing someone of the caliber you want to take over. I'm not sure I would wish to stay if the synagogue were divided. It's in your interest as incoming president to help me get us through this. But I will not put myself or Tom Johnson through gossip mongering."

Mel stared at the rabbi.

"Do we have an understanding?" Deborah asked.

Mel grimaced, nodded and left.

***

Despite her talk with Mel, Deborah delayed calling Tom. She didn't want to take advantage of his helpful nature or put him in a position where he felt he was being disloyal to a former client. She took a deep breath and dialed. She'd work out those issues with him when they met.

He answered the phone with a tired, "Hello," making Deborah regret the call.

"Hi, Tom."

"Deborah, how are you? Is everything going okay?" His cheerier tone made her feel less like an interloper.

"I don't know enough to answer. Police investigations and the like are outside my knowledge base."

Before Tom could respond, she rushed on, "If I promise to honor any boundaries you set concerning Jerry Evans, might you find time to enlighten me about some of the legal matters surrounding Roberta's death?"

"If in return you'll answer some questions I have about Jewish practices, you've got a deal."

"Of course," Deborah said, relief coursing through her. "I'll bring lunch and we can eat in the rose garden outside my office tomorrow."

"I'm out of town then."

"Going to Japan to see your daughter?" For his sake, Deborah hoped the answer was yes, but if so, he'd probably be gone for weeks.

"We haven't set a date yet. I'm making a quick jaunt to the Nasher Sculpture Garden in Dallas. There's an exhibit I want to see that's leaving at the end of the week."

"Ah. The advantages of being retired," Deborah said.

"If you're calling from your office and you have the time, I can come around now." Tom hesitated. "Unless that's going to be a problem."

"Mel Freed and I have reached an understanding."

"Is thirty minutes okay?" Tom asked.

"That would work. I don't have an appointment for an hour."

Deborah considered how today worked out better than tomorrow. Margo was coming in late this morning so Deborah wouldn't have to explain that Tom's role was adviser and not potential boyfriend.

Her door was open when he appeared wearing khaki pants and a maroon pullover. She returned his gap toothed smile with a grin.

Deborah stood. "It's lovely out. How about the rose garden?"

He made a mock bow and let her precede him.

Once they were seated on the swing, Deborah said, "I respect the fact there are limits to any discussion we have about Jerry Evans. I want to make sure I understand them."

"I can talk about anything that's been revealed publicly. For example, anything said at the trial or reported in newspapers."

"What about his wife?"

"I can't discuss anything she told me about Jerry or her belief in his guilt or innocence."

"I'm wondering about her physical description. Tall, short, fat, thin?"

"Taller than Jerry, and unfortunately just before the trial and during the trial she lost so much weight that she had to be hospitalized. I hope by now she's regained it."

"I was angry about her letter and forgot to consider all she'd gone through."

"What letter?"

"Dr. Krause found one she'd written to Roberta about her wish that Roberta's family would someday know the pain of losing a member. Do you think she could have been the person described at the scene as a tall, thin guy?"

"Do I think that a witness could have described a woman like that? Witness identifications are notoriously suspect, so it's possible. Your role is to make sure Dr. Krause gives the letter to the police who will look into it."

"I plan to visit him. See how he's coming along. I'll check on the letter then." Deborah clasped her hands together. "There is a more immediate matter."

Tom leaned towards Deborah. "Tell me about it."

"I'm sure members of Roberta's committee will ask for advice in handling their police interviews. I think they'll want me to go beyond saying, 'just tell the truth.'"

Tom spoke firmly. "They need to provide information, not speculation."

Deborah nodded.

"For example, if Roberta gave everyone two minutes to suggest a dinner menu and then told Leigh she'd gone over her time and asked her to sit down, Leigh might have said, 'I hate you for treating me like that.' If so, the women should provide that information. However, if she said nothing, they shouldn't speculate that she hated Roberta for what had just happened."

Deborah relaxed her hands. "Makes sense."

"If enough incidents like that are presented factually, rather than as suppositions, the police can draw their own conclusions."

"I guess they'll be trying to determine if Leigh had a motive."

"In Texas you don't need a motive to convict someone of murder."

"That's surprising."

"But realistically the accident division won't take a case to the homicide division if they don't find a motive."

"You're a fount of information. I'm very grateful."

A touch of pink appeared on Tom's cheeks. "How else can I help?"

"It's your turn. I have to be in my office for an appointment in ten minutes. Ask me a question you have about Judaism before I go."

"Okay, we can meet again to go over other issues that concern you." The pink color on Tom's cheeks deepened.

Deborah smiled. "Thank you."

Tom hesitated. "I don't want this to come across as criticism."

"Don't worry. Whatever it is, I'm sure I've heard it before."

"Why do so many Jewish people object to intermarriage?"

"Fair question. We have the practical problem of self preservation. Only about a third of the children raised in intermarriages are raised as Jews. We're about two tenths of one per cent of the world population and about two per cent of the U.S. population. We don't have numbers to spare."

"Yet you discourage conversion for all the reasons you've told me."

"If after all that discouragement, someone still wants to convert, I remind them of the months of study ahead, tell them they can quit at any time or finish and decide not to convert. My experience is those who follow through and become Jewish by choice are the most adherent members of the faith."

"I appreciate the explanation. Since you're the one who's working and I'm the one who's retired, I'll look forward to your calling me about when we can meet again. We'll need some time to discuss other legal issues surrounding Roberta's death."

They stood simultaneously and shook hands a little longer than necessary.

Deborah entered her office feeling more confident that she could handle whatever was thrown at her.

She arrived as her phone was ringing.

"Rabbi Stein, this is Lydia at Dr. Wright's office." Her next sentence made Deborah's heart race. "He'd like to meet with you privately when you bring Isaac in for his next appointment."

***

When Deborah arrived home, an email from Miriam was waiting for her.

Hi, Deborah,

Wanted to check in with you. How are Isaac's sessions with the psychologist going? How's your congregation handling Roberta's death?

Thinking of you,
Miriam

Dear Miriam,

The good news is that Isaac is willing to continue seeing the psychologist, who wants to meet with me before their next session. Hope there's not some big problem.

As to Roberta's death, now that I'm dealing with the police I'm even more grateful to Tom Johnson who's guiding me though the process. Even though he's far from his eighties, don't worry about him. Just today we discussed all the reasons Jews oppose intermarriage.

Love to you and your family,
Deborah

Dear Deborah,

I'm sure the psychologist's meeting with you is routine. He must be doing a good job if Isaac isn't refusing to see him. As to Tom Johnson, if he brought up the topic of intermarriage, don't assume it was due to intellectual curiosity.

Love, Miriam

Chapter Twenty-Two

She shouldn't have let Dr. Krause run off each day after evening services. He was a mourner who needed comforting, so Monday Deborah called him and told him she'd like to stop by.

"Of course. I've been meaning to talk to you. I wanted to get my thoughts together first."

Dr. Krause greeted her with a hug as she entered his home. The little that was left of his hair looked windblown, and his jacket was hiked up on one side.

The house felt empty even though Deborah noticed no furniture missing when they sat in the living room, taking opposite ends of the couch. Roberta had been such a force of nature that her home seemed inordinately affected by the physical space she no longer took up.

"I keep thinking about Roberta's last hours. When I left her that morning, she was still in bed but awake so she knew I kissed her and heard me say, 'I love you.'" Dr. Krause wiped a tear from his cheek.

"When I read in her letter that what bothered her most about dying was leaving you, I understood how fortunate she was to have gone through her life with a man she loved so much."

Deborah still felt cheated at how little time she and Dov had had together. Yet she knew that even if they had been blessed with thirty-five years like the Krauses, she would have felt it wasn't enough.

"Leigh Goldsmith has tried to turn Roberta's beautiful letter into a suicide note." Dr. Krause turned his hands into fists and pounded them against each other.

"I can't fathom the extent of your anger," Deborah said.

Dr. Krause nodded.

"As a psychologist, how would you advise someone hurting the way you do?"

"If we can get this matter settled, I won't need to see a colleague."

"I've spoken to Tom Johnson. It's not going to happen that fast. The police will talk to members of Roberta's committee and likely interview Jerry Evans and perhaps his wife."

"I gave them the letter his wife wrote to Roberta."

"Why do you think she never showed it to you?"

"Didn't want me to worry. Yet she kept it which tells me she was concerned about it."

"I understand Mrs. Evans got ill during the trial. Do you think Roberta might have felt bad for her and, after getting the letter, met with her?"

"If so, she never told me." Dr. Krause smiled. "That was Roberta. If she thought I wouldn't approve of something, she did it without mentioning to me."

"You said she was in bed when you left. She was supposed to have lunch with Tom Johnson and me but canceled because she wasn't feeling well. Yet she was in the middle of taking a walk when the thunderstorm suddenly came up."

"She was suffering from a complete lack of appetite, making eating lunch a problem. Though I suspect…"

"What?"

Dr. Krause looked sheepish. "She might have wanted you and Tom to have lunch alone."

Deborah felt herself blush.

"But it may have been her lack of appetite."

Needing to switch subjects and still thinking about the call from Dr. Wright's office, Deborah said, "Your recommending that Isaac see Dr. Wright seems to be working. Isaac has already visited him twice."

"I'm glad."

"He wants to meet with me privately when I bring Isaac in next. I hope that's routine."

Dr. Krause hesitated. "Could be, probably is."

Deborah, though disappointed that Dr. Krause hadn't given her more reassurance, said, "Of course. I'm a mother. Worry comes with the territory."

***

Walking to her car, Deborah thought about Roberta and Jerry Evans' wife. If the two had met, she could picture Roberta logically explaining to Mrs. Evans why she had testified, that she held no personal animus against Jerry, and therefore, Mrs. Evans should bear none towards her. If that were the case, once a second trial was scheduled, Mrs. Evans would know that nothing she said would stop Roberta from testifying again.

What didn't fit Roberta's unremitting rational outlook was hoping Deborah, a rabbi, and Tom, who wasn't Jewish, would become a couple. Not that it mattered. Except for her rabbinical duties, Deborah planned to concentrate only on Isaac. She'd sensed that Dr. Krause had tried to hide his surprise when she'd mentioned Dr. Wright wanted to meet with her after just two sessions with Isaac. Did he suspect the psychologist wanted to discuss a major issue? She would know soon enough.

Tomorrow she and Isaac were going to Dr. Wright's office.

Chapter Twenty-Three

Someone was following her.

Deborah's uneasy feeling began shortly after she started driving. She decided at the last moment to turn left instead of right so she could stop at the grocery store. The car behind her also changed lanes.

When she parked, the other vehicle pulled in next to her. The driver got out and tapped on her window.

Leigh Goldsmith.

Deborah opened her window. "You frightened me. I didn't know who was following me."

"Let me in." Leigh moved to the passenger side of the car as Deborah unlocked the door.

"Don't ever do that again," Deborah said.

"If you'd give me your cell phone number, I wouldn't have to."

"You know that's limited to Isaac, Margo and his school."

"I'm the one who has the right to be angry."

"Why?"

"I saw you leaving Roberta's house."

"Of course, I was there. Dr. Krause is in mourning."

Leigh tapped her silver polished fingernails against the dash. "He's turning you against me. You don't want to hear my side."

"If you want to talk about the accident, I have some questions."

"Like what?"

"You thought someone might have pushed Roberta in front of your car. Why?"

Leigh stopped tapping and folded her arms across her chest. "It happened fast, but it seemed like the front of her body came first, like would happen if someone had pushed her in front of the car."

Deborah nodded.

"Wait. My attorney told me not to discuss the accident with anyone. Are you trying to trick me?"

Deborah shook her head. "You can't believe that."

"He also told me to go to the anniversary celebration meetings. I should be in charge now that Roberta's gone. He said people need to see that as an innocent person, I don't hide."

Deborah suspected the reason he wanted Leigh at the meetings was the hope her presence would intimidate the other women into not speaking against her during their police interviews.

"I'm sorry. I wouldn't have asked about the accident if I'd known about your attorney's advice."

Deborah exited her car and when Leigh did, too, she locked the door and headed to the supermarket, still feeling unnerved by the encounter.

***

Deborah put two bags of groceries on the kitchen table and unloaded their contents into her refrigerator and pantry. Isaac wasn't home, likely having gone out for pizza with the team after basketball practice.

She kept thinking about why Leigh believed Roberta could have been pushed in front of her car. The police investigating the accident might have been able to tell from the way Roberta fell whether that was a good possibility.

Deborah took Officer Lana McKee's card from her purse. Though unlikely she'd be in her office this late, Deborah punched in her number.

She picked up after one ring.

"It's Deborah Stein. You gave me your card when you visited me at the synagogue. You're working late."

"You know the expression. 'There's no rest for the wicked or the weary.'"

Deborah laughed. "I put you in the weary category."

"Do you have some information?"

"Leigh Goldsmith mentioned that though she can't be sure of what she saw, it seemed as though the front of Roberta's body is what she glimpsed first which is why she had the sense she might have been pushed. I was wondering if the position of the body made that likely."

"The good Samaritans moved the body so we couldn't judge."

"The good Samaritans?"

"The neighbors who were leaving their house as it happened. They're both doctors who moved the body as they tried to determine if she was alive and what aid they could give. The wife is the one who thought she might have seen someone fleeing the scene."

Deborah remembered Reverend Williams telling her that two of his congregants, both physicians, had moved near her neighborhood but still drove to his church every Sunday.

"Are you talking about the Scotts?" Deborah asked.

"That's their names. How do you know them?"

"I'm friends with Reverend Williams, and he's mentioned them."

"I'm not criticizing them. They were right to do whatever they could, though at that point she was beyond saving."

After the phone call, Deborah considered all the information the Scotts could provide. Tomorrow she'd get in touch with Reverend Williams and ask him to smooth the way for her to talk to them.

Chapter Twenty-Four

"Deborah, you made my day by calling."

No wonder she was so fond of Reverend Williams.

"How did your wife like the bracelet?"

"She said in all our years of marriage, she'd never seen me display such good taste. I confessed it was your influence. Was your mother happy with her gift?"

"Yes."

"We need to go shopping together more often."

Deborah laughed. "I agree."

"What can I do for you?"

"Remember how you mentioned your church members, the Scotts?"

"Yes, they moved not that far from you. You're not trying to poach them for your synagogue, are you?"

Deborah pictured Reverend Williams' impish grin as he spoke.

"It turns out they moved on the street where Roberta Krause, one of my members, lived. They tried to help her when she was hit by a car."

"Sounds like them. Is Ms. Krause okay?"

"She died."

"I'm sorry."

"I'd like to talk to them. Could you see if they'd be willing to let me come by?"

"How lovely. You want to thank them."

"That and…"

"Yes?"

"I'm also going to ask them what they observed. The vehicle that hit Roberta was driven by another synagogue member who considered Roberta a kind of enemy. When questions were raised about whether this was an accident, the driver claimed Roberta either jumped in front of her or was pushed. It's tearing the congregation apart."

"You've got your hands full. You think it's possible someone pushed her, meaning to kill her?"

"I do. That's why I'm anxious to know what the Scotts saw."

"I'll get them in touch with you, but only if you promise to be careful."

"What do you mean?"

"Deborah, you and I don't have the skills to go after a killer, and we'd be amiss to think we could protect ourselves if one came after us. If you learn anything, you need to go to the police, not pursue this yourself."

"I hear you."

"I'll take that as a promise and ask them to get in touch with you."

***

After her call to Reverend Williams, Deborah left her office and picked Isaac up at school for his appointment with Dr. Wright.

He entered the car, grunted a greeting and was about to put buds in his ears, when Deborah said, "Please don't. Let's talk."

Isaac looked straight ahead and said nothing.

"How was your day?"

"Fine."

"Anything special happen at school?"

"No."

"Who did you hang out with?"

"The usual."

"Some of the guys on the basketball team?"

"Yeah."

"I spoke to Reverend Williams this morning."

A faint smile. "I hope he speaks at shul again. His talks are interesting."

"I'm happy to hear your suggestions on how I can improve mine."

Another grunt. When Isaac went to put his ear buds in, Deborah didn't stop him. Silence accompanied the rest of their drive.

Soon after they arrived at Dr. Wright's, the psychologist greeted them in the waiting area.

"Sometimes parents need advice," Dr. Wright told Isaac, "so I'm going to talk to your mom for a few minutes."

Deborah followed Dr. Wright and sat down on his office couch. He took the chair across from her as he had at their first meeting. She hoped all he wanted to do was give her advice.

"I'm the son of a minister so I have a sense of what it's like to be the child of clergy. Isaac has the added burden of being the son of a war hero."

"His father was never a burden to anyone. To the contrary, he was the kind of man who lifted our burdens."

"You're making my point. Imagine how difficult it is to have idealized parents. How hard it must be for Isaac to live up to what his parents represent."

"I've not asked him to or expected him to be perfect."

"Of course not. The circumstances of his birth have made him do that to himself and to be unhappy with himself for not living up to what he wants to be."

"How can I help him?"

"Don't put any added pressure on him."

"I try not to."

"Of course."

Deborah told herself not to be defensive, but it was hard.

"We'll both do the best we can for Isaac. However, I want you to know that I may decide he needs an anti-depressant. If so, he'll have to see a psychiatrist who can prescribe them."

"How likely is that?"

"I'll know after the next few visits. I'm raising the possibility now to give you time to consider it. I've asked my secretary to give you some information about anti-depressants and adolescents. I won't recommend it unless I feel strongly he needs them."

"What's the downside to his taking them?"

"Some studies indicate an increase in suicidal thoughts and behavior in adolescents who use them, but sometimes if they don't take them, the danger is greater."

"Dear God, not again."

"Isaac's attempted suicide before?"

"No, thank God. Poor Joel, my first boyfriend." Deborah took a deep breath. "He was the same age as Isaac is now. Hung himself. So many blamed me." Deborah stared into the distance.

"Some people blamed you for his suicide?"

"We were supposed to go to a dance. I got violently ill that afternoon – vomiting, diarrhea and had to back out. The next morning his mother found him. I can't tell you how many times I've thought about our last conversation. I don't remember him sounding upset, but then I was so sick I just wanted to get off the phone. He must have sensed that."

"What a terrible experience for you."

"It got worse. At school the gossip was that I hadn't been sick, that he knew I just didn't want to go out with him, and that's why he did it."

"You understand that's ridiculous."

"Now as an adult I accept it wasn't my fault, but things were so bad then that my parents sent me to an eight week sleep away camp far from home." Deborah paused. "It worked. By the time I returned no one was talking about Joel anymore. But I still think about him."

"Isaac is not Joel. You've sought help for your son. We're going to make the right decisions about his care."

Deborah looked at the man across from her, sitting at the edge of his chair, and prayed that together they could do that.

Chapter Twenty-Five

Deborah didn't try to engage Isaac in conversation as they drove home from Dr. Wright's office. She was mired in self-castigating thoughts. What kind of mother doesn't recognize depression in her own son? The signs were there. Isaac slept a lot, was frequently uncommunicative and, except for school and the basketball team, didn't spend time with friends. She'd been too young all those years ago to see the signs in Joel, but she had no excuse as a mother and as an adult for thinking she was dealing with normal adolescent behavior with Isaac.

She'd considered how difficult it was for Isaac to be the son of a rabbi but had never thought about the effect of having a father like Dov. As much as Deborah had loved her husband, that love had been magnified by his early and heroic death. She'd thought telling Isaac about his father's feats would make him feel less fatherless – that Dov would seem like a presence in Isaac's life. Instead she'd given her son an impossible role model to live up to.

A more realistic role model was Deborah's father. While his ethics were impeccable, he was imperfect in many ways. He had no athletic ability which Isaac tried to remedy without success, told terrible jokes which his grandson found hilarious and impressed Isaac with his ability to burp on demand. Being with Grandpa always cheered Isaac up. As much as he and her mother had avoided visiting Houston where they would have to recognize Deborah as a rabbi, if she told them how Isaac and she needed them, they would come.

Having a plan of action inspired Deborah to engage Isaac in conversation. She looked over to the passenger seat and saw him with his math book open in his lap.

"It's almost dinner time. Where shall we go to eat?"

"You don't want to cook?"

"Tell me what you want and I'll make it, or you can pick a restaurant."

"Spaghetti with meat balls."

Deborah added garlic bread and salad to the meal she prepared. When she and Isaac were seated at the table, she said, "Purim's almost here, and it's such a fun holiday I thought we should ask Grandma and Grandpa to come to Houston to celebrate with us."

Isaac grinned. "Grandpa will wear some outrageous costume at services."

"That's a time his kind of silliness is encouraged."

"Do you think they'll come?"

"If we both let them know how much we want them to."

"Let me talk to Grandpa. I'm his favorite."

"That would be great."

"I've got to study for my math test now. I'll call them tomorrow."
"Sure."

Deborah smiled. Maybe she wasn't a complete failure as a mother.

Deborah cleaned up the kitchen and listened to her cell phone messages. Margo's assured her all had gone well while she was away from her office and mentioned that a Dr. Patricia Scott had phoned to say she and her husband would be happy to meet with the rabbi and had left their number which Margo recited.

With Isaac busy studying for his math test, Deborah called to find out if tonight would be a good time for the Scotts to meet with her.

***

Deborah drove her car onto the circular drive in front of the Scotts' red brick one-story home. A dark complexioned woman, her black hair in a bun, opened the door and introduced herself as Patricia Scott. Her husband, whose darker hued skin was set off by gray sideburns, joined her in the foyer. Both looked to be in their fifties with the physiques of people who exercised regularly.

Following introductions, the couple led Deborah into their den, the walls of which were decorated with abstract paintings in primary colors while the end tables had photos of the Scotts with George and Barbara Bush as well as other Republican luminaries.

The couple motioned Deborah to one of the beige leather chairs that surrounded a square game table before sitting themselves.

"I remember you from when you spoke at our church about the relationship between Dr. King and Rabbi Heschel," Patricia said. "I'd seen that iconic picture of the two of them marching together in Selma, but I hadn't known they were such good friends that Rabbi Heschel delivered a eulogy at Dr. King's funeral. I especially liked your examples of how the Book of Exodus played an important role in the speeches and writings of both men."

"Thank you. Reverend Williams spoke at our synagogue where he was a big hit. Who can help but be crazy about him?"

"He's very fond of you, so, of course, we agreed when he said you wanted to talk to us," Arthur said.

"First I want to thank you for the aid you rendered to Roberta Krause. She was one of my congregants. I sorely miss her, but knowing you did all you could for her brings me comfort."

"We both thought she was dead when we got to her, but we tried cardiac resuscitation none the less," Arthur said.

"Terribly tragic," Patricia added.

"What's added to the tragedy is the question of whether it was an accident," Deborah said.

"We figured there was a problem by the way the police questioned us." Arthur pursed his lips. "We explained we'd come out of the house to try to find our cat which was probably moments after it happened."

"Because of the rain, I had a hood over my head which is why I could only give a vague description of someone I saw hurrying away. Seemed like a tall thin guy," Patricia added.

"By the time I got to Patricia, she'd already turned the victim over. We started CPR but soon realized it was useless."

"Useless. That describes the driver. She kept saying, 'I can't believe this is happening to me.' I had to remind her to call 911."

A calico cat walked into the room and went to Arthur who picked her up and put her on his lap.

Deborah turned to Patricia. "Was there anything about the way the body was lying when you got to her that made you consider how the accident happened?"

"I was only concerned about trying to save her. Later when I thought about seeing someone who hadn't tried to help but instead took off, I wondered if we'd been at the scene of a murder."

Chapter Twenty-Six

Thoughts of someone fleeing the accident scene kept Deborah awake.

Even though Patricia Scott had described the person as tall and thin, which seemed to rule out Jerry Evans, she'd said her rain hood had affected her view. Besides, Tom had told Deborah how unreliable eye witness testimony was.

Assuming Patricia's description was somewhat accurate, Jerry's wife was the more likely suspect. And she'd written to Roberta which meant she knew where she lived.

Deborah considered Tom's cautionary advice that the person who left the scene might have been a witness who didn't want to become involved.

Deborah's falling asleep late resulted in her waking up after Isaac did. She walked into the kitchen to find him pouring a second helping of Cheerios into his bowl. His open math book was on the table.

"Ready for your test?"

"Yeah, and when it's over I'm going to ask Grandma and Grandpa to come for Purim."

Deborah couldn't take the chance her parents would turn Isaac down so as soon as she arrived at the synagogue, she called her father.

When she heard his voice, she pictured him with his legs, crossed at the ankles, resting on his desk while his office chair was in a semi-reclining position. She suspected that when his phone rang, he'd removed one of the cigars he chomped on and rested it on the edge of that desk.

"Hi, Dad."

"Deborah, is anything wrong?"

"Can't a girl call her father even if nothing's wrong? Besides, Mom's always out volunteering while most days I can catch you at your office."

"Isaac's fine, too?"

"He's going to invite you to come to Houston for Purim."

Deborah's father didn't reply.

"He'll be devastated if you turn him down." Deborah heard the catch in her voice which meant her father had as well.

"We want to see you both. It's just that…"

"Purim starts on a Sunday night. You could spend the Sabbath in Pittsburgh and fly to Houston Sunday morning."

Deborah felt sure her father understood her meaning. That way he and her mother wouldn't have to watch their rabbi daughter conduct Sabbath services.

"I'm sorry we're not more supportive. Your brother Jacob has become ultra-Orthodox which puts a lot of pressure on us, especially your mother."

Deborah sighed. Her folks adored her brother's seven children who lived in Pittsburgh. They knew that if they weren't as religiously observant as her brother was, he might consider them a bad influence on his brood and limit the time they could spend with them.

"You and Mother won't be here on the Sabbath, and you can drive to the synagogue on Purim. Talk to Mom, and if you envision any problem, tell me, and if we can't solve it, I'll discourage Isaac from inviting you. I'd rather he not ask you than be rejected."

"We love you both. If for any reason your mother can't make it, I'll come myself."

"Thanks, Dad."

"Is Isaac having problems?" her father asked.

"Nothing like in California, but enough that he's seeing a psychologist."

"You told the psychologist about what happened there?"

"No, I thought it would be better if Isaac told him," Deborah said.

"Has he?"

"I doubt it."

"You might have to reconsider if Isaac takes too long to confide in him," her father advised.

"I know."

"What happened in California was not your fault."

Deborah ignored his remark.

If she hadn't been so careless, if she'd paid more attention to the paperwork, if she hadn't made Isaac feel as though he was not her priority…

She knew she deserved the guilt she felt.

Chapter Twenty-Seven

The rabbi assumed Ann Kaplan had asked for an appointment to talk about her daughter Mindy's upcoming engagement to Sam Krause and the appropriate time to wait for the wedding.

When Ann came in chewing her lower lip, Deborah realized they would be discussing a less joyful subject. She suggested they go to the rose garden, having found that setting to be soothing.

Ann was as short as Deborah but weighed a hundred pounds more. She was wearing a green flared dress which made her appear to be walking in a tent.

With effort Ann bent down to smell the roses. "These are exquisite."

"Roberta tended them."

"She was always lovely to Mindy. Sam's heartbroken she won't be at their wedding."

"But she knew how happy they were," Deborah said.

When the women sat down, Ann and her apparel took up most of the swing, leaving Deborah squeezed into one end.

"I came to talk to you about Roberta's death. Leigh Goldsmith is my dearest friend, and I can't bear the accusations people are making about her."

Ann's eyes filled with tears. "You can't imagine how good she was to me…to our whole family when my husband Ted had his cancer surgery. Mindy was four and her brother Jonas three. Mindy and Jenny Goldsmith were already best friends."

Ann took a tissue out of her dress pocket and dabbed her eyes. "Leigh picked up my children after pre-school every day and brought them to her house where she watched them and fed them until I came home from visiting Ted at the hospital. When he died, she was there for me."

Ann raised her voice. "I know she's not perfect. People complain she always wants her own way. Well, most of us do. She's just honest enough to say so."

Deborah picked up a box of Kleenex from under the swing and handed it to Ann who removed one before continuing. "When Leigh feels attacked, she lashes out. She's emotional when she should be rational. The opposite of Roberta, who was rational when you'd expect her to be emotional."

Deborah nodded.

"But, Rabbi, whatever Leigh's done to offend anyone, she doesn't deserve to have them accusing her of being a murderer."

Deborah put her arm around Ann. "I've recently reminded some members of the horror of gossip. I gave a sermon about it less than six months ago, but perhaps it's time for another."

"I know you can't stop it, but it makes me feel better to talk to you."

"Since you and Leigh are close, you could remind her how painful it is for the Krauses when she says Roberta may have intentionally jumped in front of her car."

"Roberta was facing a horrible death."

"Ann, you can't believe…"

"I'm not criticizing Roberta. I know how Ted suffered. If I were in that situation, I'm not sure what I'd do."

***

Margo walked into Deborah's office. "How did your visit with Mrs. Kaplan go?"

"She had nice things to say about how helpful Leigh was when she needed her."

"I've heard the devil is good to his mother."

Deborah chuckled.

"The bad news is?"

"She thinks it's possible Roberta committed suicide and wouldn't blame her if she did."

"You sure have a divided congregation."

"Maybe if I could come up with the perfect sermon."

"Good luck with that."

"My dad might have a suggestion. He's a mediator as well as an attorney, and he's coming for Purim."

"Great. What about your mom?"

"She'll probably want to spend Purim with my brother and his family like always."

Margo walked behind Deborah's desk and gave the rabbi a hug. "We can honor our father and mother and still resent the way they favor a sibling."

***

Dear Miriam,

What's wrong with me? I'm forty-five and still haven't recovered from my brother's birth. When I invited my folks to come for Purim, the only reason my dad accepted is because he's concerned about Isaac. I'm sure my brother and/or his kids will need something from my mother so she won't come. Sometimes I think Jacob became ultra-Orthodox and had all those kids just to have a hold on our parents. He's even taken away any pride they might have had in my becoming a rabbi by convincing them that as a woman I shouldn't be one. You know the joke – How long did Cain hate his brother? As long as he was Abel. Pretty terrible for a rabbi to admit that she can't overcome jealousy.

Love, Deborah

Dearest Deborah,

What you're really admitting is that even though you're a rabbi, you have human emotions. How shocking! It's your imperfections that make you empathetic when others seek your guidance. Enjoy your visit with your dad. I'm sure you'll feel his love then.

Your very loving friend,
Miriam

***

Upon seeing a smiling Isaac when she entered their home, Deborah said, "Your math test must have gone well."

"Yeah, and Grandpa's coming for Purim. Grandma can't make it. She promised to take your brother's brats to a Purim carnival."

Deborah ignored the name calling and instead considered how to make sure Isaac didn't feel bad about her mother's upcoming absence.

His next words relieved her of that burden.

"Worked out perfectly. I get to be with Grandpa and don't have to put up with Grandma's millions of questions."

Deborah reached up and tousled her son's hair. She couldn't wait for all the good things her dad's visit would bring.

At that moment she forgot her grandmother's favorite expression.

"Man plans. God laughs."

Chapter Twenty-Eight

"Rabbi, do you have time to talk to me?"

Deborah turned around and saw Ida Marks, an eighty-year-old congregant, rushing down the synagogue hallway towards her. The rabbi stopped and assured Ida, "You can slow down. I'm waiting for you."

Ida, breathing a little too hard for Deborah's comfort, caught up with her and let the rabbi guide her to her office where they sat next to each other in front of the desk.

Ida patted her short white hair and smoothed her beige skirt. "I took very seriously your sermon about the dangers of gossip though I wasn't as successful as I would have liked about completely stopping."

"I realized how much you were trying when you came to see me about your concerns that talking to the police about Roberta and Leigh would constitute gossip."

"When they interviewed me, one a tall black woman and the other a shorter white man…" Ida reached into her large brown purse, dug out two business cards and read them. "Officer Lana McKee and Officer George Stanford."

Deborah nodded. If they were still investigating, it meant they hadn't turned the accident over to the homicide division.

"I tried to do what you said and only tell them what I saw and heard at our gala planning meetings and not attribute motives to anyone."

"Good."

"I said I tried." Ida reached back into her purse and pulled out a handkerchief which she twisted as she held it between her hands.

"They kept asking me what I thought each woman really meant. I got scared. I didn't want to get in trouble with the police."

"Of course not."

"Or they would say, 'Did Leigh seem angry?' I couldn't lie to them so I had to tell them she did. They wanted to know if I thought Leigh hated Roberta." Ida smiled at the rabbi. "I told them what you said to – that I couldn't attribute motives to anyone."

"Good."

Ida wrapped the twisted handkerchief around one hand. "Most of it wasn't good. Most of it was me having to admit that Leigh got upset every time Roberta disagreed with her."

"You did the best anyone could have."

"You really think so?"

"I do." Deborah tamped down the anger she felt towards the police for picking on this elderly woman. If she let her feelings come out, Ida might think they were directed at her.

When Ida next spoke, Deborah realized the eighty year old hadn't been singled out.

"The other women I talked to said the police treated them the same."

"While we don't understand, the police must feel it's the best way to do their job."

Ida untwisted her handkerchief and returned it to her purse before adding, "They asked the oddest question about Roberta."

"What was that?"

"They wanted to know if she ever talked about committing suicide."

"That is odd." Deborah tried to maintain a placid expression.

"I told them that was ridiculous."

"Good for you."

Ida stood. "Thanks for listening."

"Come by my office any time. May I walk you to your car?"

"Goodness, no. I'm needed at the gift shop. I volunteer there three days a week."

After Ida left, Deborah tried to digest everything she'd heard and figure out where the investigation was going. She was at a loss.

Tom could help her piece it all together.

She heard his voice after two rings. "Deborah, nice to hear from you."

"How did you know it was me?"

"The synagogue's number showed up on my phone."

Deborah laughed. "I've been calling you too much if you can recognize that number."

"Not at all."

"I can use your expertise again."

"Lunch today?"

"You pick the place. Don't worry. I can always find something to eat."

"Giovanelli's at noon?"

"Perfect."

Chapter Twenty-Nine

Tom's grin indicated he was happy to see her. Deborah smiled in return. Though she was a little early, he'd arrived at Giovanelli's before her. Even dressed casually in a beige pullover and blue slacks, he looked stylish. Not having known that morning that she'd be meeting him, Deborah was in her usual uniform of a white blouse and black skirt.

At Tom's request, the hostess seated them at a corner table towards the back of the restaurant.

"You're still worried about ruining my reputation with Mel Freed," Deborah teased.

"As a recently retired defense attorney, I know to keep away from possibly incriminating witnesses."

"That's the expertise I'm here for."

The waiter, his gray hair in a pompadour, rushed to their table. "Mr. Johnson, I'm happy to see you. It's been too long." He gave Deborah an appraising look. "And the lovely lady?"

Deborah held out her hand to shake his but instead the waiter brushed it with his lips. "I'm Deborah Stein, and you are?"

The gentleman responded with a slight bow. "Carmen Giovanelli." He addressed Tom. "I would be honored to prepare your favorite veal dish for you and your guest."

"I'm in the mood for your special vegetable pizza."

"Sounds delicious," Deborah said.

"And would the lovely lady care for a glass of wine?"

"None for me. I have to go back to work. You go ahead, Tom."

"Oh, he never drinks," Carmen said.

Tom watched the owner walk away. He gazed at Deborah. His chest heaved. "My grandfather was an alcoholic. My dad knew that can run in families so he never drank and urged me and my older brother Ed to abstain. Ed didn't listen. He stole from my parents, sold his clothes to buy liquor and became an underground street fighter to get money. He'd come home with a black eye or a bloody nose or a broken arm. That was enough to convince me to listen to my dad."

"It must have been difficult growing up in a home where you always had to worry about what your brother might do next."

"The least stressful times were the three when he was in different rehabs. When they all failed, my parents considered throwing him out but they couldn't bear thinking of him sleeping on the streets. He eventually went to jail for a DWI. He'd found the keys and had taken my parents' car."

"Is he out now?"

"Probably has been for years, but fortunately he's never contacted me. I understand alcoholism is a disease, but after what Ed put my parents and me through I couldn't have him near Denise or Courtney. Though Denise was so kindhearted that she would have let him into our lives if he'd tried."

"She sounds like a really special person."

"She drew people to her. Carmen was so fond of her that he came to her funeral. It had been too hard to come here without her, but then I thought about how you could eat the vegetable pizza she and I both loved, so I suggested it."

"It was a great idea. Roberta spoke of your devotion to her when Denise was so ill. I'd like to share something Roberta told me."

Tom leaned over his side of the table.

"If it's too painful, please stop me," Deborah said.

"Okay."

"I don't believe Roberta committed suicide, but there's one thing that's bothering me." Deborah hesitated. "When Roberta talked about how much your late wife suffered and how difficult that was for you, she commented that if Denise had realized what was going to happen, to spare you, she could have done something about it."

"I can understand why that disturbed you. I was the one who stupidly encouraged Denise to try any available, even experimental treatment. I didn't want to lose her. In retrospect, early hospice care would have been the more humane solution. I was just too selfish."

"I'm sorry I brought it up. I should have realized Roberta had hospice care, not suicide, in mind."

"It could be either, and don't feel bad about raising the topic. I need to talk about it."

"Your wife must have been comforted to have lived her last months knowing you loved her so much you wanted to try anything to keep her." Deborah reached over the table and put her hand on Tom's. When she looked up, she saw Carmen carrying their pizza on a tray.

Deborah quickly removed her hand and felt a blush creeping over her cheeks.

Carmen put the pizza and plates on the table. Before leaving he said in a stage whisper, "Glad to see you with such fine company."

Deborah's blush deepened.

"Subtlety is not Carmen's strong suit," Tom said.

"I guess he's your version of Mel Freed," Deborah whispered.

They laughed and helped themselves to pizza.

When Deborah saw Tom picking up his slice, she put down her fork and knife and adopted his method.

After she took a few bites, Tom said, "You've got some sauce on your cheek."

"Yikes!"

Tom smiled. "Don't worry. It looks good on you."

Deborah took her napkin and dabbed at her cheek until Tom's nod indicated she'd succeeded.

"You must have brought up the issue of the outside possibility of Roberta's committing suicide for a reason," Tom said.

"One of my congregants told me the police asked her if Roberta had ever spoken about committing suicide, and she replied she hadn't. But I wondered if Roberta had made other questionable comments, and if the police heard about them, what they might do."

"They'd have too little to go on to make a suicide accusation. But they'd use the information to convince themselves it wasn't foul play on the part of Leigh Goldsmith or some unknown person and would end their investigation."

Deborah and Tom helped themselves to more pizza.

"I met with the Kings, the two doctors who tried to save Roberta. They mentioned Leigh kept saying, 'I can't believe this is happening to me.' Besides sounding self-centered, it seems like something a person would say if she were surprised at what had happened as opposed to someone who had planned to have her vehicle hit Roberta."

"Or it could be someone who planned that reaction to reinforce the idea it was an accident."

"True. You can see how my congregants can take any fact and use it the way it agrees with their theory about Roberta's death. It's causing a lot of dissention. I'm hoping my dad will think of a way I can help keep the peace. He's coming for Purim."

"I have a book about the Jewish holidays, but I haven't read about Purim yet."

"I can give you the short version."

"First have another slice of pizza."

Though she almost never ate three pieces of pizza, this one was so tasty with its thin crust, spice laden tomato sauce and generous portions of cheese and vegetables that Deborah complied.

Tom took the last slice, commenting, "Five is my limit."

Deborah finished eating and wiped her fingers and face with her napkin.

"The King of Persia banished his wife Vashti because she refused to dance naked in front of his friends. His second wife had to be the most beautiful woman in the kingdom. She turned out to be the Jewess Esther, cousin of Mordecai. Haman, the king's second in command, wanted everyone to bow down to him. Mordecai refused, saying he only bowed down to God. Haman convinced the king, who didn't know his wife was Jewish, to sign an edict allowing the slaughter of all the Jews in the kingdom. Esther risked her life to go to the king without his summoning her so she could plead for the lives of her co-religionists. The Jews were saved and Haman and his sons were hanged on the gallows he'd planned for Mordecai."

"A happy ending."

"We celebrate raucously. We read the story from a scroll called the *megillah* and every time we hear Haman's name, we drown it out with noisemakers. We eat triangular filled pastries, which represent the hat Haman wore. Almost everyone comes in costume with many dressing as one of the story's characters and others come disguised any way they want."

"Sounds like fun. Do you have to be Jewish to attend?"

"You're welcome to join us. Most of the boys and men come as the king or as Mordecai. Most girls and women come dressed as Queen Esther but Roberta always came as Vashti whom she admired for refusing an immoral order and paying the price." Deborah sighed. "I really miss her."

A short wiry middle aged man with slick backed black hair walked by, turned around and came over to their table. Ignoring Deborah, he greeted Tom. "I thought that was you, you lucky retired guy. I've been wanting to talk to you."

Tom pulled a card from his wallet. "My cell phone number's here. Call at your convenience."

The intruder sat down. "This will only take a couple minutes."

"Deborah, this is Maurice Dunham. Maurice, my guest is Rabbi Stein."

Maurice turned to Deborah. "Rabbi? I didn't know you people allowed women to do that sort of thing."

"I'm proof we do."

"Can't imagine you hanging out with religious types, Tom. Retirement must have gotten to you."

"We could have a good conversation if you called. How about this afternoon?"

"Guess you heard I'm representing Jerry Evans in his new trial."

"I did."

"I'm going to win this one. Talk about good luck. The witness who got him convicted last time is dead. A car ran her over."

Deborah tapped Maurice on the shoulder. When he turned towards her, Deborah's words spurted out of her. "Was it good luck or a good push from someone with a motive to have her dead?"

"What?"

Deborah stared at him.

"If you're implying something about my client…"

"Or someone close to him."

"That's why people get sued for slander."

"There was a witness to Roberta Krause's death."

"There was?"

Tom stood, towering over Maurice. "Please leave."

"With pleasure." Maurice disappeared as quickly as he'd appeared.

Deborah took a deep breath. "I'm sorry. I embarrassed you in front of a former colleague. I usually think before I talk. I don't know what got into me."

"It's my fault. I know how nasty Maurice is. I should have tried harder to shoo him away before he got near you."

"How can anyone call a death 'lucky' especially when he's talking about Roberta. Still, I have no excuse for what I did."

"It's fine. It's just that…"

"Yes?"

"I hope he doesn't think you're the witness."

Chapter Thirty

"I need Maurice's phone number," Deborah said.

"No." Tom spoke firmly and with a slightly raised voice.

Carmen, who was headed towards their table, reversed course.

"Nothing good can come of your calling him," Tom said.

"As horrible as his remark was, I had no right to make the accusation I did. I have to apologize to him, and, if he tells Jerry Evans and his wife, apologize to them."

"Maurice is spiteful, Jerry is desperate and his wife has severe emotional problems. You can't get involved with them."

Deborah had never heard Tom speak so vehemently.

"I have to ask for forgiveness," Deborah insisted.

"I've read enough about Judaism to know you can wait until the Day of Atonement. That's months away. By that time the trial will be over and Maurice and Jerry will be in a mood to forgive you."

"I don't have an excuse to wait."

"Kindness. That's your excuse."

"I'm not following you."

"Rabbi Telushkin's book on Jewish ethics. He writes about the importance of kindness. Be kind to me and wait to call him."

"That's what I get for recommending a book to an attorney."

"You'll wait?"

Convinced Tom wouldn't drop the subject until she agreed, Deborah said, "Okay."

"I'm ordering cannoli. One bite will cheer you up."

Before Deborah could taste dessert, her cell phone rang.

"What's happened, Margo?"

"Mindy Kaplan called. Her mom Ann's in Methodist hospital. She was too upset to give details."

"Let her know I'm on my way."

Deborah told Tom she had to go, apologized and headed towards the door.

Tom watched Deborah as she hurried from the restaurant. She had to honor her agreement to have no contact with Jerry Evans, his wife or his attorney until after Jerry's new trial. Tom had first-hand knowledge of how desperate Jerry was and how emotionally fragile his wife was. It had never been clearer than when they were waiting for the jury's verdict in Jerry's trial.

***

"We want to be nearby so when I get the call the jury has come in, we can get to the courthouse quickly." Tom spoke as he shepherded Jerry Evans and his wife into a coffee shop a half block from the courthouse.

Jerry, short and brawny, had his arm around his taller wife who had a waif-like appearance. She kept muttering, "He's innocent. He's innocent."

Tom led them to a corner booth so their conversation wouldn't be heard.

When Mrs. Evans' began speaking more loudly, Jerry took her hands in his and said, "It's okay, sweetheart."

"You know he's innocent." Mrs. Evans' remark was directed at Tom.

As a good defense attorney, Tom had never asked Jerry if he was innocent. Had Jerry responded that he was guilty, Tom couldn't have put him on the stand to have him declare innocence. That would have been suborning perjury.

Jerry's testimony, trying to explain away what looked like embezzlement, was no match for Roberta Krause's whose charts and numbers had likely proved it beyond a reasonable doubt. Tom had to prepare his client for the likelihood the jury had viewed it that way.

"We can hope that the jury finds him not guilty, but we have to understand it could go either way."

"It's because of that lying woman, isn't it?" Mrs. Evans tapped her foot.

"The problem is that she believes she's telling the truth which made her an effective witness," Tom said.

Mrs. Evans sobbed. Jerry put both arms around her, murmuring, "Shush, shush."

Tom gave her his handkerchief.

She wiped her eyes, moved her scraggly brown hair off her face and left for the ladies' room.

The waitress came by and Tom ordered three coffees.

"You think the jury's going to find me guilty, don't you?" Jerry asked.

"It's more likely than not," Tom said.

"It's all because of Roberta. No one else would have figured it out."

That was the closest Tom's client had ever come to admitting his guilt.

Jerry stroked his grey crew cut. "I'm afraid my wife won't survive if I'm in prison." His eyes filled with tears.

"Is there someone who can look in on her?" Tom asked.

"We don't have any children. Maybe her sister could, but I'm the only one who can calm her when she gets upset."

"If it comes to it, I'll request that you be sent to the Huntsville prison, it's a little more than an hour away. She'll be able to visit every weekend."

"I need time to prepare her."

"I'll request probation. It's your first offense and a white collar crime. Judge Schultz likely won't buy it, but he'll wait for a pre-sentencing report from the probation office before he makes his decision."

Jerry put his elbows on the table, entwined his fingers and rested his chin on them.

"Will anyone be watching me during that time?"

Tom leaned across the booth so that his face was almost touching Jerry's. "No matter who is or is not watching you, you must never consider running away. Fugitives get caught and get very long prison sentences. If this jury finds you guilty, we'll appeal."

"But while you're appealing, I'll be in prison, away from my wife, who needs me. You can see how much she needs me."

"You'll have time to make arrangements with her sister, with whomever else you think of."

Mrs. Evans returned to the booth. "I'd rather die than be away from you," she said to her husband.

Tom's cell phone rang.

The jury was in.

***

Tom pushed his cannoli away.

It was imperative that Deborah stay away from Jerry and his wife.

Chapter Thirty-One

Deborah parked her car and treated herself by entering Methodist Hospital through Dunn Tower. It was a hospital entrance like no other, outdoing most resort hotels. Its vastness was filled by upholstered couches and chairs and fine end tables, many sporting flower arrangements. Potted plants, some the size of small trees, were spread throughout. Marble floors added to the elegance.

One of Deborah's favorite works of art, a bronze statue of Arion riding a dolphin and playing his lyre, sat in the middle of a pool of water. The myth of Arion being kidnapped by pirates and saved by dolphins had resonated with her as a child. The sculptor Walter Hancock had depicted the last part of the story the way she'd always imagined it.

Smaller painted clay sculptures were displayed in cabinets which lined the walls.

As an added treat, an African-American gentleman in a black tuxedo sat down at the baby grand piano and began playing DeBussy's *La Mer*.

Deborah listened for a few minutes before rousing herself to go to the reception desk and find out which room Ann was in. As she suspected, it was not in the too expensive for insurance Dunn Tower.

When she arrived on Ann's floor, she saw Leigh Goldsmith and Sam Krause sitting diagonally across from each other in the visitors' waiting area. They both stood and came over to her.

"How's Ann doing?" Deborah asked.

"She fainted. They're getting her diabetes under control. Turns out she took insulin and forgot to eat," Leigh said.

"Leigh's assuming that was an accidental forgetting. In this case, she's not accusing anyone of attempted suicide," Sam said.

Leigh's face turned as red as her dress. "You don't suffer from diabetes the way you do from cancer," she hissed.

"That's why we have hospice care," Deborah said, "so our suffering is abated and we can have peaceful deaths."

"Don't you dare side with him."

All three stopped talking when they saw Mindy, her black wavy hair cascading down her back as she walked towards them. Sam rushed to embrace her. "Is everything okay with your mom?"

"Yes, thank God. Rabbi, I'm sorry I panicked when I spoke to Margo. I was afraid my mother had collapsed because she'd had a heart attack. They have her on some intravenous solution which should take care of what turned out to be dangerously low blood sugar."

Mindy stood on tiptoes and kissed Sam on the cheek. "This sweetheart dropped everything to bring me to the hospital. And, of course, as soon as Leigh heard, she rushed over."

"I'd like to see her," Leigh said.

"So would I," Sam said.

"Rabbi, if you can help me keep the peace between these two, we can all go together."

Deborah put her arm around Mindy as they walked towards Ann's room. Mindy, about to become engaged to Sam and being attached to Leigh as her mother's best friend, illustrated on an individual level what the congregation was going through on a larger level.

When Deborah and Mindy walked into Ann's room, she smiled, only to change her expression to one of concern when she saw Leigh and Sam.

"Don't worry, Mom, they promised to be on their best behavior."

Ann was as Mindy described her with an intravenous line in her arm.

"I was lucky I didn't break anything, just a few bruises on my other arm and a small gash on that hand."

Leigh and Sam stood in opposite corners of the room, like boxers waiting for the bell to ring.

After the rabbi and Ann spoke a little longer, Ann said, "I know you need to get back to the synagogue. And Sam, I appreciate your getting Mindy to me quickly, but you have to work. I'll have Leigh drive Mindy home soon. I'm pretty tired."

Deborah bent down and kissed Ann on the forehead while Sam hugged Mindy.

When they were in the hall, Sam said, "What you said about hospice care gave me an idea. I'm going to my dad's house to check it out."

***

Dr. Krause called that evening. "Rabbi, you're brilliant."

"That's nice to hear, even if it's not deserved."

"It's what you said about hospice care. Sam came over and we went through more of Roberta's papers. She was such a planner that I should have suspected. Turns out she'd arranged for hospice care. That's not what someone contemplating suicide does. I can't wait to rub Leigh's face in it."

"It's more important you tell the police officers. If they think suicide, they'll end their investigation. They need to understand how unlikely that is."

"Brilliant again."

"The credit goes to Tom Johnson. He suggested hospice care."

"I talked to him today. He calls often, has been a big help. He understands what it's like to lose a wife prematurely. He seemed embarrassed he'd invited himself to Purim services. I assured him he was welcome and that he could come with me."

"I'm glad. I bet Tom would join me in urging you to tell the police about the hospice care soon."

"Of course."

The more Deborah thought about her encounter with Jerry Evans' attorney and his gloating about Roberta's death, the more she wanted the police to look into the possibility of murder.

Chapter Thirty-Two

"I told you we'd be late," Isaac said.

"I explained I had to cover Mr. Shaw's Sunday school class. Once Grandpa gets off the plane, he has to walk to baggage and wait for his suitcase. Our timing will be fine."

While talking to her son, Deborah almost missed the ramp to the parking lot for Terminal C at Houston's George Bush Intercontinental Airport. She pulled into a space in the short term section of the lot and had barely stopped the car when Isaac jumped out.

"Wait for me."

Isaac, acting like he hadn't heard, kept going.

Deborah caught up with him at baggage claim, where he was checking the marquee to find out on which conveyor belt the suitcases from the Pittsburgh flight would come in.

As Isaac headed towards it, he said, "There he is."

Deborah's father waved. He and Isaac greeted each other with fist bumps, followed by a bear hug. The top of the older man's head came up to his grandson's chin. When the two unclenched, Grandpa said, "You get handsomer every time I see you. You know what that proves."

"What?" Isaac asked.

"You take after me."

Isaac and his grandfather bumped fists again.

"Deborah, you look lovely, as usual." Her father hugged her.

"It's because of her we're late."

"I'm sure she had a good reason. No problem since my bag hasn't arrived yet."

"I'll get it for you when it does. What color is it?"

"It's black. You'll recognize it by the huge purple ribbon Grandma tied around it."

Isaac moved to the part of the conveyor belt that was spewing out suitcases.

"Dad, you look like you've lost a few pounds."

"I'm a bit less rotund, but I've lost more hair than pounds." He bent his head, displaying a fringe of gray that stopped him from being completely bald.

"You look distinguished."

Isaac returned, wheeling his grandfather's case.

"I have our Purim costumes in there."

"What are they?" Isaac asked.

"A surprise."

"When will I see them?"

"Not until you've heard a few of my jokes."

"Oh, no," Deborah said as she led the way to the car.

"Your mother never appreciated my superb humor."

"I'm ready," Isaac said.

"Ask me about diversity."

"What's diversity?"

"De verse city I was ever in was Detroit."

Isaac's laughter pealed through the parking lot.

"Do you know what you should do if you have ringing in your ears?"

"What?"

"Don't answer."

More laughter.

"I think your grandmother must have Egyptian blood."

"Why?"

"Every time I kiss her, she says, 'Tut, Tut."

Isaac gave his grandfather a light punch on the arm. "I bet Grandma doesn't like that one."

When they arrived at the car, Isaac put his grandfather's suitcase in the trunk. Deborah assumed her father would join her in the front seat. Instead he opened the back door to sit with Isaac.

"How's mother doing?" Deborah asked.

"Fine. Feels bad she can't be here, but she promised the little ones…"

Isaac interrupted, "We have a basketball net up over the garage. You can't leave until you make ten free throws."

"If you can teach me that, I'll teach you how to burp on demand."

"Thanks, Dad. That's what I need him to learn." Deborah felt like she was dealing with two adolescent boys whenever her father and Isaac were together.

"We have to do something about your mother's lack of a sense of humor."

"It's because she's a rabbi. I don't think they're allowed to laugh."

"Enough, you guys." Deborah tried to sound exasperated, but failed.

***

When they arrived home, Isaac rolled his grandfather's suitcase to the guest room and put it on one of the twin beds.

"Let's see the costumes."

Deborah stared at the Superman outfit, complete with red boots.

"Bet you didn't know they made this in plus sizes," her father said.

"You actually plan to wear those blue tights?"

"If I wrap the cape in front of me, no one will notice my beer gut."

"You are going to be killin' it in that, Grandpa."

"And you will be killin' it in this." Deborah's father dug into his suitcase and pulled out a Batman costume. "We're super heroes!"

Isaac grabbed his gift and hugged his grandfather.

Deborah left the room to answer the phone. She tried not to sound surprised when she heard Tom's voice.

"I'm going to miss your Purim celebration tonight. I should never have invited myself."

"It'll be worth coming to see my seventy-year-old father in his Superman costume. Besides, Dr. Krause is counting on your sitting with him."

"Well…"

"I'll take that as a yes."

As soon as their conversation ended, Deborah had second thoughts about having encouraged Tom to come. Her father didn't understand that men and women could be friends without romantic entanglements. It would be best if he and Tom didn't spend time together.

Deborah assured herself there was no reason they would.

Chapter Thirty-Three

"I can't wait to show you your costume," Deborah's dad said.

Deborah had returned to the guest room to find out what her father and son wanted for lunch but now was so curious that food preparation left her mind.

"I'll give you a hint," Isaac said. "Meow."

"Close your eyes," her father said.

When Deborah opened them, she saw, laid out on a twin bed, the black pieces that were to constitute her attire for Purim services. She gazed at the jumpsuit with attached boot tops, the molded eye mask with attached headpiece, the molded belt and the gloves.

"You expect me to go as Cat Woman to the synagogue?"

"No one will know it's you," her father said.

"She's a villain," Deborah reminded him.

"She only steals from gangsters and mobsters," Isaac assured her.

"That's a relief," Deborah said.

"No one will expect you to come as someone like that. You'll fool them all."

"Dad, you can't be serious."

"I told you she'd spoil all our fun, Grandpa. Since she has to be perfect, she can only dress like someone who's perfect."

Dr. Wright's warning about how difficult it was for Isaac to deal with a rabbi mother and a deceased hero father came back to Deborah. She picked up the costume. "I can at least try it on and see if it fits."

It did, though the form fitting outfit accentuated her bust line and forced her to hold her stomach in. She wondered what Tom would think when he saw her, but quickly erased that thought from her mind.

She returned to her dad and son. "Margo told me I needed a makeover."

Isaac hugged his black clad mother. She couldn't remember the last time he'd done that.

After lunch she watched through her kitchen window as Isaac demonstrated over and over to his grandfather how to make free throws. After twenty minutes they came inside.

"Grandpa made one. Nine more to go."

"Time to try something I'm good at. Get your chess board."

Deborah, knowing the two would be occupied for a while, took a book and snuggled into a corner of the living room couch. Isaac and her dad were in the next room, playing chess on the dining table. She couldn't see them, but she could hear them. After thirty minutes, her father exclaimed, "Checkmate."

"Best of three," Isaac said.

"Just so we have time for dinner and to get into our costumes."

Isaac chuckled. "Mom doesn't need a mask. When people see that outfit, they won't believe it's her."

"Boychick," his grandfather said, using a Yiddish term of endearment. "It's hard being a rabbi. Everyone expects you to be perfect, and when you're not, they can't wait to talk about it."

"Same's true of a rabbi's son. We had to move from California because of what I did."

"It wasn't so terrible. Your mother rushed off for fear people wouldn't be understanding."

"Yeah. One guy said they should bring charges so I'd go to juvy and learn a lesson."

"That guy was a putz."

"What's a putz?"

"It's Yiddish for a prick."

Isaac roared with laughter. "Grandpa, you're the best."

"Have you told Dr. Wright what happened?"

"Not yet."

"Maybe your mother should tell him."

Isaac raised his voice. "If she did, I'd never forgive her."

Chapter Thirty-Four

"Mommy, help. It's Cat Woman." The little girl buried her face in her mother's skirt.

Deborah, who'd just walked into the synagogue with her son and father, crouched down to the child's level. "I'm not a mean Cat Woman. I'm always nice to little children."

The girl's slightly older brother, looking at Isaac, said, "It's okay. Batman's here to protect us."

Staring at Deborah's father, he added, "I didn't know Superman was fat."

"Matthew," the children's mother said, "that's not polite."

"My stomach's sticking out because Cat Woman made me a big dinner."

"She gave you food? Maybe she's not bad," the little girl said.

"You're a beautiful Queen Esther," Deborah told her. "Did you make the crown yourself?"

The little girl nodded.

"And your brother's crown tells me he's Ahasuerus, King of Persia."

The little boy's eyes widened. "I didn't know Cat Woman was Jewish."

"What do you mean?" his mother asked.

"How else would she know the Purim story?"

Deborah stood up and covered her mouth, afraid her smile would turn into a laugh.

The three super heroes were walking down the hall to the sanctuary when Deborah's father stopped in front of a wall holding ten framed needle points, each depicting a Biblical scene.

"Reminds me of your mother's needlepoint. I appreciate the skill that went into producing these."

"A member made them to celebrate the synagogue's anniversary. She turned each Bible story into a happy one."

As an example, Deborah pointed out how the scene in the Garden of Eden depicted Adam and Eve before the snake's scheme destroyed their idyll in Paradise. They were hiding behind trees, seemingly playing a game. Another was of Sarah laughing as the angel told her she and her husband would produce a child in their old age.

Deborah moved in front of her favorite. "Instead of depicting Abraham raising his knife to Isaac, this shows the father and son embracing when their ordeal ended."

Her son Isaac waved and joined a group of his classmates who were strolling by. Deborah heard one say, "Is that really your mom?"

As she and her dad entered the sanctuary and walked to the first row, she registered snippets of conversation.

"That can't be the rabbi."

"Never guessed she had that good a figure."

"Is the man she's with her boyfriend?"

Services started with the head of the Hebrew and Sunday Schools explaining that a number of fourth and fifth graders had learned to read from the *megillah* and that, as they took turns doing so, the rest of the congregation could follow in Hebrew or English in the booklets at their seats.

Everyone had a *grogger,* a noise-maker rattle. Each time Haman was mentioned in the reading, the *groggers* were used to obliterate his name. In their excitement, some of the children used them more often.

Over an hour later, the last words recited, Deborah walked up the three carpeted steps to the *bima*, the elevated platform from where she conducted services each Saturday. She took off her mask and heard reactions from, "I told you it was the rabbi," to "I can't believe it's the rabbi."

When she'd prepared her remarks, she'd been thinking of the adolescents and pre-adolescents who would be at services.

"We can learn a lot from the stars and featured players in the Purim story. Vashti stood on principle and refused to act immodestly.

Her banishment led to Esther's becoming queen which led to the Jewish people being saved. Mordechai also followed his principles and refused to bow down to Haman as he only bowed down to God. In contrast, we have King Ahasuerus who, instead of following principles, listened to so-called friends. First a group of them convinced him to banish Vashti, claiming that otherwise all the women in the kingdom would say that if the queen didn't have to follow the king's orders, none of them had to follow their husband's orders."

Women in the audience groaned.

"Next the king listened to Haman…"

Deborah had to stop and wait for the noise to end.

"Who told him the Jewish people in the kingdom weren't loyal to him and had to be destroyed. It's easy to do what our friends suggest without sticking to our principles and thinking of the consequences, which is exactly what the king did. He didn't have the courage to refuse what he should have known was wrong. With Mordechai's encouragement, Esther had the courage to risk her life by appearing before the king without being summoned, though she knew this breaking of protocol could cost her life. We understand that life is a gift from God which we only risk for the greater good, such as saving all the Jewish people in Persia, which Esther accomplished. Then there is Haman."

At the mention of his name, the *groggers* blasted again. When they stopped, Deborah continued. "There are evil people in the world, but with our principles and our courage, Purim demonstrates we can defeat them." She paused, smiled and said, "Time to eat *hamantaschen*."

The congregation streamed from the sanctuary into the social hall where tables were set up with the three cornered pastries, filled with a jam like center made of sesame seeds or prunes or cherries or apricots or chocolate.

Deborah and her father were waylaid by people complimenting her on her remarks and her outfit and those wanting to meet her dad.

She had just finished eating a chocolate filled *hamantaschen* when Dr. Krause and Tom Johnson approached. The former was wearing a crown and a purple robe. The latter sported a fake white beard. Deborah remembered Dr. Krause wearing it last year in an effort to portray Mordechai. She guessed he'd loaned it to Tom.

"Both you and the kids did a great job tonight," Dr. Krause said.

"This is my father Sid Stein. Dad, meet Douglas Krause and Tom Johnson."

The men shook hands.

"A rabbi dressed as a villain. I never expected that," Tom said.

"My daughter has to spend most of her time being a goody two-shoes. I bought her the costume to give her a break."

"Great idea," Tom said.

Deborah willed herself not to blush under Tom's admiring glance and hoped her father hadn't noticed it.

Tom continued. "Besides all the fun costumes, some people have handed me small bags filled with candy."

"Purim's the traditional gift giving holiday. In countries like the U.S. where most children get Christmas presents, Chanukah became the time for presents," Deborah explained.

"Both Purim and Chanukah have the same theme," Sid said. "They tried to kill us. They failed. Let's eat."

Isaac appeared holding a *hamantaschen* in each hand. "In Israel at Purim there are stores filled with baskets of treats which people buy and give to their friends."

Many hamantaschen later, Deborah said, "Time for us to go home."

"We're leaving, too," Dr. Krause said.

The five walked to the parking lot. Deborah's car was parked in the space marked, "Reserved for Rabbi." When she and her dad and Isaac were about to get in, Tom noticed her left back tire was flat. He bent down to examine it. "That's odd. The cap on the valve stem is gone."

"I never noticed," Deborah said.

"If you give me the spare, I can change it."

Despite Deborah's protests and her suggestion she call AAA road service, Tom insisted. Dr. Krause offered to take Sid and Isaac home and to wait there for Tom to give him a ride to his house.

Tom handed Deborah his jacket, which felt so soft that she guessed it was a silk blend. His short sleeve shirt revealed the muscles of someone who worked out.

He finished quickly. She reached into her purse for a packet of tissues which Tom used to wipe his hands. On the way to her home, they bantered about how he could have a second career as an auto mechanic.

When they arrived, Deborah's father, Isaac and Dr. Krause were sitting on Deborah's small front porch.

"What's going on?" she asked.

Sid stood and put his arm around his daughter.

"We're waiting for the police."

Chapter Thirty-Five

"The police? I don't understand," Deborah said.

Then she saw it.

A swastika painted in red emblazoned on her front door.

In an effort to make sure Isaac didn't get upset, Deborah said, "Let's go inside and wait. We don't want to overreact because a hateful person thought this would scare us."

"The police want us to stay outside until they've checked the house," her father said.

Deborah guessed they wanted to make sure no one was inside.

"I called Laura McKee and George Stanford, the officers who've been investigating Roberta's death," Douglas Krause said. "They're on their way."

"But they handle traffic accidents," Deborah said.

"They decide whether to turn an investigation over to homicide detectives," Douglas responded.

"Maybe I'm tired and that's why I don't see the connection between the swastika and Roberta's death."

Before speaking again, Douglas looked at Tom who nodded.

"Tom told me about your encounter with Maurice Dunham, Jerry Evans' attorney. When you mentioned there was a witness to Roberta's death, Tom was concerned Dunham thought you were referring to yourself."

Isaac interjected, "Someone saw a witness?"

"There's a possibility it was the person who pushed Roberta in front of the car," Douglas said.

Even under the dim bulb in the porch light Deborah could see Isaac's distressed appearance so she directed her comments to him.

"We don't know that she was pushed, and we only suspect that the person leaving the scene saw something."

Deborah's father tightened his grip around his daughter's shoulder until it became uncomfortable. He looked from Tom to Douglas. "Is my daughter in danger?"

"Dad, this is clearly the case of one anti-Semite who could have picked the door of any rabbi in Houston."

Not to be placated, her father continued, "And you had a flat tire tonight."

"That could be a coincidence," she said, looking at Isaac who was chewing his lower lip.

A police car pulled in front of the house. Officers Lara McKee and George Stanford exited and walked to the porch.

Tom had pulled off his fake beard and Douglas had taken off his crown and purple robe. The officers turned their attention to Deborah, her son and father. As they gazed at Cat Woman, Batman and Superman, their expressions indicated they were suppressing laughter.

"Are you coming from a costume party?" Stanford asked.

"Sort of," Deborah replied.

Stanford turned his eyes from the super heroes to the swastika. "Don't clean this off until we get some pictures."

While he headed to the car to retrieve a camera, his partner stood in front of the door as though concerned the group before her had soapy wet cloths hidden and ready to use.

After Stanford returned and finished photographing the evidence, Officer McKee ordered, "Wait right where you are while we check the house."

Deborah handed over her key.

In the few minutes it took them to carry out their inspection, Deborah succeeded in stopping her father from discussing the evenings' events by nodding towards Isaac who was staring at the ground.

When the officers gave the all clear for them to enter the house, Isaac asked if he could go to his room. After a few questions about when he first saw the swastika, the officers said they didn't need him anymore. Avoiding eye contact with anyone, Isaac left the group. Deborah sat on the couch with her dad next to her. Tom, Douglas and the police continued standing.

Officer Stanford took notes as Tom told them about Maurice Dunham's visit to their lunch table, and how he'd gloated about Roberta's death which he was convinced meant his client Jerry Evans wouldn't be convicted.

"His attitude caused me to say something I immediately regretted," Deborah added. "I suggested someone who would benefit from her death could have pushed Roberta in front of Leigh's vehicle, and I announced there was a witness."

"I was concerned Dunham thought Deborah was the witness and would tell Evans so that in the unlikely event he or his wife was involved…"

"You took my daughter to lunch and introduced her to someone who posed a danger to her?"

Deborah felt bad seeing how abashed Tom looked.

"Tom tried to get rid of Dunham before he introduced him to me, but the guy sat down and refused Tom's offer to talk later."

"I introduced Deborah as Rabbi Stein, another mistake. That made it easy for him or his client to find her."

"Officers, can you please tell these gentlemen how it could be coincidental that an anti-Semite struck shortly after my run-in with Evans' attorney?"

"What about the tire?" her dad responded.

Tom explained how he'd found the cap off the valve stem of Deborah's flat tire, making him concerned that someone had removed it and pressed the button under it to let the air out.

"How would they know it was her tire?" Officer Stanford asked.

"It was parked in a space reserved for the rabbi," Douglas said.

"It's possible the cap came off before and I never noticed."

The officers exchanged a glance before Lara McKee said, "We'll go to the synagogue parking lot and check if the cap is near where you parked."

"And, if it is?" Deborah's father asked.

Deborah tried not to show how unnerved she was by McKee's response.

"We'll turn the investigation into Mrs. Krause's death over to homicide."

Chapter Thirty-Six

"You need to be prepared when reporters call."

Deborah turned to Tom who'd sat down next to her on the couch.

"How will they find out?" she asked.

"They use radio scanners to listen to police calls. Besides, your neighbors will see the swastika, and one is sure to call a reporter."

"I might have some turpentine. We can wipe it off."

"The better way is to sand off the swastika and then repaint that part of the door. I'll bring my electric sander tomorrow and buy the matching paint."

Deborah's father sat up straighter. "I'll still be here tomorrow. I can do it."

Tom looked around Deborah to her father, but before he could speak, Deborah said, "Dad, I don't have an electric sander. Perhaps you could get the paint while Tom does the sanding."

Sid nodded.

"As to the reporters, I'll call Marci Dennison. She handles media relations for the ADL," Deborah said.

"What's the ADL?" Tom asked.

"The Anti-Defamation League is a civil rights organization that's over one hundred years old. Anti-Semitism is one of the issues it deals with."

Deborah left the men, walked into the kitchen and called Marci who insisted that, since she lived a block away, she'd come over.

Deborah went to her bedroom where she changed out of her Wonder Woman costume and into a beige blouse and black slacks. Upon her return to the living room, her father, sitting at the opposite end of the couch from Tom, told her he'd checked on Isaac and found him asleep. She was about to sit down when the doorbell rang, so instead she opened the door to Marci Dennison, decked out in a fuchsia dress with matching high heels. Her reputation as a petite dynamo was realized as she barreled into the hall and then into the living room where the rabbi introduced her to her father, Tom and Douglas.

"I've already taken pictures of the door. Do you want to refer any reporters to me?" Marci asked.

"Yes, please," Deborah said. "My message is that Houston is a tolerant and diverse city that occasionally has a hateful person act out."

Marci took a seat across from the couch, a round table with a lamp separating her from where Douglas was sitting. "Sounds good. Usually when someone paints a swastika, they want lots of people to see it so they tend to be in public places. Having it on a private door's a bit unusual." Marci paused. "There's no reason to think this could be something personal, is there?"

Before anyone else could speak, Deborah said, "I'm a female who's the senior rabbi of a synagogue. Likely it's someone who dislikes both Jews and women."

"Could be," Marci said. "I'll get in touch with Dan Stevens, the police officer who liaises with the Jewish community. He'll keep me informed, and I'll keep you informed."

"The less in the news the better. Isaac was pretty shook up," Deborah said.

"I'll do my best," Marci assured her. "I'll use the quote you gave me."

Deborah walked Marci to the door. As she was returning to the living room, Douglas took her aside. "Isaac seemed pretty upset. When's his next visit with Dr. Wright?"

"Tuesday."

"It would be a good idea for you and Isaac to meet with him before Isaac's session begins to make sure your son addresses what happened tonight."

Deborah sighed. "Isaac has made it clear that only he's to report important information to Dr. Wright. I don't want him to get angry and refuse to see the therapist."

"If you tell Isaac the situation has bothered you, you have an excuse to share it with Dr. Wright."

"Good idea."

As Tom and Douglas were about to leave, Deborah thanked them again for all they'd done. While her father was talking to Douglas, Deborah managed to quietly ask Tom when he thought the police would get back to them about her tire.

"We might not find out unless and until homicide detectives turn up at your house."

***

"I hate to think about how I've endangered Deborah. If I hadn't introduced her to Dunham, he and his clients wouldn't have known who she was." Tom spoke as Douglas was driving him back to his house.

"She may be right that we're dealing with an anti-Semitic incident. And, if not, what happened isn't your fault. She said you tried to shoo that damn attorney away and that she never should have spoken to him."

"I've been attempting to guide her through the maze of police procedures. Instead I…"

"You've been a help in more ways. Before you met Deborah she'd shied away from male companionship when it could broaden both her and her son's horizons. She clearly enjoys yours."

"And I'm safe because I'm not Jewish so there's no chance of romance."

Hearing how thwarted Tom sounded, Doug wanted to say something to encourage him, but he stayed silent rather than raise false hope.

***

The next morning as Deborah was about to enter her office, she was startled when Margo jumped from her desk, rushed to her and hugged her.

"Are you all right?" she asked the rabbi.

"I'm fine. Why are you worried?"

"I've been answering calls from synagogue members who heard on the local news this morning that a swastika was painted on your door. Everyone's concerned about you."

"I didn't think the news would get out that quickly. Please blast an email to all our congregants telling them I'm fine, that the police are looking into the matter and that we shouldn't let the actions of one anti-Semite make us lose sight of what a tolerant, diverse city we live in."

"You must have been shocked when you saw it."

"It really affected Isaac. He insisted on staying home from school today to help my dad and Tom get rid of the swastika and repaint the door, and I capitulated."

Margo smiled. "Tom?"

Deborah felt herself blushing. "I had a flat tire last night. He changed it, gave me a ride home and saw the swastika."

"And now he's at your house again with your dad and Isaac?"

Deborah would have been relieved that this discussion was ending except that it was Mel Freed who interrupted them.

His face was red, he was baring his teeth and he was wearing a blue shirt. If he'd had a white beard and a star spangled hat, he would have looked like a furious version of Uncle Sam.

"I'm about to become president of this congregation, and I have to hear on the news about my rabbi's door being defaced by a swastika. Why didn't you call me last night?"

Deborah led Mel to her office and closed the door. When he refused to sit, she stayed standing.

"I'm sorry. I planned to call you this morning. If I'd known there'd be an early news report, I would have called you last night."

Mel scowled. "We don't need bad publicity for the synagogue."

Deborah straightened up to her full height. "You're blaming me for being the victim of an anti-Semitic incident?"

"Why did they choose you?"

"Why do you think?"

"I'm not sure."

Deborah gazed at Mel. "Have you considered that it may be someone who's unhappy that the rabbi of this synagogue is a woman? People like that say ugly things which is a step away from doing ugly things."

Mel clenched his teeth. "Don't count on this getting you sympathy that will mean your contract is renewed."

"I don't recall ever formally requesting it be renewed."

As she spoke, Deborah considered the possibility of giving up her pulpit and moving back to Israel like Isaac wanted. He'd either be happier or, if he weren't, he'd be more willing to make a commitment to return to and stay in the States. But she'd miss so many people here. One of the first to come to mind was Tom.

"You'd better let us know soon," Mel sputtered.

As he stormed from the rabbi's office, he almost collided with Leigh Goldsmith who was on her way in, even as Margo was saying, "She has someone in there."

Leigh was breathless. "I heard it on the news. Seems whoever pushed Roberta in front of my car is after you, too."

Deborah studied Leigh. Her being so animated over the possibility of the rabbi's being in danger was unusual, even for her.

After Leigh and Deborah were seated in front of the rabbi's desk, Deborah said, "It's more likely the act of an anti-Semite."

"Nah. This was directed at you. Why else would you have a flat tire the same night?"

"That wasn't in the news report." Deborah guessed that was true since neither Margo nor Mel had mentioned it.

"I…I saw your flat tire as I was leaving the synagogue last night."

Deborah tried to remember whether she'd seen Leigh at Purim services. She didn't think she had, but Leigh could have been in a costume that made her unrecognizable.

Deborah looked at Leigh who wouldn't meet her gaze.

The rabbi felt guilty thinking that Leigh could have been responsible for what happened the night before. But it would be to Leigh's advantage to have people believe that Deborah was being personally threatened because she was trying to figure out who was responsible for Roberta's death. Between the swastika and the flat tire, it would be easy for Leigh to spin a story that whoever had pushed Roberta in front of her car was now after the rabbi.

Then no one would blame Leigh for what had happened to Roberta.

Chapter Thirty-Seven

Deborah saw Tom before he saw her. His back was to her as he used an electric sander on her door.

She tapped him on the shoulder. "Tom."

He turned around quickly and switched off the sander.

"Deborah, I didn't think I'd see you. I figured you wouldn't be home until dinner time."

She laughed. "At my synagogue they let the rabbi eat lunch. I came by to prepare some for you and my dad and Isaac. Where are those two?"

"The store gave them the wrong paint color, so they had to go back."

Deborah studied the door. "You got the swastika off. Thank you."

"I'll unplug the sander and help you make lunch."

Moments later Tom followed Deborah into her house, through the hall and den into the kitchen. After they'd both washed and dried their hands, Deborah asked, "Does tuna salad work for you?"

"One of my favorites."

Deborah brought two large cans out of the pantry. While Tom used the electric can opener, Deborah took four eggs out of the refrigerator. She put them in a pot and was running water over them when Tom said, "Just like Denise."

Deborah turned and looked at Tom.

"I always boil the water first and then put the eggs in but Denise, my late wife, insisted the way you're doing it is better."

"Oh, no. It must be a guy thing. Dov, my late husband, always boiled the water first, too."

Deborah smiled, feeling good to be sharing memories with Tom. His return smile indicated he was having a similar thought.

"I'm going to leave after lunch. I don't think your dad wants me looking over his shoulder when he paints the door," Tom said.

"I hope he's been treating you okay. Dad can be cantankerous."

"I don't blame him. I'm probably the reason for what happened last night. I should have found a way to keep Jerry's attorney away from you."

"That encounter may have had nothing to do with it."

"What do you mean?"

Deborah sat at the kitchen table, and Tom joined her.

"People heard about the swastika on radio news this morning. Poor Margo was inundated with calls from congregants worried about me. Leigh Goldsmith came to see me about the report. She claimed what happened proved whoever had pushed Roberta in front of her car was after me, but…"

"But, what?"

"I feel bad to even think this, let alone say it. But she knew about the flat tire, and it seems that wasn't on the news. She said she'd noticed it when she left the synagogue last night, but I don't remember seeing her there."

"Why wouldn't she have told you about it when she saw it?"

"That may be why she couldn't look me in the eye. She may have been embarrassed that she didn't."

"Or…"

"Yikes. The water's boiling over." Deborah grabbed a pot holder from the drawer, took the pot of boiled eggs off the stove top and put it in the sink.

When Deborah was seated again, Tom said, "Or she knew because she'd done it."

"Would I rather be the prey of a killer or the victim of a very misguided woman?" Deborah sighed. "I almost have to hope we're dealing with a case of anti-Semitism."

"I know you hate to think this but the very misguided woman and the killer may be one and the same."

Deborah sighed. "You're right; I hate it every time I think that."

She got up from the table and took mayonnaise out of the

refrigerator and a large bowl from a cabinet while Tom peeled the eggs.

They worked in companionable silence which was broken when Tom asked, "Any other fallout from last night?"

"After the president of the congregation practically accused me of being responsible for what happened, I reminded him that I hadn't asked to have my contract renewed."

"But surely you want it to be."

"I wonder if Isaac would be better off if we left here and went to Israel."

Tom stopped slicing the eggs, gazed at Deborah and said, "You… you're seriously considering that?"

"For a fleeting moment."

Tom smiled. "Good. You should stay here." A slight blush caressed his cheeks. "What I mean is that you do such a good job for your congregation, it would be a shame for them to lose you."

"Thank you."

By the time Sid and Isaac, carrying a can of paint, walked into the kitchen, Deborah and Tom had the tuna salad made and bread on the table for sandwiches.

Sid looked from Tom to his daughter. "How long have you been here?" he asked her.

"Maybe thirty minutes. I'll head back to the synagogue as soon as we're finished eating."

During lunch Deborah reminded Isaac to find out about the schoolwork he'd missed.

"My friends have been texting me, asking what happened last night."

"Maybe you want to go back to school now and tell them."

"Do you mind if I leave the painting to you, Grandpa?"

"That's fine."

"I'll drop you off at school on my way to the synagogue."

"Let me take him. You have to get back to work, and I'm retired," Tom said.

Deborah looked at Isaac, who nodded.

"Thanks," she said.

When Tom and Isaac left, Sid said, "That was a very bad idea."

"Letting Tom take Isaac to school?"

"No, being alone in the house with him all that time. Your neighbors saw his car and your car. What do you figure they're thinking?"

"Dad, you're from a different generation. Today people understand a man and woman can just be friends."

"Just friends? I guess you're naïve because it's been so long since you've allowed yourself to be courted by any man."

"What do you mean?"

"Tom can't take his eyes off you, and he pays attention to every word you say. No matter what generation you're from, you know what that means."

Chapter Thirty-Eight

"I feel terrible leaving when you're in danger."

"Dad, I'm fine," Deborah said as she drove to the airport.

"I can't help being angry with your friend Tom, considering he's the one who introduced you to that criminal's attorney."

"He did his best to get the guy away from me. And the swastika may have nothing to do with that encounter."

"And the flat tire?"

"Could have been a coincidence."

"And if it's not, how are we going to make sure the police protect you?"

"Tom will give me guidance. He was in the D.A's. office and then a defense attorney. He's familiar with the drill."

"I know you won't listen to me, but I have to say it. The less time you spend with Tom, the better."

"Dad…"

Before she could say more, Deborah slammed on the brakes to avoid hitting the car in front of her. It had stopped suddenly due to an unexpected traffic jam. They were a few miles from the airport, but if gridlock continued, her dad might miss his plane.

Her father, sensing how tense Deborah was, stopped talking. For the next five minutes Deborah's car crawled along the highway and then, as quickly as it started, the traffic jam cleared.

Before Deborah could start a new conversational topic, her father went back to the old. "You want your contract renewed. If there's a scandal over a man, and one Douglas Krause has confirmed is not Jewish, you'll be looking for a new position, which won't be easy to find."

"Tom's not being Jewish…"

"Does matter. We tell our children to marry within the faith so they have Jewish children to perpetuate that faith. The rabbi has to set an example."

Deborah was relieved when they arrived at Terminal C. As she stopped the car, she said, "I'm not even dating Tom, let alone marrying him."

"You're fooling yourself about how you feel about him because the truth would complicate your life."

Deborah quickly got out of the car, slammed the door and opened the trunk. She was about to pull out her dad's suitcase when he joined her and beat her to it. He hugged her.

"I'm coming back soon."

***

When Deborah arrived at the synagogue, she saw three people standing near Margo's desk.

"Rabbi, we'd like to talk to you," Richard Golub, wire rimmed glasses sliding down his nose and gray hair gracing his neck, spoke for the group. Deborah had helped him reconcile with the son he'd originally rejected when the young man came out as gay.

With him were Bonnie Spokane, who'd survived her divorce with help from the rabbi, and Joyce Loftus for whose disabled daughter Deborah had found a residential facility.

The rabbi ushered them into her office. Richard brought in a chair from the reception area, allowing all three guests to sit in front of Deborah's desk while she sat behind it.

They looked at the rabbi sheepishly. Joyce cleared her throat. "We're on the committee that's to decide whether we invite you to renew your contract or search for a new rabbi."

When Joyce said no more but instead looked at her two companions as though willing one of them to continue, Deborah decided they'd been given the task of telling her they were searching for a new rabbi. Until now she hadn't realized how much she wanted to keep her position. Trying not to make their task more difficult, the rabbi smiled and said, "Go on, please."

Bonnie rubbed her hands together. "It was presumptive of us, but we assumed you wanted to stay."

"Of course, I do," Deborah said.

"You do?" They replied in unison.

Richard said, "Mel Freed reminded us that you've never officially requested a renewal. We thought you'd taken another position."

"I plan to stay as long as you want me. Consider that my official request."

The two women got up, rushed to Deborah's desk and hugged her.

Richard stood. "I know Mel's trying to convince the other committee members to look for a new rabbi, but this latest ploy of his…"

"It's my fault. I said something that was easy for him to misunderstand."

"That's like you, to be forgiving," a now red faced Joyce said.

"Really, it is in part my fault."

Her three guests exchanged glances. Richard said, "We'll do our best to handle Mel before he causes any more damage."

When they left, Margo said, "You have some loyal supporters."

"And at least one really strong non-supporter."

***

When Deborah picked Isaac up to take him to Dr. Wright's, he greeted her with, "You should have let me miss school to take Grandpa to the airport with you. I hardly ever see him."

"He said he's coming back soon."

"I guess that's one advantage of some creep being after you."

Rather than expressing her anger, Deborah decided to use Isaac's comment to help her accomplish her goal.

"While I don't think anyone's after me, I am upset about what happened. Could we take a little of your time with Dr. Wright and talk to him about it?"

While Deborah kept her eyes on the road, she could sense Isaac studying her. After a few moments he said, "Okay."

***

When they arrived at the psychologist's office, Deborah told his receptionist that she and Isaac would like to visit with Dr. Wright before her son's session. The woman nodded, sent an email to her boss and then ushered mother and son into his office.

Just as the first time they'd visited, Deborah and Isaac sat on a couch across from the therapist.

"Isaac, since you saw the door first, perhaps you can start the story of the events of Sunday night," Deborah said.

"You start. Since the flat tire comes first," Isaac insisted.

"As we were leaving the synagogue a friend noticed I had a flat tire. He fixed it and drove me home where Isaac, my father and Douglas Krause were waiting for us."

"I saw the swastika painted on the door and told the others. They called the police who were on their way when Mom and her friend arrived."

"That must have been a pretty upsetting sight," Dr. Wright said.

"More for Mom and Grandpa than for me," Isaac insisted.

"Did none of it bother you?" Dr. Wright asked.

"When Tom, Mom's friend, said someone might have made my mother's tire go flat and Dr. Krause said it might have been the same person who pushed Mrs. Krause in front of a car, I didn't like that."

"That's all wild speculation, though I can understand how it affected Isaac," Deborah said.

Her son raised his voice. "You told that murderer's attorney there was a witness who saw someone push Mrs. Krause in front of the car, and now the killer thinks it's you and will be after you. Why did you have to say anything?"

Before his mother could respond, Isaac burst into tears.

Chapter Thirty-Nine

"Rabbi Stein, please leave now," Dr. Wright instructed.

"No," Deborah said as she put her arm around her son.

Isaac stopped crying and looked at his mother. "I know I'm not supposed to skip school."

This was likely the least of the problem, but Deborah was determined not to rush Isaac so she merely nodded.

"And I picked the worst day possible to cut out early."

Deborah handed him a tissue, and he wiped his cheeks.

"It was raining. But that wasn't the bad part."

Dr. Wright sat forward in his chair.

"To get home, I walked on the street where Mrs. Krause lived."

More of Isaac's tears fell. Deborah reached for additional tissues with one arm while keeping her other arm firmly around his shoulder.

Isaac took a deep breath. "That's when I saw it."

With great effort Deborah stayed silent.

After what seemed like a long time, but was only seconds later, Isaac said, "Someone pushed Mrs. Krause in front of this big SUV, which turned out to be Mrs. Goldsmith's."

Deborah's heart pounded.

"I'm the witness, not you, but now the murderer thinks you are and is after you. If you get killed, it's all my fault."

Isaac shuddered as he cried.

As Deborah hugged him to her and reassured him no one was going to harm her, she thought about the call she'd received from Alison Eisen, the principal at Isaac's school, telling her that Isaac had left school early the day Roberta had died. Aware her son's walk home went through Roberta's street, she'd been grateful he hadn't been the accident victim. Despite knowing the route he took, she'd never considered he might be the witness.

"I should take over now," Dr. Wright said.

Deborah ignored him.

"And you decided not to tell me because?" Deborah did her best to speak in a non accusatory way.

"I didn't want you to know I'd cut school. But mainly I thought you'd make me go to the police, and after the trouble in California…"

"The police never got involved then."

"But some people said they should. I was afraid the police here would talk to the police there, and I'd be in big trouble."

"It doesn't work that way, sweetheart. There was no police report for them to access."

"You're going to make me go to the police here?"

Her son's fear pierced her, but Deborah resolved to tell the truth.

"There's no choice. We have to help catch Mrs. Krause's murderer." Deborah took a deep breath. "They should understand that someone your age… And we'll get Tom's help. He knows lots of police officers." Deborah spoke reassuringly even as she feared the trouble that could befall her son.

"Rabbi Stein, I think it's best for Isaac if I take over now," Dr. Wright said.

Deborah stood to go.

Isaac jumped up. "I'm going with my mom." He put his arm around her and gently moved her towards the door.

The logical part of Deborah told her she should insist Isaac stay. This might be a chance for a breakthrough. Maybe he'd even talk to the psychologist about California.

But the emotional part of her was so filled with joy that Isaac had finally chosen her that she couldn't do it.

As she left with her son, Deborah knew that if her decision made his situation worse, she would never forgive herself.

***

"Are you going to take me right to the police station?" Isaac asked as his mother was pulling out of the parking lot.

"I think it would be better to go after we've spoken to Tom."

"Grandpa doesn't think you should see him, especially not alone."

"Sometimes Grandpa gives bad advice, and anyway you'll be with me."

As soon as they arrived home, Deborah called Tom.

"Hi. It's Deborah."

Her tone must have revealed her anxiety because Tom responded, "Is something wrong?"

"Any chance you could come over now and talk to Isaac and me?"

"I'll be right there."

Tears of relief sprang into Deborah's eyes.

Fifteen minutes later an unshaven Tom in cutoff jeans and a short sleeve sweatshirt entered the Stein home.

Deborah ushered him into the living room where a somber Isaac was waiting on the couch. Deborah sat next to him while Tom sat in a chair across from them.

"I messed up badly," the teen said.

"Most mess-ups are fixable," Tom assured him.

Isaac hung his head. "Maybe not this one."

Tom looked at Deborah, but she said nothing, instead waiting for Isaac to speak.

He looked up. "I saw someone push Mrs. Krause in front of Mrs. Goldsmith's SUV, but I didn't tell the cops. I didn't even tell my mom until today. I want everyone to know I'm the witness so no one hurts her."

"How did you happen to see it?" Tom asked.

Isaac told the story of his skipping school and being on Mrs. Krause's street on the way home.

Tom spoke in a stern voice. "You are sure this happened? You're not saying it to protect your mother?"

"It happened. I wish it hadn't, but it did." Isaac bolted from the room.

Deborah bit her lower lip. "I'm sure he's telling the truth. His school's principal told me he cut a class that day which would have put him on Roberta's block at the right time, but I never considered…"

"I'm sorry, Deborah. I didn't mean to upset him, but I had to make sure he was telling the truth. Lying to the police would get him in big time trouble."

Deborah sat forward. "I've been afraid he'll be in big trouble for not telling them immediately."

"They won't be happy about it, but the larger concern is that they won't believe him."

"Why wouldn't they?"

"Roberta's being pushed solves your problems."

"What do you mean?"

"That eliminates one of your congregants as a possible murderer and stops rumors of another being a suicide."

Deborah collapsed back into the couch. "They might think I made up the story for him?"

"Let's not get ahead of ourselves. You need to call Lana McKee and George Stanford. I suspect after they hear what Isaac has to say, they'll turn the matter over to the homicide division. Once that happens…" Tom paused.

"Then what?" Deborah asked.

"I still have my attorney's license. Of course, I wouldn't charge you, but perhaps I should sit in when the homicide detectives interview Isaac."

Deborah could hardly breathe. Tom wouldn't have made the offer unless he was concerned the police might consider Isaac a suspect rather than a witness.

Chapter Forty

Deborah opened her door to Officers Lana McKee and George Stanford who looked intimidating. It wasn't McKee's height or Stanford's powerful build, but rather their stern demeanors which affected her.

She thanked them for coming and invited them into the living room where they refused her offer to sit.

"You said your son had something to tell us," McKee said.

"I'll get him." Deborah went to Isaac's bedroom where he was supposedly studying for the next day's science test but was instead staring at the wall.

"It's okay. I'm with you," Deborah said.

She wished Tom were with them, but he'd considered it a bad idea for the officers to think Isaac needed an attorney at this point.

When Deborah and Isaac entered the living room, she reminded the officers they'd met her son the night the swastika was painted on their door.

"Are you here to tell us you painted it?" Stanford asked Isaac.

"Of course not," Deborah said in a tone so angry that she was surprised when she heard herself.

"Then why are we here?" McKee asked. "You wouldn't tell us on the phone."

Deborah motioned Isaac to the couch where she joined him. "I thought it was better for you to hear what Isaac has to say in person."

As Tom had rehearsed with him, Isaac started by telling the officers how he'd skipped school the day Roberta Krause died.

"I didn't tell my mom because I didn't want to get in trouble with her." He looked at Deborah. "And I knew she'd tell the school, and I'd get in trouble with them, too."

Isaac took a deep breath. "I walked home on Mrs. Krause's street. That's when I saw someone push her in front of a big SUV."

If the officers were surprised, they didn't show it. Instead, McKee said, "You had an obligation to tell us."

"I…I didn't think it would help. I was behind the person."

"Height, weight, sex," Stanford barked.

"And it was raining hard."

"You must have some idea," McKee insisted.

"He was wearing a black hooded cape."

"You're sure it was a man?"

"No."

"Height?" Stanford was practically growling.

"Shorter than me. It was over in a couple of seconds and then I took off."

"You didn't try to help her?" McKee sounded incredulous.

"I saw someone come out of a house, so I knew she'd get help."

McKee stopped writing on her notepad and turned her attention to Deborah. "This is certainly convenient for you. No more blame for anyone in your synagogue,"

Deborah stood. "If you have an accusation you can back up, make it. Otherwise I think it's time you leave."

Isaac got up and put his arm around his mother. "I'm the witness, not my mom."

"Do not put my son in danger by releasing his name as the witness."

Stanford smirked. "That will be up to Conway and Vega, the homicide detectives."

Chapter Forty-One

"But I want everyone to know I'm the witness." Sleep hadn't changed Isaac's insistence. Now he was disturbing his mother's breakfast with the same mantra she'd tried to dissuade him from after the police had left the night before.

"I know you want to protect me, but I'm not in danger. Even if the murderer knows there was a witness, he must realize the witness saw him from behind and, therefore, can't identify him or her."

"Then why the flat tire and swastika?"

"Maybe the timing was coincidental, maybe to scare us or maybe... There's someone else I suspect."

"Who?"

"I need more proof before I tell you."

"Tom."

"What?"

"It made him a hero, didn't it? He fixed your tire and got to spend time with you when he got the swastika off the door."

"Isaac, how can you say such a thing when Tom's been so helpful to you?"

"Sorry."

Deborah put her cream cheese covered bagel down. She felt as if she'd choke if she took another bite.

Isaac stood. "I'm going to school."

Still so angry about what Isaac had said about Tom, Deborah didn't offer her son a ride.

No sooner had Isaac left than all the thoughts Deborah had tried to keep at bay assaulted her.

Isaac had hidden the fact he'd witnessed a murder, and not any murder. The murder of one of his mother's congregants which had led to accusations that the victim had committed suicide or that another congregant had purposefully hit her with her SUV. Worse, he hadn't stopped to help Roberta.

Deborah had known Isaac had skipped school and had been walking in the area when the accident occurred, but she hadn't considered he could have been the witness. If she had, they could have immediately gone to the police. What haunted her more was the thought that, if the Kings hadn't come to Roberta's aid, Isaac still might have fled.

No matter what she told Isaac, she feared he could be in danger if word got out he was the witness. The police were almost sure to tell Douglas Krause. He had the right to know. How would Isaac cope when everyone in the congregation found out?

***

Deborah, dressed in a black and white striped blouse and a black skirt, walked to her front door. She touched its handle, but didn't turn it. She went back to the living room where she sank into the couch.

After a few minutes of her mind being blank, she heard her phone ring and went into the kitchen to answer it.

"It's Tom. I wanted to make sure everything had gone okay last night with McKee and Stanford."

"I'm sorry. I should have called and told you."

Deborah related how Tom had been correct that the officers would question the truth of Isaac's assertion that he was the witness, had berated him for not staying to offer aid and had said they were turning the matter over to homicide.

"Your son is a teenager. Most boys his age would have reacted the same way. They get scared, can't think straight and then don't know what to do when they realize they've made a mistake. Just because he's the son of a rabbi doesn't mean he can be expected to act like an adult."

Deborah sighed. "Isaac can't identify anyone since he was behind the killer who was wearing a black hooded cape. But still I'm afraid if the police reveal Isaac's name…"

"Who are the homicide officers?"

"Conway and Vega."

"Conway's an old-timer. Was there when I was an assistant D.A. He owes me some favors. No promises, but let me see what I can do. And, if you're willing, I think it would be a good idea if I'm there when they interview Isaac."

Deborah's gratitude was boundless, but all she managed was a quiet, "Thank you."

***

As he'd suggested, Tom answered the door when the police officers rang the bell at Deborah's home.

Archie Conway's bald head capped a long wrinkled face. Deborah guessed he was a little older than Tom. His partner Burt Vega looked young enough to have recently graduated from the police academy. Thick black hair and bushy eyebrows were his most prominent features.

"You son of a gun," Archie said to Tom in greeting. "Been a while since I've seen you."

"I'll never forget your coming to Denise's funeral," Tom said.

"We go back far enough that it was the least I could do." Archie looked at Deborah who was standing behind Tom. "Hope things are going better for you now."

Tom nodded and introduced Deborah to the detectives.

Vega took out his notebook and asked Tom, "Are you here as the boy's attorney?"

"Here as a family friend unless you guys force me to be his attorney."

"I think it's important…"

Conway interrupted Vega. "Cool it for now. Tom was one of us for a long time, and then played fair when he wasn't."

"I'll get Isaac," Deborah said.

She went to her son's room where he'd gone when he'd returned from school.

"Remember what Tom said. Answer their questions honestly, but briefly, and to the point, even if they stay quiet to tempt you to fill the conversation void."

Isaac nodded, followed his mother from the room and shook hands with each of the officers when Tom introduced them.

Tom and Deborah sat on the couch with Isaac between them. The officers took seats on chairs across from them.

Conway took out a notepad and read a synopsis of what Isaac had told McKee and Stanford.

Isaac confirmed that conversation.

"You know, son, we could have started looking into who pushed the victim in front of the SUV a lot sooner if you'd come forward when you should have," Conway said.

"I know, and I'm really sorry." Isaac's voice cracked and his eyes filled with tears.

"And you're sure you can't describe the killer?"

"No, sir. I was behind the person and anyway, he was wearing like a black hooded coat."

Deborah chewed her lower lip. A black hooded coat. Was that what the black clad stranger at Roberta's burial had been wearing?

"How do you know it was a he?" Vega asked.

"I don't. Everyone says he when you don't know the person's sex."

Vega sat so far forward in his chair that he looked like he was about to jump out of it. "You admit to being at the scene and to fleeing from it. Are you the one who pushed her?"

Deborah gasped.

"No, sir, I am not."

Tom spoke. "Since Isaac's a witness, his mother and I are concerned that if his name is revealed, he could be in danger. It's important you make sure it's not given to anyone outside the police department."

Vega opened his mouth but before he could speak Conway said, "Of course, that's standard procedure in a case like this."

When the officers stood to leave, Vega asked Isaac, "Is Mrs. Goldsmith or one of her children a friend of yours?"

"I can't stand the woman," was Isaac's quick response.

"Isaac!" Deborah said.

"You told me to tell the police the truth."

Conway's smile indicated Isaac's spontaneous honesty had paid off.

Vega remained stern faced. "We need to verify your son's story about cutting class the day the victim died. You can either give us permission to see your son's school records, or we'll subpoena them."

Deborah, mouth agape, looked at Tom.

He gazed at Vega. "Your odds of getting a subpoena, especially that broad, are almost non-existent. However, Rabbi Stein might agree to having the school principal send her a letter listing any dates when Isaac cut class. She'll turn it over to you once she receives it."

Deborah nodded.

Conway stood. "That should do it."

Vega had the last word. "We'll get back with you after we've verified your son's story. Depending on what we learn, the next interview could be at the police station."

Chapter Forty-Two

Deborah couldn't sleep as she agonized over what would have happened if Tom hadn't been with her and Isaac during the police interview. Not knowing any better, she would have been frightened into permitting the officers to request copies of Isaac's school records. She couldn't bear to imagine Alison Eisen's reaction to having homicide detectives ask for them. Could she have blamed the principal if that had led her to believe Isaac was a suspect in Roberta's murder?

If the police had all of Isaac's school records, they'd see he was disciplined for threatening to punch another student, giving them the wrong impression that he was violent. Considering Officer Vega's question about whether Isaac had pushed Roberta in front of Leigh's SUV, that information could be damning.

It had been years since Deborah had relied on someone the way she was relying on Tom. With Dov's death she'd had to accept sole responsibility for herself and Isaac. She couldn't burden her in-laws who could hardly bear their loss. She'd stopped depending on her parents after they'd disapproved of her becoming a rabbi. The circumstances of Roberta's death had forced her to turn to Tom. It felt good to not have to be one hundred percent self-sufficient, and such a relief to have someone help her where Isaac was concerned.

Deborah got out of bed, went to her computer and emailed Miriam about all that had happened since Isaac admitted to being the witness and how grateful she was to Tom.

Deborah woke up to find a return email from Miriam.

Dear Deborah,

I understand the shock and fear you felt upon learning Isaac is the witness. I also understand your worry, but a suspect who was hidden by a hooded coat and knows he was only seen from behind has to realize that no witness can identify him. I'm glad you have Tom there to help. You need to be honest with yourself about whether you were really forced to turn to him or whether you want to turn to him.

Love, Miriam

***

That morning, knowing it would be tricky asking Alison Eisen for the letter, a nervous Deborah called the principal.

After the usual greetings, she said, "Could you send me a letter stating how often and on what dates Isaac cut class?"

"I can tell you it was just the once, the day Roberta was killed."

"I know it's an odd request, but could you put that information in the form of a letter to me?"

"Ah…I guess so." The principal paused. "Does this have something to do with Isaac's visits to the psychologist?"

"Sort of."

"It doesn't matter why you want it. Of course, I'll do it."

"Thanks."

The officers would soon have confirmation that Isaac was at the scene when Roberta was killed. But after yesterday's interview, Deborah couldn't be sure they'd believe his role was that of a witness.

***

Douglas Krause stood aside as other congregants spoke to Deborah after evening services. When they were gone, he said, "Can I visit with you in your office?"

"Of course." Deborah tried to speak in a casual tone to conceal her concern about the purpose of their meeting.

Douglas closed the door to the rabbi's office. The two sat down next to each other in front of the desk.

"Two homicide detectives came to my home earlier today. Conway and Vega. The other officers had given them the copy of the letter Jerry Evans' wife had sent Roberta. They asked me to look through her things and see if there were any other letters from Jerry or his wife."

Deborah bit her lip, waiting for Douglas to tell her that homicide officers were involved because Isaac had confessed to being the witness to the murder. She had no excuse to give him about Isaac's conduct.

"They wouldn't tell me why the case was transferred to them. I suspect it's because of the swastika on your door and your flat tire, which means you could be in danger. You need to insist they give you protection."

Instead of feeling relieved that Douglas didn't know about Isaac's role, his concern about her made Deborah feel even worse about her son's inaction.

"I couldn't find additional letters at home, but I wondered if any might be here mixed in with the papers Roberta kept about her synagogue work," Douglas said.

"I'll look for them and let you know," Deborah assured him.

"Thanks, and remember what I said about getting police protection."

***

Since Isaac was working on a science project at a classmate's home, Deborah stayed at the synagogue to look for any documents Roberta might have left.

She opened her desk drawer where she'd put Roberta's anniversary party preparation schedule. She read through it carefully, appreciating Roberta's neat handwriting. All Deborah gleaned from it was that Roberta's schedule was being met.

She walked down a narrow hallway to where the synagogue president had a small office. Since Mel Freed had not yet officially been named president and Roberta was gone, the office, except for a small desk and one file cabinet, was empty.

Wanting to be thorough in the search she'd told Douglas she'd undertake, Deborah sat at the desk and opened the top drawer. She found Roberta's Daily Planner. Going through it made her realize she hadn't fully appreciated all Roberta had done. The entries weren't limited to the work for the anniversary party. Roberta had read reviews of books to advise which ones the synagogue's library should order. She'd made sure that there were enough volunteers at the gift shop each day. Thanks to her efforts, every Friday night there were flowers in the sanctuary. The more the rabbi read, the more she realized how the smooth running of the synagogue had depended on her detail-oriented friend. If she'd recognized this sooner, Deborah could have expressed her gratitude to Roberta.

Since it was unheard of for Roberta to be late, an entry which started, "Was almost late for the anniversary party meeting," caught Deborah's attention. This was followed by a phone number and continued with, "Prior meeting lasted longer than I anticipated. Guess I should have figured logical arguments wouldn't work when someone's freedom is at stake."

Deborah read the words three times. The person whose freedom was at stake had to be Jerry Evans, which likely meant that the meeting was either with him or his wife. Perhaps Roberta had logically stated that she had no choice but to tell the truth about Evans's illegal activities and that she would do the same at another trial. If Deborah was right, the meeting had gone badly.

Chapter Forty-Three

Deborah copied the phone number she'd just read, took Roberta's Daily Planner and went to her car.

She arrived home to find Isaac in the kitchen, eating ice cream out of the carton.

"Did the science project meeting go well?" she asked.

"Yeah."

"Look at this," she said, putting the planner on the kitchen table and opening it to the last page she'd read. She pointed to the entry she thought was significant. "What do you make of this?"

Isaac put the carton on the sink and came over to the table. He studied what his mother showed him. "You think whoever met with her killed her later?"

"Possibly. I need to take this to Dr. Krause, who'll give it to the police."

Isaac met his mother's gaze and then looked down at the floor. "You want me to go with you and tell him I was the witness."

"Yes."

"He'll be really angry."

"Perhaps."

"When do we have to go?" Isaac spoke in a monotone. His face was pale.

"Now if he's home."

Isaac watched as his mother dialed Dr. Krause's phone number. When she said, "We'll be right over," he took a deep breath and followed her out the door.

Mother and son didn't speak on the drive to the Krause home. Dr. Krause ushered them into his living room where he and Deborah sat next to each other on the couch. Isaac stood at the edge of the room near the hall until Dr. Krause, in the booming voice of a good host, insisted he sit down.

Deborah and Douglas looked at the planner. He said, "She has to be referring to meeting with Jerry or his wife or both, but she never told me she was going."

"She probably figured you'd worry."

"And I would have been right to."

"I'm suspecting the phone number belongs to one of the Evanses."

"I can do a reverse lookup with the number and see if it's theirs. Give me a minute. The computer's in the other room."

When Douglas left, Isaac stood and looked towards the hall. "I don't think I can do this."

"You can."

Douglas returned and said, "No luck. I was looking for a land line and that could be a cell phone number. The number wasn't in the letter I gave the police. They must have contacted her again, maybe by phone or maybe by a letter we haven't found."

"The police should be able to discover to whom the number belongs."

"Unless it was one of those throwaway cells," Douglas said.

"Let's both look again in case there was another letter. Also, the police can get phone records from your home and the synagogue and Roberta's cell to see if she was contacted by this number before."

Douglas nodded and looked at Isaac as though he was just registering how odd it was that Deborah had brought her son along. "Is Isaac going to help us with our sleuthing?" he asked.

The teen sat down. He looked from his mother to Dr. Krause and took a deep breath. "I'm here to tell you …" His eyes filled with tears. "I'm here to tell you that I'm the witness." The tears flowed down his cheeks. "I'm sorry."

Deborah fought her instinct to go to Isaac.

"I don't understand," Douglas said.

"I skipped out early from school, and I was there when someone pushed Mrs. Krause in front of the SUV. I should have stayed to help, but I saw this woman coming out of her house, so I thought everything would be okay. I should have told you and my mom and the police right away. I'm sorry."

Douglas's gaze went from Isaac to Deborah. He stood and paced back and forth from one end of the living room to the other. That and his silence unnerved Deborah almost as much as it did Isaac.

He left the room and came back sipping water from a large glass. He sat down and put the glass on the table in front of the couch.

"The psychologist in me understands how an adolescent boy could make such a poor choice. The husband in me finds it hard to forgive."

"I bear part of the blame," Deborah said. "Alison Eisen told me Isaac skipped out early from school that day, but I didn't consider…"

Douglas spoke sharply. "You do your son no favor when you try to take responsibility for his actions."

Deborah's hands shook as the psychologist's words reverberated.

Douglas continued. "Isaac should have stayed to help Roberta. He had no way of knowing the woman coming to her aid was a doctor. And by waiting to tell the police, he was complicit in letting people think Roberta had committed suicide."

Isaac was bent over, his head almost in his lap.

Douglas continued. "I know you were scared, as I would have been at your age."

Deborah hoped Dr. Krause's next words would make Isaac feel better, but instead he said, "Maybe someday I'll be able to deal with what you did, but for now, it's best if you and your mother leave."

Chapter Forty-Four

"I'm always ruining your life." Isaac spoke as he and his mother were in the car on their way home from Douglas Krause's house.

"Don't ever say that. You *are* my life. Nothing in this world is more important to me than you."

Isaac shook his head. "I'm always screwing up."

"You took responsibility tonight, and it was more difficult than either of us imagined. But you did it."

"It was really hard," Isaac said.

He didn't speak again until they were home. "Things are going to get worse when Dr. Krause tells everyone I'm the witness. They'll all be as mad as he is."

Mother and son went into the kitchen where she poured him a glass of milk and sat down at the kitchen table across from him.

"He's not going to tell anyone," she said.

"How do you know?"

Deborah hesitated. She didn't want to frighten Isaac with the truth; Dr. Krause would be concerned that would put the teen in danger. Instead she said, "He could mess up the police investigation if he did."

"Except for the police and Dr. Krause, it's only you and me and Tom who know?"

Deborah nodded.

"I should tell Grandpa."

Deborah reached across the table and put her hand over Isaac's. "I'm proud of you for thinking of it, but it's an hour later in Pittsburgh so he's likely in bed. Call him at his office tomorrow when you get home from school."

Deborah felt guilty about her ulterior motive. A call to her father and mother's home meant her mother would become involved. This way her dad could keep the news to himself.

***

The next afternoon as she was about to leave her office, the rabbi's phone rang. She could hear the anger in her father's voice from the moment he said, "Hello, Deborah."

Before she could greet him in return, he said, "What's the matter with you? Putting your son in danger by telling people he's the witness."

Though at first taken aback, Deborah quickly recovered. "He told the one person who deserved to know. He needs to be praised for taking that responsibility."

"I didn't raise my daughter to be a fool. You need to understand you're both in danger and insist the police give you protection."

"I'll talk to them."

"You'd better," he said and hung up.

A few minutes later when Deborah saw Tom at the door to her office, her first instinct was to get up from her desk, run to him and literally cry on his shoulder. Instead she motioned to him to close the door and sit down.

"I understand you and Isaac had a rough time last night."

"How do you know?"

"I periodically call Douglas to see how he's doing. When he said you and Isaac had left after giving him disturbing news, I asked if it dealt with whom the witness was. He seemed surprised I knew, so I explained you'd wanted my advice."

"I don't blame him for being angry. The good news is Isaac took responsibility. He learned the hard way there are consequences to his actions, and that's an important lesson."

"You're doing okay?"

Deborah smiled. "With a good friend to look after me, of course I am."

A blush tinged Tom's cheeks.

"My dad called. He's convinced I've endangered Isaac by having him inform Douglas he's the witness."

168

"I'm sure Douglas won't tell anyone."

Deborah got up from behind her desk and sat next to Tom. "Dad wants me to ask the police for protection."

"I've already talked to Officer Conway about that possibility. He said if you or Isaac received a direct threat, the best we could hope for is a patrol car making a few passes around your house each night. I could start doing that now."

Deborah put her hand on his arm. "That's not necessary. But thanks for offering and for talking to Conway. Now I can tell my dad the police have been approached." She quickly removed her hand and bit her lip.

"What's wrong?"

"I guess I should have Isaac tell Leigh Goldsmith. She needs to know she's no longer suspected of intentionally running over Roberta."

"If that's your reason, don't do it."

"What do you mean?"

"Archie Conway told me his partner is big on conspiracy theories and is trying to find a connection between Jerry Evans and Leigh Goldsmith."

Chapter Forty-Five

Isaac met Deborah at the door when she came home, something he hadn't done since he was in elementary school. He started talking before she entered the house.

"I had the weirdest conversation with Grandpa when I called to tell him I was the witness everyone's been looking for."

Deborah dropped her purse on the long narrow wood table in the hall and walked into the living room where Isaac followed her. She motioned him to join her on the couch. Instead he took the chair across from her and sat on its edge.

"What happened?" she asked.

"Grandpa stuck up for me, saying, considering my age and how frightened I must have been, most kids would have run off."

Deborah nodded.

"When I told him I'd let the police and Dr. Krause know, instead of saying he was proud of me, he got upset and asked if 'that god damn Tom' had put me up to it."

Deborah took a deep breath.

"I explained you'd suggested it."

Deborah chuckled. "Thanks."

"He said, 'Shit,' and hung up."

Deborah understood how much his grandfather's approval meant to Isaac. She should have spoken to her father before Isaac had.

What's going on?" Isaac asked.

"Grandpa didn't think this through. Instead he had a knee jerk reaction, assuming the police and Dr. Krause would tell everyone you're the witness and fearing that would endanger you."

"How do you know that won't happen?"

"When you told Dr. Krause, he was surprised because the police hadn't let him know. If they didn't tell him, they won't tell anyone."

"And Dr. Krause?"

"Tom talked to him, and he didn't mention it. Instead Tom had to bring up the subject. That's a good sign he's keeping the information secret."

Not as confident as she sounded, Deborah said a silent prayer for her son's safety.

***

When Deborah couldn't sleep that night, she got up and went to her computer.

Dear Miriam,

I live in fear Roberta's killer will figure out Isaac was the witness to her death, and he fears the killer thinks it's me. His concern makes me understand that, despite all the mistakes I've made as a mother, he still and truly loves me. But what if I fail in a mother's most important task – protecting her child? I must find a way.

Love, Deborah

After finally getting a few hours of sleep, Deborah woke to find Miriam's reply.

Dearest Deborah,

What you must do is leave your and Isaac's protection to the police. Though it was years ago, I've never forgotten the incident at the Malha mall when we saw four huge Jewish Israeli teens taunting two smaller Israeli Arab boys. When the four started moving towards them, you jumped in front of the two boys. The would-be attackers, realizing their blows would fall on you, stopped in their tracks. If you were that quick to put yourself at risk to protect strangers, I'm afraid of what you might do to protect Isaac.

Your worried friend,
Miriam

***

Later that day Deborah stopped by the synagogue gift shop to thank the three women who were volunteering there.

"Don't thank us, buy something," the one with the New York accent teased.

"We don't pay her enough for her to afford our prices," the tallest one joked.

Ida Marks, at eighty, the oldest of the three said, "Rabbi, I'm finished here for the day. Do you have time to talk to me?"

Deborah had learned from her last encounter that Ida didn't need any assistance walking to her office. When they arrived, Deborah closed the door, and she and her congregant sat down next to each other in front of the rabbi's desk.

The last time they'd visited, Ida had told Deborah about the police interview in which accident investigators had asked her about the relationship between Roberta and Leigh. Now that they were off the case and homicide officers were on it, Deborah became concerned they were talking to the synagogue members. That would mean they thought Leigh was still somehow involved.

Ida twisted her short white hair around her finger. She fidgeted in her chair. The longer she waited to discuss what was bothering her, the more uneasy Deborah became.

The older woman gazed at Deborah, blushed and blurted out, "Someone wants to marry me."

Deborah hugged Ida.

"Who's the lucky man?"

Ida pursed her lips. "Someone my children don't want me to marry."

Deborah couldn't imagine this down-to-earth woman choosing an inappropriate mate.

"They're using your sermon to make their argument."

Before the rabbi could figure out which one she was referring to, Ida said, "You told us we should marry within the faith because only one third of the children born to interfaith couples are raised Jewish, and we're too small a group to survive if that continues."

Deborah nodded.

"Bill's not Jewish, but I told my son and daughter not to worry because, unlike Sarah in the Bible, I don't plan to have any post-menopausal children."

Deborah smiled at the vehemence with which Ida spoke.

"What other objections are they raising?"

"My son fears Bill's a gold digger, but I have no gold for him to dig."

"And you could always have a pre-nuptial agreement."

"My son admits that, but the real problem is my daughter. She thinks I'm being disloyal to her father, who's been gone for almost two years." Ida took a handkerchief out of her serviceable brown vinyl purse and dabbed at her eyes.

"You took such good care of him when he was sick."

"I did all I could." Ida sighed. "Thank you for listening. I'm going to get things worked out with the kids. I deserve to be happy."

The older woman stood to leave. When she reached the door, she turned back to Deborah. "You're probably getting too old to have children, so you shouldn't limit yourself to Jewish suitors."

Taken aback by Ida's statement, it took the rabbi a few moments to respond. "The young people to whom I was addressing the sermon and their parents would call me a hypocrite and accuse me of setting a terrible example."

As she spoke, an image of Tom flashed through her mind. Knowing the truth of her words, sadness enveloped Deborah.

***

Deborah sat at her desk and sent Miriam an email.

Dear Miriam,

As usual, you know me better than I know myself. I was just with an eighty-year-old congregant who should be an inspiration to me. She's found a new love since her husband's death and is determined to overcome all obstacles to make a life with him. I'm so sad that I can't do the same because, of course, you were correct about how I wanted to turn to Tom. It's not just because he's not Jewish that I'm trying to keep my emotional distance. To care about any man except Dov, the love of my life, makes me feel disloyal. So I tell myself that all I'm feeling is gratitude for the help Tom's giving me and Isaac. Yet, if it's only gratitude, why do I come up with excuses to call him or be with him? I've really made a mess of things.

Love, Deborah

Miriam's response was quick in coming.

My dearest friend,

I pray everything will work out for you, and you will again know joy.

Love, Miriam

Chapter Forty-Six

The midsize black car appeared behind her shortly after Deborah drove out of the synagogue parking lot.

When she was close to home she remembered how low she was on groceries. Since the store was between her house and the synagogue, Deborah turned around, only to notice the same car behind her.

Or was it?

She wasn't good at identifying the makes or models of automobiles. Maybe it was a different car that just looked like the other.

Still, she felt relieved when it didn't follow her into the supermarket's parking lot. She found a space close to the door and parked.

She entered the store and heard, "Rabbi Stein, I'm glad to see you." A hug from Ann Kaplan followed. Feeling her congregant's bulk against her, she suspected she hadn't lost any weight since being in the hospital, where Deborah had last seen her. When Ann released her and she got a good look at her, Deborah's conclusion was confirmed.

"Mindy and Sam will be coming to visit you soon about their wedding plans. They don't want to set a date until they're sure you're available to marry them."

If Dr. Krause was willing to have her officiate at his son's wedding, perhaps he wasn't as angry with her as she thought.

Ann lowered her voice. "And the good news is that Roberta's death has been turned over to homicide detectives because a witness saw someone push her in front of Leigh's car. So Douglas Krause has no reason to be mad at Leigh."

Deborah didn't correct Ann, who was euphoric in her belief that her best friend and her daughter's future father-in-law would now get along. She was ignoring the anger Douglas still felt toward Leigh for the way she'd insisted his wife's death was a suicide. And, if Tom was right, at least one of the police officers had still not given up on Leigh as a suspect, possibly as one who'd conspired with the person who had pushed Roberta.

Ann dropped her voice to a whisper. "The police wouldn't tell Leigh who the witness was. They must think he's in danger."

Deborah swallowed hard.

"Gotta go. You can look forward to seeing the kids soon."

Fifteen minutes later Deborah left the store with a bag of groceries. Twilight had turned into dusk, making it difficult to be sure no one was near her car. Rather than go to the back and put the groceries in the trunk, she managed to get herself and the overstuffed bag into the driver's side of the car and then put her bundle on the seat beside her.

She was on the road for just a minute when she noticed a black midsize car behind her.

She was probably being paranoid, but she wasn't going to take a chance that the car would follow her to her house, where Isaac was waiting for her. Deborah drove a few blocks to a police substation. As soon as she pulled into the parking lot, the other car sped away.

Deborah took a deep breath and held her shaking hands tightly against the steering wheel. She debated with herself about whether she should go inside and file a report. But what could she report? That maybe the same car had followed her or maybe it was three separate cars.

She made up her mind. If she didn't see a midsize black car on her street when she arrived home, she'd stop worrying.

If she saw a car like that, she'd grab Isaac from the house and head back to the police substation.

Deborah pulled out of the parking lot and took a circuitous route home, all the while checking to see if she were being followed. She drove up and down her own street a few times before pulling into her garage.

When she entered the kitchen, Isaac, who was sitting at the table, dipping tortilla chips into salsa, greeted her with, "What took you so long? I'm starving."

Deborah went to him and kissed the top of his head.

"What's that for?"

"I love you."

"Then feed me."

"I'll warm up the salmon burgers and have the salad ready in ten minutes. You can put the chips and salsa away."

Isaac dipped three more times before complying.

Deborah wondered if Isaac had seen the car she had, either at school or on the way home or on the block, but she didn't want to frighten him by asking directly. As casually as she could she said, "Anything unusual happen today?"

Isaac put down the milk carton he was drinking from. "Like what?"

Deborah turned from the sink where she was rinsing off lettuce. "Like anything."

"Nah." After another swig of milk, Isaac said, "Oh, yeah, there was something."

Deborah's heart rate sped.

"Ian Freed was caught with marijuana. He's suspended for three days." Isaac laughed. "His grandfather, your soon to be synagogue president Mel, came and got him. His face was so red it looked like it was on fire."

Isaac put the milk back in the refrigerator and took out the salad dressing. "Now he knows his grandson's not perfect."

Chapter Forty-Seven

"No, no, no. I cannot put up with it any longer."

The rabbi got up from her chair and walked over to Margo, who was standing in her doorway. "What's wrong?"

"Another day. Another white blouse and black skirt. We're going shopping at lunch."

Deborah glanced at Margo's outfit – her dress a swirl of reds, greens and yellows and her stiletto heels a shiny maroon. "Maybe we can find something in between what I'm wearing and what you're wearing."

Margo's laugh rang out. "I'm not planning to make you my clone, but for goodness sakes, we can do better than that."

***

Margo was back in Deborah's office at eleven.

"Kind of early, isn't it?" Deborah asked.

"I'm taking you to Dillards, and you know how crowded the Galleria gets at lunch time. We need to head out now."

Deborah grabbed her purse and followed her assistant through the hall and out to the sparsely filled outdoor parking lot, where the only black vehicle she saw was a large SUV. Margo, with the rabbi close behind, jogged to her red Miata convertible, the top already down. As Deborah lowered herself into the passenger seat, she considered that she didn't have a scarf for what was bound to be a windy ride. Nonetheless, she was glad they were in Margo's car. If someone had been following her car last night, they wouldn't expect her to be in this one.

She told herself to get a grip. No one had followed her from her home to the synagogue this morning, and she'd taken a circuitous route and made two u turns to be sure.

Though they were less than three miles from the department store, there was enough traffic to keep them on the road for fifteen minutes, during which time Margo switched lanes so often, Deborah felt a little nauseated. All the while she listened to her assistant telling her they were not returning to the synagogue until Deborah had a least two new outfits.

They found a parking spot in the lot in front of Dillards. Deborah followed Margo up the escalator to the women's clothing area where Margo pawed through the racks of dresses. "Depending on the manufacturer, you could be a size six or you could be an eight. Try these on while I look for more."

Deborah took the clothes Margo handed her into the fitting room. One dress had a yellow, purple and pink impressionist design, another sported an aquamarine background with purple flowers, and a third exhibited a flame stitch in a multitude of colors. Deborah couldn't imagine herself wearing any of them, but not wanting to hurt Margo's feelings, she tried them on and was relieved when none fit.

A quick knock on the fitting room door, followed by Margo holding a handful of dresses. The two that fit were two Deborah could wear without feeling conspicuous. One was navy blue and white checked with a large blue band at the waist and the other had a brown, black and white zebra pattern.

After reminding Margo she had navy blue shoes to wear with one and black shoes with the other, her assistant agreed they could go back to the synagogue.

"Let me treat you to lunch first. It's the least I can do," Deborah said.

They went a little out of their way to Fadi's Mediterranean Grill where they ordered a vegetarian platter to share. They dipped their pita bread into smooth hummus and baba ghanoush, the choppier tabouli and muhummara which, with its walnut and roasted red pepper flavors, was Deborah's favorite of the Middle Eastern treats.

When only a few smears were left on their platter, Margo said, "I'm concerned you might have a congregant with significant memory issues."

Deborah dabbed her mouth with her napkin. "What makes you think that?"

"It's this odd mail you've received."

"Like what?"

"Yesterday and the day before, an envelope came in the mail addressed to you. When I opened each to put the letter on your desk, nothing was in either."

"How do you know they were from the same person?"

"The block printing on the front looked the same."

"No return address?"

"No. I'm thinking someone meant to send you a letter and forgot to put it in, and then the same thing happened the next day. It seems the person can't remember to do something that simple. That's why I'm worried."

Deborah thought of Martha Radinsky. After she couldn't find the synagogue ladies' room, though she'd been in the building every Saturday for years, the rabbi had called her children in Tulsa and suggested they have their mother evaluated to determine if she should still be living alone. But Martha had never sent her a letter and was unlikely to start now.

A scarier thought hit Deborah. No letter was needed to let her know that someone who could harm her knew where to find her. But if she were right, the envelopes might be the way to prove who the sender was.

"Give me the envelopes, and I'll try to figure it out." Deborah spoke as calmly as she could while getting excited the police might be able to discover who sent them. Perhaps DNA where the person licked the flap or maybe some fingerprints.

"Sorry. I threw them out."

Deborah tried to hide her disappointment.

"Is something wrong?"

"No. But if another one comes that looks the same, give it to me without opening it. Could help me guess who sent it."

When the women returned to the synagogue parking lot, they transferred Deborah's new clothes into her car. Deborah looked around and saw no suspicious black vehicles.

***

Thirty minutes later Leigh Goldsmith swung open the door to Deborah's office. Margo must have gone to the women's room just when Deborah needed her to intercede.

"Oh, my god, you're not going to believe what's been going on in my life."

Leigh appropriated one chair while putting her lavender leather purse, which matched her dress and nail polish, in the adjoining one.

"The police told me they have a witness who saw someone push Roberta in front of my Range Rover. They refuse to say who it is, though I certainly have a right to know."

Pausing for a response from the rabbi and getting none, Leigh continued. "Like they think I'm going to try to find him or something? The police are so incompetent."

"They must have their reasons," Deborah said.

Leigh drummed her fingers on the rabbi's desk. "One of them is such an idiot. He thought I'd agree to let him get a record of all incoming and outgoing calls on my land line and cell. My attorney said that without my agreement, he needs a subpoena, which he'll never get."

Considering her own experience with Officer Vega, Deborah suspected Leigh was talking about him.

"I asked my attorney why the police would want that, and he said…" Leigh stood up and closed the door. "You're not going to believe this either. My attorney said they must have a suspect in mind and want to see if I've been in contact with him."

Deborah nodded. Tom had told her Officer Vega was into conspiracy theories.

"Well, aren't you going to say how ridiculous that is?"

Leigh spoke so loudly that Deborah wondered whether Margo was back and could hear her through the closed door.

"Of course it is."

"If that creepy cop comes asking you any questions about me, you'll tell him that."

A few minutes after Leigh left, Margo came into Deborah's office. "Sorry. I was in the parking lot getting something out of my car, or I would have saved you from Leigh."

"I survived."

"She was parked next to me and started complaining about how she'd been given such a small car as a loaner while hers was being fixed. It was quite a bit bigger than my Miata, but I didn't argue with her. It would have been pointless.'

"What color's her car?"

"Black."

***

After Margo left, Deborah put her face in her hands. She had to start thinking clearly instead of fearfully.

All that Leigh's driving a black car proved was that lots of people drove vehicles that color. While Deborah still considered Leigh a suspect for her flat tire and the swastika on her door, she could understand the motive behind that. Leigh would have wanted Deborah and the police to think that someone had pushed Roberta and to believe that person was now after Deborah.

That had led to Isaac's admission of witnessing Roberta's death. Now homicide officers were involved, just as Leigh had wanted. With that being accomplished, there was nothing Leigh had to gain by following her and mailing her empty envelopes.

The person who painted the swastika on her door knew where Deborah lived. If she could convince herself that Leigh was responsible for that, then she could believe it was a second unrelated person who followed her from the synagogue which is also where the envelopes had arrived. Whoever was trying to scare her might know where she worked but not where she and Isaac lived.

Then she could keep her son safe.

Chapter Forty-Eight

Deborah was sitting in the synagogue garden having lunch when Officers Conway and Vega appeared.

"We'd like to talk to you," Conway said. His face gave no hint of a smile.

Deborah offered to move over so they could sit on the swing with her, but both refused, leaving them to tower over her.

"Why didn't you tell us about the connection between Leigh Goldsmith and Jerry Evans?"

Deborah found Vega's question more humorous than shocking. "Leigh and Jerry Evans? Leigh thinks most of the people at the synagogue are beneath her. She would hardly cavort with a criminal."

"What about her daughter?" Conway asked.

"Jenny's always doing good works." Deborah paused. "She may have done some tutoring at a prison. But an educated man like Evans would hardly need her help."

Vega looked down at Deborah. "He volunteered to assist her when she tutored at Huntsville where he was incarcerated."

Deborah tried to hide her surprise but when Vega smiled triumphantly, she knew she'd failed.

She gazed at the officer. "You want to turn a good deed into something nefarious."

He walked closer to the swing. "Makes her an excellent conduit."

"Makes for an unfortunate coincidence."

"You're claiming you didn't know about this?"

"No. And I don't see how you can make this into anything more than a coincidence." Deborah's tone reflected the anger she felt at the thought of anyone besmirching Jenny's good name and good deeds.

Vega took another step closer. His legs were almost touching Deborah's. "She tells her mother Evans is helping her. Mother finds out Evans' connection to Mrs. Krause. He gets out of prison awaiting his second trial. Mother contacts Evans and the rest, as they say, is history."

Deborah stood, forcing Vega to step backwards. "You actually believe that?"

"Working on getting enough evidence to get a subpoena for Mrs. Goldsmith's phone records."

Deborah shook her head.

Vega sneered. "You ought to be glad we're looking into this. Remember your son has placed himself at the scene. If we weren't checking out Evans and Goldsmith, he'd be our prime suspect."

***

Though the officers had been gone for ten minutes, Deborah didn't move. She hardly breathed. Should she have insisted her son speak to the police? He couldn't help them because he couldn't give them anything but a rudimentary description. The only good that had come of it was that everyone knew that Roberta had not committed suicide. But was that worth the price Isaac might pay?

***

"Deborah. Rabbi."

When Deborah realized Margo was talking to her as she passed her assistant's desk, she turned in her direction but didn't speak.

"Is everything all right?" Margo asked.

"I need to go into my office and work on my sermon. Please don't let anyone disturb me." Deborah closed her door and sank into her desk chair.

After a few minutes she turned to her computer and typed "Sermon." Thirty minutes later nothing more appeared on the screen.

She heard a knock on her door and stayed silent, hoping whoever it was would go away. The door opened a crack and she heard Tom's voice. "May I come in?"

"Sure." Her voice sounded as desolate as she felt.

Tom closed the door and sat in front of Deborah's desk. "Margo called me. She said you were bummed out after the police visited you."

The words spilled out of her, first telling Tom about the connection the police had found between the Goldsmiths and Jerry Evans. "How would they have discovered that?"

"Best guess is they checked the visitor logs at Huntsville and also a list of his approved activities. They came to the tutoring program and saw the Goldsmith name. They looked into Jenny and found her mother was Leigh."

"And they're going to drag Jenny into this?"

"Anyone would realize Jenny was an innocent conduit, but…"

"Yes?"

"If they can't find any evidence to prove an actual connection between Leigh and Jerry Evans, they might try to get a confession out of Leigh by claiming that otherwise they'll go after Jenny."

"I can't believe this is happening."

"They also wanted to shake you up so you'd give them any information you had."

Deborah's eyes filled with tears. "They've done that."

"What happened?"

"They said…they said…" Deborah's sobs stopped her efforts to explain.

Tom came behind her desk, kneeled beside her and put his arm around her shoulder.

With him that close, Deborah realized how much she'd missed the smell of a man – the whiff of salty perspiration, the slightly perfumed scent of shaving cream and the spicy fragrance of after shave. So reminiscent of Dov. She rested her head against Tom's chest. After a few moments she stopped crying, smiled at Tom and said, "Thanks. I'll be okay."

He walked slowly back to his chair and waited for her to speak.

"Vega told me that if they weren't looking at Evans and the Goldsmiths, they'd be looking at Isaac as the prime suspect."

"That bastard."

"I shouldn't have insisted he tell the police he was the witness. Nothing good has come of it. And it placed him at the scene."

"You'd never have forgiven yourself if you'd withheld information you thought could help the police. And though it isn't obvious to us now, at some point it might lead to a breakthrough. If you hadn't made sure Isaac spoke to the authorities, and later the truth came out, the assumption would be that you hid the fact because you thought your son was guilty."

Deborah sighed. "I suppose you're right."

"I am. I did criminal work for a long time."

Deborah wasn't sure if Tom was as confident as he seemed or if he was so determined to make her feel better that he'd say anything to accomplish that.

"I have an idea," Deborah said. "As Isaac's parent, I can give his psychologist permission to tell the police what Isaac told him, can't I?"

"Yes."

"Isaac and I were with his psychologist when he confessed to being the witness. So if I asked the psychologist to go to the police, I'm sure he could convince them Isaac was telling the truth that his only role was that of a witness."

"As a friend, I understand why you want to do that. As an attorney, I have to advise against it."

"Why?"

"You aren't privy to what Isaac has told the psychologist in their private meetings. There could be something unrelated but still harmful that you wouldn't want the police to know."

Chapter Forty-Nine

As Deborah drove to pick up Isaac at school for his appointment with Dr. Wright, she reconsidered her decision to avoid telling Tom about her safety concerns. She'd refrained from mentioning the possibility that she'd been followed or her theory that the empty envelopes had come from Jerry Evans or his wife as a warning. She'd been concerned that talking about them would make her sound either like she was paranoid or that she considered herself a damsel in distress who wanted to be saved by Tom. Yet, if she'd mentioned the incidents, he could have advised her whether her worries were needless. She'd have to figure that out for herself.

Isaac was waiting in front of the school. He got into the car and slammed the door behind him.

"Bad day at school?" his mother asked.

"Why am I still going to Dr. Wright's? I confessed to being the witness. What else do you want from me?"

"With all we've both been going through, I need all the help I can get. He wants to see me before your visit with him."

"Haven't you figured it out? He's going to ream you out for not leaving last week when he told you to."

"You're probably right."

"I can come in with you and tell him you should have stayed."

Deborah suppressed a smile. Her son wanted to protect her. "Thanks. I think I can handle it."

Ten minutes later as she sat in Dr. Wright's office, Deborah learned she'd been too optimistic about how tough their meeting would be.

Dr. Wright leaned so far forward in his chair that Deborah felt her space was been invaded even though her chair was a few feet across from his.

"Do you want me to continue seeing your son?"

"Yes, of course."

"Then you can't work at cross purposes with me."

"I'm sorry I didn't leave when you asked me to, but my mother's instinct told me to stay."

"And that took precedence over a psychologist's judgment?"

"Some good has come from it."

"Such as?"

"Isaac took responsibility and told Dr. Krause that he was the witness."

Dr. Wright's frown softened. "How did that go?"

Deborah sighed. "Very hard on Isaac. I should have prepared him for how angry Dr. Krause would be."

"Reasonably so."

"Isaac also told the police who were also quite rough on him."

"He's gone through a lot this week."

Deborah took a tissue from her skirt pocket and dabbed at her eyes. "Yes."

"And you feel it's your fault."

"Yes."

"Even though you know he did what needed to be done."

"Yes."

"Did he do what needed to be done in California?"

"What…what do you mean?"

"Last week he said he'd been afraid to get the police involved here because of what happened in California. I need to explore that with him."

"Please. Only if he brings it up."

"I don't understand."

"That incident was nothing as serious as this situation, but the fewer people who know the less chance that the police find out about it and get the wrong impression about Isaac."

Dr. Wright gazed at Deborah. "You do realize that if he brings it up, I will pursue it."

"Yes," Deborah whispered.

***

Mother and son walked into the house to the sound of a ringing phone. Isaac ran into the kitchen to get the call.

Deborah saw her son's grimace and heard his side of the conversation.

"Yes, I'm doing well at school."

"Yes, I'm still playing basketball."

"Yes, I enjoyed Grandpa's visit."

Deborah took pity on Isaac and grabbed the phone from him. "Hello, Mother. How are you and Dad doing?"

After hearing what each of her brother's seven children was accomplishing, Deborah got an answer to her question. "Your father and I are doing fine. You must have shown him quite a good time. He wants to come back to see you and Isaac soon."

Deborah interpreted that to mean her father was going to return to Houston to provide his version of protecting Isaac and her whether she wanted him to or not.

"Won't Isaac be out of school during Passover?"

"Yes."

"We're coming during the middle four days."

"You're both coming?"

"Yes."

Under normal circumstances Deborah would have been thrilled that her parents cared enough about her and Isaac to travel to Houston. Now all she could think about was how she could keep her father from "protecting" her and her mother from finding out why he felt he needed to.

***

The next call came shortly after dinner.

"Deborah, if you and Isaac are both home, I'd like to come by and talk to you," Douglas Krause said.

"Please do," Deborah responded.

She went to her son's room where an open American history book lay in front of him on his desk while he swayed to the music being delivered through his ear buds.

Deborah spoke loudly enough for her son to hear her over whatever he was listening to. "Dr. Krause is coming over."

He took the ear buds out. "Oh, shit."

"He wouldn't have asked permission if he were planning to be unpleasant."

"I have lots of homework."

"I'm sure he won't stay long."

Fifteen minutes later Deborah opened her door for their guest. He wore a green cardigan, reminiscent of those worn by Mr. Rogers, Deborah's favorite television personality throughout her childhood. Douglas Krause's wasn't buttoned correctly, making the left side longer than the right.

She motioned him to her living room. "Take a seat. I'll get Isaac."

Moments later she returned with Isaac, gently pushing him from the hall into the living room.

When mother and son were seated across from him, Douglas said, "I'm sorry I was hard on you, Isaac. It took a lot of courage for you to tell me what happened. Once my shock and anger abated, I realized that even an adult could have been so frightened of whoever pushed Roberta that he might have fled."

"I was afraid, but honest, I would have forced myself to stay and help if I hadn't seen this woman coming out of her house."

"I needed to know that," Douglas said.

"And I heard something about Mrs. Goldsmith talking about Mrs. Krause and suicide, but she's such a nut case, I never thought anyone would believe her."

Douglas smiled. "That's what I thought at first, too."

"Can I go now?"

Douglas nodded.

When Isaac left the room, Deborah said, "Thank you for coming."

"It was unfair of me to blame a fourteen-year-old boy for all my troubles."

"He understands what he did was wrong."

Douglas patted down his few strands of hair. "I also came to tell you that I gave the police the phone number you found among Roberta's papers. Unfortunately the police said it was to one of those throwaway phones, so they can't tie it to Jerry Evans or his wife."

"How disappointing."

"Speaking of phone calls, I got the strangest one from Leigh Goldsmith. She was so hysterical that at first I couldn't understand what she was saying. It was crazy. She said that if I sent the police after her daughter Jenny, there would be hell to pay."

Deborah hesitated to relate what the police had told her. She didn't need any more needless hatred among her congregants. But her family had withheld information from Douglas before. She couldn't let that happen again.

"What I'm about to say is confidential."

"Of course," Douglas replied.

"The police came by the synagogue today and told me about the strangest coincidence," she began and continued to tell him what they had said.

Douglas formed his hands into fists. "The kind of coincidence Leigh would take advantage of."

***

Deborah didn't trust her judgment any more.

Despite what Tom had said, had she made a mistake when she insisted Isaac tell the police and Dr. Krause that he'd witnessed Roberta's death?

Was her latest mistake having told Dr. Krause about a possible connection between Jerry Evans and Leigh Goldsmith?

Was it a mistake to have failed to tell Tom about the empty envelopes and her concern she was being followed?

The question that haunted her the most as she lay in bed wide awake was whether she was doing all she could to protect Isaac.

Every day before and after she got home she drove around her block a few times to make sure there were no strange cars. Without fail she changed her route between the synagogue and her home and made at least two U turns before she arrived at her house. If she'd been followed, it had been on a Sunday, so perhaps that's the day she would have to be particularly cautious.

She hated living this way. And there was no end in sight. Whoever pushed Roberta in front of Leigh's Range Rover appeared to have been too clever to leave evidence. The witness was the only threat to him or her.

The thought that initially gave Deborah comfort was that, since the empty envelopes had come to the synagogue and the possible car that followed her did so from there, the murderer didn't know where she and Isaac lived. Or was she fooling herself in believing it was Leigh who'd painted the swastika on the door of their house? If she was wrong, the murderer knew where to find both Isaac and her.

But even if the killer were only after her, what would become of Isaac if something happened to her?

He claimed he wanted to return to Israel, but, without her, who would take care of him there? His paternal grandparents, having become parents for the first and only time when they were in their forties, were now both close to ninety. There were no aunts or uncles for him to rely on.

Deborah hated to imagine how miserable Isaac would be if he had to live with her parents. He complained that Deborah's mother's constant questions made him crazy. As much as he enjoyed his grandfather, Deborah had grown up in that home, so she knew that her father consistently capitulated to his wife's wishes. That would mean Isaac would be forced into a level of religious observance he wouldn't tolerate. The only thing worse would be if her parents felt Isaac was too much to handle and asked her brother to raise him.

She thought of writing to Miriam and asking if she could name her as Isaac's guardian. But then her friend would know how frightened Deborah was.

And yet, Deborah had nothing tangible to go to the police about.

She shivered as she realized something specifically dangerous would have to happen before she could expect any help.

Chapter Fifty

Wednesday, Thursday and Friday Deborah's rabbinical duties kept her so busy that she wasn't constantly consumed with safety worries. Beyond the usual was the additional work that came from Bret Singer's Bar Mitzvah preparation. The thirteen year old had convinced himself he wasn't ready to lead services Friday night and Saturday morning. His mother took the frantic child out of school and brought him to Deborah's office where the two of them begged Deborah to go over all his Hebrew parts as well as his speech with him.

The rabbi looked at the pair sitting across from her desk, the teen whose face bore both acne and sweat and his mother who was literally wringing her hands.

"Bret," Deborah asked, "do you know what Bar Mitzvah means?"

"Son of the commandment," he responded in a near whisper.

"You know that you become one when you turn thirteen, even if you don't go through a ceremony."

"Yes."

"What counts is that you are now morally and ethically responsible for your decisions and actions."

"I know."

"But," Mrs. Singer interjected, "he doesn't want to make a fool of himself."

"He and I have worked together long enough that I know that won't happen," the rabbi said.

Seeing Bret was on the verge of tears, she added, "But if it will make you feel better, we'll spend some time today, tomorrow and Friday practicing."

The extra hours of instruction paid off. Bret led the Friday night services with some semblance of confidence and Saturday morning his Hebrew was flawless as he read from the Torah, and when he chanted from the Haftarah, the Book of Prophets.

Friday night Deborah thought she'd caught a glimpse of Tom at the back of the synagogue, but a little later she couldn't find him in the social hall at the dessert reception.

Saturday morning she spotted him at services. Afterwards, as she carried a paper plate with tuna salad, fresh fruit and a bagel from the buffet table in the social hall, she saw him speaking to Bret's father who said, "Rabbi, I'd like to introduce you to my friend Tom Johnson."

"We've already met," they answered simultaneously.

When Mr. Singer left to greet another guest, Tom said, "I'd never seen you wearing a dress until last night, and now you have another lovely one on this morning."

Deborah felt the warmth of a blush cover her cheeks. "That's Margo's influence."

"You're not upset with her for calling me to visit with you last Tuesday?"

"No, she did the right thing. Talking to you helped."

"Are you coming to the party tonight?"

"Sure."

"See you there."

***

Deborah had a black sheath which she dressed up for Bar Mitzvah parties. Tonight she added a black lace shawl. Instead of just her usual makeup of foundation, lipstick and mascara, she also put on blush, eye liner and coral eye shadow.

She went into Isaac's room and found him playing a video game instead of getting dressed.

"We need to leave soon."

"Why are you making me go? Bret's a loser and almost none of my friends will be there."

Deborah couldn't tell him she was afraid to leave him alone in the house for the evening, so all she said was, "Please get ready."

When he came out of his room twenty minutes later in a navy blue short-sleeved shirt hanging out of blue jeans, she decided his far too casual dress was not worth an argument and ushered him to the car.

They arrived at the Singers' large home to find it crowded with guests. The long table in the dining room was filled with chafing dishes from which the catering staff was serving meat balls, salmon, chicken and other delights.

Isaac found some friends and disappeared.

Mrs. Singer appeared with her father in tow. When she introduced him to Deborah, she said, "Mother died a year ago and we've been encouraging Dad to leave New York and move to Houston. We've told him there are lots of lovely widows here. He's such a young sixty-five." She smiled at Deborah as did her gray haired father who insisted on handing the rabbi a plate and following her in the food line.

He found two seats at one of the round tables that filled a living room from which all of the other furniture had been removed. His daughter glanced at them and smiled again.

As Deborah listened to her companion's tales of the dental practice he'd have to give up if he moved to Houston, she surreptitiously looked around hoping to see a congregant about to rescue her. When she saw none coming her way, she feared she was trapped for the evening.

The person seated on the other side of Deborah took his plate and left. Tom slipped into the seat and said, "Hi."

She introduced him to her dinner companion and mentioned she was thirsty. Dr. Singer stood up and announced he'd get her some wine.

Tom smiled. "I don't think you've ever been so happy to see me."

"Thanks for rescuing me."

"We once had a cat that ran up a tree when a dog chased her. The look on your face reminded me of the look on hers that day."

Deborah laughed. "I know how she felt."

"Is Isaac here?"

"Yes, I suspect he and some of the guys are off somewhere playing video games. He didn't want to come, but the thought of leaving him alone in the house all those hours at night…"

"Would you feel better if you had an alarm system?"

"I suspect when Isaac's home alone, he wouldn't use it."

Deborah spotted Mrs. Singer introducing the newly divorced Elizabeth Sussman to her father. As the two became engaged in conversation, they sauntered off, the dentist seemingly have forgotten his errand to get wine for Deborah. She smiled and nodded in the couple's direction.

"I think I'm safe now," she said to Tom. "Go get something to eat."

"Okay. I'll be right back."

Moments after Tom vacated his seat, Mel Freed pounced on it, splashing drops of wine from his glass onto the white tablecloth.

"How are you, Mel?" Deborah asked.

"My wife and I just got back from California."

"I hope you had a good trip."

"I had a very good trip."

Mel took a long sip of wine.

"One day when I sent Florence off shopping, I made a point of visiting the synagogue where you used to be the rabbi." He paused. "I had a good talk with a former board member."

Mel's smirk revealed the name before he spoke it.

"Earl Lipsky."

Deborah's heart rate accelerated. Lipsky had wanted the police brought in when Isaac had his problem.

"You and I will have to talk soon." Mel left as quickly as he'd come.

Deborah rushed from the table to find Isaac. He was in the dining room grabbing a brownie.

"We've got to go."

"First you make me come. Now you make me leave when I've had just one dessert."

As Deborah prodded Isaac to the front door, she saw a surprised Tom looking in their direction.

Chapter Fifty-One

After all the Sunday School teachers and students had left the synagogue, Deborah sat in her office expecting Mel Freed to come by and tell her what he'd learned in California and what he planned to do about it.

While trying to decide how to handle what she expected to be an unpleasant confrontation, she heard a knock on her door.

"Come in," she said in the tone of a condemned prisoner.

Instead of Mel Freed, the person who walked through the door was a stranger. She was wearing a blonde wig of poor quality and was quite thin. Deborah immediately suspected the middle aged woman was a cancer patient going through chemotherapy.

"Please sit down," she told her guest. "I'm Rabbi Deborah Stein."

"I'm Gladys Jones. I'm trying to find out about forgiveness. What do Jews say about it?"

Deborah guessed her visitor, fearing death, wanted to make sure all whom she'd offended had forgiven her before she was gone. Her first instinct was to see if Gladys had her own member of the clergy and suggest she talk to him or her, but, if Gladys had tried that, it must not have worked or the woman wouldn't be here. Deborah would help her any way she could.

"For sins against God, at Yom Kippur, our Day of Atonement, we advise prayer, fasting and performing good deeds."

"Sins against a person. Can those be forgiven?"

"For most sins, you must ask forgiveness."

"If the person won't give it?"

"If after you've asked three times and he still hasn't given it, he's the one in the wrong."

"You said most sins."

"If the sin is one you can't make amends for…an example would be that you'd slandered someone. You can't undo that since what you've said has been spread, and the harm can't be undone. In a case like that, the person can choose whether to forgive you."

"Are there any sins a person can't forgive you for?"

"Perhaps when your parents were alive, you treated them badly. When they're dead, you go to your sister and say please forgive me for treating our parents as I did. She can only forgive you for hurting her because of the way you treated your parents. Only they can forgive you for what you did to them and, since they're dead, that's now impossible."

"That's terrible. There must be a way."

"We believe you can only forgive someone for what they did to you, not for what they did to someone else."

Gladys stood. "You have such a harsh religion."

Before Deborah could respond, her visitor took off.

Deborah was puzzling over this strange encounter when Jenny Goldsmith appeared at her door and asked if she could come in.

"Of course."

"A woman I've never seen before almost knocked me over in the hall."

"First time I ever saw her. I'm afraid I didn't help her."

Jenny sat down. "Maybe you can help me."

Deborah got up and took the chair next to her. "The police have been bothering you?"

Jenny nodded.

"No one will believe you could have anything to do, even indirectly, with Roberta's death."

"That's what I thought, so I spoke to the police even though my mom and her attorney didn't want me to."

Deborah put her arm around her.

"I explained that because my mother was unhappy about my tutoring at the prison, I never told her anything about it. One of the officers, Vega, made it clear he didn't believe me."

"A friend, who used to work with the police, told me Vega is big into conspiracy theories. But once he has no evidence, he'll have to accept the facts."

"I hope you're right. I had no idea there was any connection between Evans and Roberta."

"He didn't talk about who put him in prison or how he felt about being there?"

"No. The only thing he mentioned was his worry about how his wife would manage with him in jail. I asked if she was ill. He called her 'emotionally fragile.'"

Deborah considered that a nice way of saying she was mentally ill – perhaps ill enough to have been a danger to Roberta and now to Isaac and her.

Chapter Fifty-Two

Early Monday morning Isaac woke up with a cough so severe that he couldn't go to school. Deborah, not wanting to leave him alone in the house all day, drove to the synagogue to pick up some work and bring it to her home.

In the dimness of the approaching dawn she saw only one car in the parking lot. Though she didn't recognize it, since it was white rather than black, she walked into the building unconcerned.

As she came to her office, she saw light creeping out under the closed door. She hesitated before deciding that she must have forgotten to turn it off when she left Sunday.

Deborah opened the door and saw a figure sitting at her desk.

Her gasp made him look up at her.

Mel Freed.

A large checkbook sat open on top of her desk.

"What are you doing?"

He hesitated as though considering whether to tell the truth or bluff. He chose the former.

"Looking at how you've spent the money from your discretionary fund."

The rabbi's chest heaved. "How dare you!"

"After what Earl Lipsky told me, can you blame me?"

"I can, and I do."

"Don't worry. I found everything in order – money given to pay bills our members couldn't – for doctors, kosher meals, prom dresses, etc."

She grabbed the checkbook. "I'm not worried. I'm outraged."

"If you gave Isaac access to your synagogue's credit card in California, how could I know if you'd given him access to our checkbook here?"

"I didn't give him access. I was careless."

"Yeah. I heard all about it."

Deborah slumped into a chair, hating to remember what had happened.

***

The California synagogue had given her the credit card to make it easy for her to pay expenses like books for the library, for kosher caterers and items for the gift shop.

Each month when the bill came in, she checked any item over one hundred dollars and barely glanced at the others. She wrote "okay" on the bill and put her initials next to that notation before it went to the synagogue's treasurer Ron Brady who paid it.

The day Ron came into her office carrying three of those bills she was puzzled. But not for long.

"Rabbi, there are some unexpected charges I need you to explain. They were from Amazon, so I did a little research to find out what they were. You'll see them circled with my note about what was purchased."

Deborah took the bills from him and looked at the items he'd circled. The first bill indicated a video game and a movie. On the second, two video games and one movie and on the third, three video games. Deborah took a deep breath. Isaac must have used the synagogue's credit card.

"You've probably noticed," Ron said, "that the video games are pretty violent."

"That's why I refused to buy them for Isaac. He knows I would never have let him watch anything like that."

"Why do you think he used our credit card instead of yours?"

"My personal credit card typically has small charges, so anything extra would have stood out. I'm sorry. If I'd kept the synagogue's card more secure and checked the bills more carefully, this either wouldn't have happened or I would have discovered it quickly. Let's settle this. We'll figure out the total charges, and I'll write you a check." As she spoke, Deborah was considering the appropriate punishment for Isaac. She pulled her checkbook out of her purse.

"It's not that easy," Ron said.

"What do you mean?"

"I had to go to the rest of the executive committee for advice. Earl Lipsky is talking about getting the police involved."

"The police?"

"He and a couple others think it would insure that Isaac never does anything criminal again."

"They're talking about an eleven-year-old boy."

"Earl said the younger they are, the more impressionable they are."

Deborah considered the argument that would affect the deliberations in Isaac's favor. If she reminded Ron of it, she was sure he'd mention it to the executive committee

"Once the police are brought in, there's no way to keep the incident quiet. I feel bad to think about the synagogue washing our dirty laundry in public. You can imagine what some people will say about us in particular and Jews in general."

Ron nodded. "We're taking a vote this afternoon. I'll let you know."

Deborah sat at her desk for hours, doing no work, thinking about everything that had led to Ron's visit. After her father had bought Isaac a PlayStation, she'd carefully monitored what video games he was permitted to buy for it. When he'd wanted some she considered too violent and she'd told Isaac she wouldn't have them in their house, he'd said, "Why can't I be like the other kids and get them? If my dad were alive, he'd let me."

"Don't you understand, violence killed him," had been her response.

She'd considered the matter settled.

But Isaac hadn't.

He'd been clever to use the synagogue's credit card instead of her personal one not only because she was less likely to notice the purchases but also because Isaac must have hoped once his actions were discovered, his mother would lose her job. To him that meant they could leave California and return to Israel.

When Ron came to tell her "the good news," her gratitude was mixed with the knowledge that hers was a Pyrrhic victory. She'd dealt with Earl Lipsky often enough to know he would wreak revenge by strategically leaking the word of Isaac's disgrace.

Deborah had been determined not to let that happen, so now they were in Houston instead of California.

***

After giving Deborah a roughly correct synopsis of what had happened, Mel finished his recitation by announcing, "Earl Lipsky wanted to bring in the police, and he was right. It would have straightened Isaac out."

Deborah gazed at her nemesis. He was clueless about the lengths she'd go to protect her son. The Houston police, already aware that Isaac was at the scene when Roberta was murdered, could turn Isaac's previous interest in violence laced videos and video games into accusations. She couldn't take a chance Mel would go to them. Thanks to what Isaac had told her the day she'd asked if anything unusual had happened, she had something to hold over the man who still sat behind her desk as if he were entitled to.

"The three day suspension your grandson was given when he was found to be in possession of marijuana at school was a joke. Even expulsion would have been too good for him. The police should have been brought in. Maybe it's not too late."

Mel stood. "You wouldn't dare…"

Deborah heard the glass shatter just before she saw the rock hit Mel.

Chapter Fifty-Three

Mel crumpled to the floor, holding his shoulder and howling in pain.

Deborah rushed to him, grateful to find him conscious. "I'll call 911. They'll have an ambulance here quickly."

"I can't wait. Too much pain. Drive me to the hospital now."

"That could cause more damage."

Mel let go of his right shoulder long enough to use his left arm as a lever to help Deborah raise him from the floor.

"No ambulance. Your car. Now."

As he walked to the synagogue parking lot, Mel held his right arm against his chest and used his left arm to support it.

When he sat down in Deborah's car, she tried to put the seat belt on him.

"I can't have that against my shoulder."

"That's why you need an ambulance."

Deborah pulled out her cell phone, but before she could use it, Mel, with tears of pain brimming in his eyes, said, "Have pity and drive."

Deborah drove slowly and carefully, afraid a sudden stop would either cause Mel to lunge forward against the dash or jostle his shoulder. When they arrived at St. Luke's Hospital, Deborah stopped her car long enough to help Mel out and walk him into the emergency room. She got back in her vehicle and parked in the indoor lot. Rather than take a chance she wouldn't have cell reception in the hospital, she called Margo before she returned to Mel.

"I'm sorry to bother you at home, but I need you to go to the synagogue as soon as possible. A rock went through my office window and hit Mel Freed. I'm at the St. Luke's ER with him now. His shoulder was hurt."

"Oh my gosh!"

"Don't let anyone clean up my office before the police come."

"Have you called them?"

"No. Call Marci Dennison at the Anti-Defamation League. She'll get in touch with the police officer who liaisons with the Jewish community, and she'll handle any publicity that comes with the incident."

Deborah was about to call home when she thought better of it. She'd wake Isaac and get him upset about what had happened.

She returned to the ER where she found Mel in a room with an IV in his left arm and his right arm in a sling under a white and blue hospital gown. It was opened enough that Deborah could see one end of electrodes attached to his chest and the other to a beeping monitor.

"We should call your wife."

"She's in San Antonio visiting her sister."

"Your son or daughter-in-law?"

"Both at work. You can stay until I'm finished with the x-rays and the doctor and then take me home."

Deborah didn't have the heart to argue with the injured man, but she decided to use her time at the hospital well. "Tina Solomon's having heart surgery today. I'm going to visit with her family in the surgical waiting room while you're being taken care of."

Five minutes later she arrived in the large area with vinyl chairs and magazines and a machine that allowed you to prepare coffee, tea or hot chocolate. Joe Solomon, his hair resembling that of Albert Einstein's, slowly got up. "Rabbi, how kind of you to come. They took Tina in thirty minutes ago. My daughters should be here soon."

It took the two middle aged women forty-five minutes to arrive, during which time Deborah assured her congregant that the surgeon they chose was excellent and that his wife's surgery and recovery should go well. Once his children came, she spent a few minutes with them before heading back to the ER, where the receptionist checked and told her x-rays had revealed that Mel had a broken shoulder and was waiting for the doctor to immobilize his arm.

She turned from the receptionist's desk and heard, "Deborah, thank God you're all right."

Tom's arms were around her, holding her in a bear hug.

So many years had passed since she'd been held by a man. Pressed against Tom's chest, she heard the rhythm of his heart beats, smelled the fragrance of a newly laundered shirt and felt the protection of his sturdy arms. She let herself enjoy all these sensations for a few moments, and then gently broke away.

She looked up at Tom who took both her hands in his. "I called the synagogue this morning. I'd been concerned ever since you suddenly left the Bar Mitzvah party. I wanted to make sure you were okay."

He gently squeezed her hands.

"When I asked for you, Margo said a rock had gone through your office window and that you were at St. Luke's emergency room. I hung up before she could say more and rushed here."

"I brought Mel Freed to the hospital. He was sitting behind my desk and had just stood up when the rock came through. He was in a lot of pain. The doctor's taking care of his shoulder."

"Isn't he about six inches taller than you?"

"Yes," Deborah answered in a puzzled tone.

"Considering your height and his, if you'd been standing behind your desk, the rock would have hit you in the head."

Deborah shuddered.

Tom spoke calmly. "We have to get the police involved."

"I told Margo to call Marci Dennison who knows the right officer to contact."

"The right officers are Conway and Vega."

Tom put his arm around Deborah and led her to a chair. He sat next to her and spoke in a near whisper.

"I'm afraid someone was aiming for you."

Chapter Fifty-Four

Deborah stared at Tom. "Conway and Vega are homicide detectives. You think someone was trying to kill me?"

"At the least they were trying to scare you and could have critically hurt you. Conway and Vega need to know."

"If you're right, Jerry Evans or his wife is the likely culprit. But how would either know where my office is?"

"Anyone is welcome during your Sabbath services."

"Yes, but my office isn't near the sanctuary. It's in the back of the building where a visitor wouldn't go. Unless…"

"Unless what?"

"You told me Jerry Evans' wife was taller than he was and had become quite thin during the trial. How else would you describe her?"

"Lots of wrinkles, brown hair."

"Covered by a blonde wig." Deborah shook her head. "I'm such a fool."

"I'm not following you."

"I had an unexpected visitor to my office yesterday. Because she was thin and her face looked drawn and she was wearing a blonde wig, I assumed she was a cancer patient in need of help. She got angry when I explained that Judaism teaches that if you've harmed someone who's died, no one else can forgive you for what you've done to that person. If her wig was covering brown hair, she could have been Jerry's wife, seeking forgiveness for Roberta's death which I couldn't give her."

"You'll need to describe her to a police artist."

"Maybe she was the figure in black I glimpsed at Roberta's burial. Perhaps she was seeking forgiveness even then."

"More likely she'd realized there was a witness and had come to see if she could spot the person."

"Thank God Isaac wasn't there."

"I'll call Conway. Go to the synagogue and wait there for him and Vega."

"But, Mel Freed…"

"You go. I'll take him home."

Deborah smiled. "Have a good time explaining *that* to him."

***

Instead of going directly to the synagogue, Deborah stopped at home.

She found Isaac, with a blanket around him, sitting in the den, eating cereal and watching television. When he tried to greet her, he coughed loud and long.

Deborah put her hand on his forehead. "Feels like you've got a temperature. I'll get you some Tylenol. Have you taken your cough medicine?"

Isaac shook his head.

"I'll get that, too."

Deborah returned with the medicine and a glass of water. After giving them to Isaac, she said, "There's been another anti-Semitic incident. Someone threw a rock that shattered a window at the synagogue."

"Shitheads!"

"Agreed. But since we know that type is on the loose, I want you to be extra careful. I've checked all the doors. Don't let anyone in the house except me. Keep a phone nearby, and if anything scares you, call 911 immediately and then me."

"Yeah. Yeah."

Deborah kissed the top of Isaac's head and walked towards the door.

"Which window did they hit?"

Deborah pretended she didn't hear, and left the house.

***

When the rabbi pulled into the synagogue's parking lot, she saw a police car near the front entrance. As she got out of her vehicle, Margo, who must have been watching for her, ran out of the building.

Her assistant caught her breath and said, "One set of police officers, who investigate hate crimes was here. They took lots of pictures of the rock and the shattered glass. Then two others showed up, and the first two left."

"What about the press and the synagogue members?"

"Marci Dennison put out a press release saying this was being investigated as a possible hate crime. I sent out an email to all the congregants saying that a rock went through a window, that the police were investigating and that you'd send out another email when we had more information. And I arranged for the window to be repaired."

The rabbi hugged Margo. "Perfect."

"I don't know why they sent a second set of police. They're waiting for you," Margo said.

Deborah entered her office to find Conway and Vega sitting in front of her desk in deep conversation. When they saw her, they both stood. She closed the door.

"Your boyfriend seems convinced the rock was meant for you," was Vega's greeting.

"I don't have a boyfriend."

"Seems to me, if he's right, it would be someone in your congregation who knew where your office is."

Vega's comment indicated to Deborah that he was thinking of Leigh Goldsmith as the culprit.

"Before you jump to any conclusions, listen to what happened yesterday," Deborah said. She told the officers about the stranger who'd visited her the day before.

"Tom suggested I work with one of your sketch artists to see if the person could have been Mrs. Evans."

"Did anyone else see the visitor?" Conway asked.

"Jenny Goldsmith came to my office immediately afterwards and said someone had almost knocked her over. I suspect it was the same person. Maybe she can describe her, too."

Vega snickered. "How convenient. The daughter of a prime suspect wants to help you shine a spotlight on someone else."

"What?"

Vega moved closer to the door where the rabbi was standing. "Another coincidence, huh?"

The door opened, barely missing her.

"What are you doing here, Johnson?" Vega asked. "Think your girlfriend needs an attorney?"

Tom walked between Deborah and Vega and glared at the officer. "I'm here to make sure you give the rabbi all the protection she needs."

Conway gently tapped Tom's shoulder. "It's hard to know whether we're dealing with a hate crime or something directed at the rabbi. The latter is only the case if we assume Jerry Evans and his wife suspect she's a witness to a crime that they may have been involved in."

"I've been worried about a couple of other things," Deborah said. She told them about the possibility that she'd been followed and about the empty envelopes.

"You're not sure you were followed and there was nothing threatening in the envelopes which your assistant threw away," Vega said.

Deborah nodded.

Tom turned to Conway. "It's a series of events, starting with the flat tire and the swastika on her door and ending with a rock aimed at her."

Conway shook his head. "You know our budgetary issues. There's no way this can result in anything more than extra patrols around the synagogue."

Tom raised his voice. "The swastika was on the door of her house."

"Everything else has been connected to the synagogue. It's even the place from which she may have been followed," Conway reminded him.

"She's your girlfriend. You protect her," Vega said.

"This is not a girlfriend issue. This is protecting a rabbi. I can picture the headline. 'Cop's stupidity causes Houston rabbi harm.'"

Vega pushed Conway to get closer to Tom. "Why you..."

Conway grabbed Vega by the arm. "We're going now. I'll arrange for the sketch artist."

When the two police officers left, Tom and Deborah sank into the chairs in front of her desk.

"I wish you'd told me you thought you'd been followed and about the empty envelopes. Promise me if anything, no matter how insignificant it seems, bothers you, you'll let me know."

Deborah hesitated. "Okay."

"Meanwhile you need to meet with the sketch artist. We've got to find out if Mrs. Evans was your Sunday visitor."

Chapter Fifty-Five

"Why didn't you tell me the rock came through your office window?" Isaac's cheeks were red enough to suggest a fever. The blanket around his shoulders slipped to the floor.

Deborah closed their front door and walked into the hall. She picked up the blanket and put it back around her son's shoulders. He shook it off.

"It didn't seem that important."

"You tell me not to lie and then you do."

"You're right. I'm sorry. The truth is I didn't want to worry you."

"The truth is you don't want me to know that someone still thinks you, not me, is the witness."

Isaac coughed so hard he had trouble catching his breath. He let his mother lead him to the den where he sat down while she went into the kitchen to get him water and his cough medicine.

When she returned, she said, "I think we're safe but, just in case I'm going to have an alarm system put in. We'll both have to be diligent about using it."

"I'll only do that if you let me know what's happening, like when you get a rock thrown through your office window."

"Who told you?"

"Bunch of my friends called. Everyone's talking about how it hit Mel Freed, and they wondered why he was in your office so early in the morning. I said they shouldn't be surprised that an old guy came up with some excuse to be alone with you."

"Isaac!"

"That was to get even with him for some of the things he's said about you."

Deborah couldn't stay angry with her son. Anyone who heard what he said would consider it a joke and not a rumor. She tried to tousle Isaac's hair which was so sticky from sweat that she didn't succeed. A sickly odor, reminiscent of stale beer, emanated from him.

"Why don't you take a hot shower? The steam might help your cough. Meanwhile I'll call a couple of alarm companies to get estimates."

"I mean it. I'll only use it if you tell me what's going on. I'm fourteen, and I've witnessed a murder. You shouldn't try to keep things from me."

Deborah took a deep breath. All she had accomplished by trying to withhold information from her son was to alienate him. "I'm going to police headquarters tomorrow to meet with a sketch artist. A strange woman visited me in my office yesterday, and we're trying to figure out who she is and if she had anything to do with the rock."

"Shit. It could have been a woman I saw pushing Mrs. Krause."

***

The next day when Deborah arrived downtown at the indoor parking lot attached to the police department building, she found a gate obstructing her entrance. She pushed a button marked "help" and heard a voice ask her whom she was there to see. After she gave Officer Conway's name, the gate lifted with a screech, and she entered to find herself on a circular ramp taking her from one floor to another with no available parking spots. Finally after traveling up six floors she found a space, left her car and took an elevator to the first floor where she entered the building. A police officer directed her to put her purse on a conveyor belt where it was scanned as she walked through an x-ray machine. A second officer asked for her driver's license and used a picture he took of it to make a badge for her.

After a ten minute wait, Officer Conway appeared and shook her hand. "Since we're still working on the premise we're dealing with a hate crime, before we take up the sketch artist's time, we want you to look at some pictures of skinheads, white supremacists and other haters."

"Okay," Deborah said as Conway led her to an elevator.

The women in the pictures she viewed were mainly young, most with tattoos which Conway explained were signs of their beliefs or affiliations.

"Many of them have an 88 tattoo. What does that stand for?"

"Since H is the eighth letter of the alphabet, it's a shortcut for Heil Hitler."

After fifteen minutes of looking, Deborah said, "None of these was my Sunday visitor."

They were back on the elevator and up a few more floors before Deborah was ushered into a room where she waited for half an hour before the door opened to reveal a woman in her sixties with shoulder length gray hair. Though a little taller and a little heavier than Deborah, she seemed overwhelmed by the kit she was carrying.

Deborah rushed to her. "Let me help you."

The woman, who introduced herself as Gail Larson, insisted she could manage.

She put her kit on the table and opened it to reveal an easel, a t-square, stencils, a drawing board, pastel paints and a catalogue featuring images of hundreds of different eyes, eyebrows, noses, lips, foreheads, hairstyles and ears.

While she set up her easel, she instructed Deborah to search the catalogue and choose each of the facial features that matched that of the woman she wanted to identify.

As she picked each portion of the face, she handed it to Ms. Larson who used it to create part of her drawing. Almost an hour later, the artist showed Deborah what she'd created.

"It's a lot like her, except she had more wrinkles."

The artist went back to work.

When she finished, Deborah said, "Amazing. That's who visited me, but I'm sure the blonde hair was a wig."

"If we've got the face right, it's easy enough to change the hair color."

She left and came back with Officer Conway who was holding a newspaper picture. He put it next to the artist's rendition.

"That's her, with brown hair instead of a blonde wig," Deborah said.

She read the caption under the picture. "Jerry Evans leaving the courtroom with his wife."

***

When she arrived home, Deborah called Tom and told him she'd identified Mrs. Evans as the woman who visited her the day before the rock went through her office window.

"What happens now?" she asked.

"The police will try a 'knock and talk.'"

"A what?"

"They'll knock on her door and say they want to talk to her. They'll give her a choice of speaking with them at her home, in their squad car or at the station."

"Then what?"

"Since her husband has an attorney, she'll either call him, and he'll tell her to refuse, or she's smart enough to know she doesn't have to talk to the police and will refuse without calling."

"She can do that?"

"Her visit to you doesn't prove anything."

"Then what did we gain by my identifying her?"

"Enough to motivate the police to try to talk to her. My hope is that once she knows the police are on to her, she'll end any plans she has about going further."

Deborah shook her head. "Going further" was Tom's euphemistic way of saying "going beyond just threatening you and Isaac."

Chapter Fifty-Six

Deborah dreaded the visit.

But considering how often she reminded her congregation that visiting the sick and comforting mourners were two of the most important good deeds they could perform, she couldn't be a hypocrite. So Tuesday morning she drove to the condominium, gave her car to the attendant and entered the sixteen story building. She went to the desk and announced she was there to see Florence and Mel Freed. After calling the couple, the receptionist buzzed the rabbi into an area that held a bank of elevators. Deborah took one, got off on the sixth floor and walked down the hall to the Freed's apartment.

Florence opened her door and hugged the rabbi. The elfin woman, at just four feet and nine inches, was one of the few people who made Deborah feel tall.

"Thank you for all you did for Mel yesterday. I came back from San Antonio as soon as I heard."

"How's he doing?"

Florence motioned the rabbi into her living room and onto a damask couch where she sat next to her.

"He seems to be doing fine until I ask him why he was meeting with you so early in the morning, and then he starts moaning and doesn't answer."

Deborah suppressed a laugh. Poor big Mel, afraid of his tiny wife's wrath.

"I'm not the only person wondering."

All mirth left Deborah. Could Isaac's offhand remark have made its way to Florence? How many other people had heard it?

"Why was he there at such an early hour?" Florence asked.

"He knows I sometimes come to shul to get work done before services, so it's a good time to catch me to discuss synagogue business."

Deborah reassured herself that, considering the importance Jewish teachings put on keeping peace in the family, her stretching the truth was necessary.

"Seems odd he didn't tell me that himself."

"He's probably in emotional shock because of all's he been through."

"Could be." Florence paused. "Our bedroom's around the corner. Why don't you go see him while I make some coffee."

Deborah found Mel in pajamas and robe sitting in a chair, staring out the window.

After asking him how he was feeling and hearing his grunt in reply, Deborah quickly and quietly let him know what she'd told his wife.

"What we're not going to tell her or anyone else is what I know about your son and you know about my grandson. We're going to let sleeping dogs lie."

Deborah managed to keep a neutral expression which hid her relief. "Agreed."

***

Deborah stopped home to check on Isaac. He coughed less often and less severely but enough that she decided he wasn't well enough to keep his appointment with Dr. Wright.

Ten minutes after she called his office, the phone rang.

"Rabbi Stein, this is Dr. Wright. "I'd like to know if you're canceling just for today or permanently."

"Just today. Isaac's ill."

"I thought perhaps you decided to stop treatment because you were concerned he was going to discuss what happened in California with me."

"No. In fact, I plan to encourage him to talk to you about it."

"That's wise."

When their conversation ended, Deborah mumbled to herself, "No time like the present."

She found Isaac in the den sitting cross legged on the couch with a blanket tucked in at his waist. She sat down next to him.

"Next week when you meet with Dr. Wright, I think you should talk to him about what happened in California."

"No!" Isaac threw off the blanket, stood and started heading out of the room.

"I'm sorry, Isaac. I made too much of the incident and made it traumatic for you."

Isaac stopped, turned and gazed at his mother.

"Please come back."

Isaac stood as though frozen and, after a long pause, walked back. But instead of taking his former seat next to his mother, he sat in a chair across from her.

"Mel Freed was in California and met Earl Lipsky who told him what happened. And you know what? The world didn't come to an end."

Isaac moved to the edge of his chair. "Freed will use it against you and you'll lose your job."

"No. He understands a lot of boys make mistakes, like his grandson having marijuana."

Isaac smiled. "You blackmailed him. Way to go."

"The point is that children make mistakes, and parents shouldn't overreact to them."

"But Mr. Lipsky told me he wanted me to go to juvy so I'd learn my lesson and not become a hardened criminal."

"Mr. Lipsky is an ass, and I wish I'd told him so."

"You didn't want him talking about me and everyone agreeing with him."

"I should have realized that if he'd done that, people would have seen it as diminishing him, not you."

"But you thought what I did was wrong."

"Of course. Using the synagogue's credit card was taking their money, just as if you'd stolen it from the premises."

Isaac shook his head. "I knew it."

"What I lost sight of was that an eleven-year-old boy, who badly wanted something his mother wouldn't give him, would figure out the simplest way to get what he wanted. And I'd made it too easy for you to use the credit card."

"It's not your fault. You didn't leave it lying around. I had to go in your purse when you weren't looking and get into your wallet to find it." Isaac's eyes brimmed with tears. "I wanted to hurt you and the synagogue."

Deborah's voice was barely above a whisper. "Because they had taken me away from you all those times you needed me."

Isaac nodded.

Mother and son got up simultaneously, met in the middle of the room and held each other while they cried.

Chapter Fifty-Seven

Deborah planned to stay home with Isaac, but when he told her he wanted to sleep, she went to the synagogue where Margo greeted her in a tone that did not reflect her usual calm demeanor.

"Your phone hasn't stopped ringing. It's worse than yesterday."

"Sorry," Deborah said. "After I visited Mel, I stopped home to check on Isaac. Thank God, both are doing well."

"I've assured the callers you're fine, that the window's been fixed and that the police are looking into the incident."

"Thanks."

"Some of them have questioned why Mel was 'bothering' you so early in the morning." Margo laughed. "They asked in a way that indicates they're wondering if he's a lecher."

"Oh dear."

"Consider yourself lucky. Otherwise they might be trying to figure out why Tom was with you at the emergency room and took Mel home."

The rabbi felt her cheeks getting warm. "What's on my schedule for the rest of the day?"

"You're going from one extreme to another. Now that Lisa Barr's conversion is complete, she and Jeremy Novak are coming to talk to you about their wedding ceremony. They're followed by Jeremy and Melody Sloan who want a Jewish divorce, as well as a civil one, and need information about obtaining it."

Deborah had been one of the three members of the *beit din*, a Jewish religious court, at which Lisa, after a year of Jewish studies, had appeared so she could offer assurances of the sincerity of her desire to convert. The rabbi sighed. She would likely be on another *beit din* when the Sloans sought their Jewish divorce.

The first meeting went as expected. The couple was euphoric as they told Deborah stories of their courtship which she'd repeat during their ceremony.

The encounter with the Sloans took a surprising turn. After the rabbi gently probed the reasons they'd decided to divorce, the couple began to question whether that was what they really wanted. They left, agreeing to meet with a marriage counselor Deborah recommended.

When they walked out of her office, Margo came in. "Tom Johnson said he was in the neighborhood, so he came by to check on how you're doing. I sent him to the rose garden."

Deborah stood to join him.

"Wait." Margo grabbed Deborah's purse and pulled out a lipstick and a small mirror and handed both to her. "First things first."

Deborah followed Margo's orders. Once in the garden she saw Tom sitting on the swing. He got up, walked towards her with his arms out as though to hug her, but quickly put them down. They sat on the swing, facing each other, not touching.

"Have you recovered from yesterday?"

"I'm fine. Thank you for taking Mel home. How did you explain your presence?"

"I said when Margo told me what happened, I went to the emergency room to relieve you since you needed to meet with the police."

"Have they spoken to Mrs. Evans?"

"Her husband answered the door and refused to let them. He said his attorney was representing both him and his wife, and any communications had to be through their lawyer." Tom paused. "I'm sorry."

"You warned me that might happen."

"The police are increasing patrols around the synagogue."

Deborah nodded.

"I'd like your permission to drive around your house a few times in the late afternoons and evenings when you or Isaac is at home."

"I couldn't let you do that."

"The police visit likely affected the Evans so that they'll stop trying to frighten you. I'll do it for a couple of weeks until we're sure that's the case."

"Thank you." Deborah put her hand on Tom's arm and quickly removed it.

"Don't worry if you see my car circling your neighborhood."

"What kind is it?"

"A black Lexus."

***

Deborah entered the house and saw Isaac napping on the couch. When the phone rang, she rushed to answer it before it woke him.

"Why didn't you tell me someone was trying to kill you? I'm your father. Did you think you could keep it from me?"

"Calm down, Dad."

"A boulder thrown through your office window."

"It was a rock."

"Saturday the congregation should say a prayer of gratitude that you weren't harmed."

"I'm sure they will."

"The man who was hurt, please tell me it wasn't that Tom fellow, meeting you alone early in the morning."

"No, Dad. It was the synagogue president. How do you know any of this?"

"How do I know? How do I know when my own daughter didn't think to call and tell me she's all right?"

"Sorry, Dad."

"My friend Lou's son lives in Houston. He called his dad who called me. Can you imagine how I felt to have a virtual stranger tell me what my daughter should have?"

"You said Lou was your friend."

"I call everyone my friend, even virtual strangers."

"Thank God, I'm fine."

"Are the police giving you around the clock protection?"

"They're increasing patrols around the synagogue."

"That's all they're doing?"

"I'm putting in an alarm system to be extra cautious."

"You put in the best one they have. I'll pay for it."

"It's okay. I can afford it."

"I should come to Houston before Passover, but your mother would get suspicious that something is wrong, and I don't want to worry her."

"Of course, you don't."

"If, God forbid, anything happens to you or Isaac in the meantime, I'll never forgive myself."

Chapter Fifty-Eight

Deborah's stomach roiled when she saw the black car passing her house for the second time. The first was when she stepped onto her front porch to pick up her mail. The next was when she looked out her window as she was about to close her living room drapes.

She told herself that just because the color was the same didn't mean it was the vehicle that had followed her previously. Nonetheless, she kept the drapes open just enough to see if it appeared again.

The third time it passed her house, she pulled out her phone to call the police, but stopped. She remembered Tom telling her he owned a black Lexus, and would be checking out her neighborhood occasionally. Grateful for his trying to protect her and Isaac, she walked outside to the front yard. When he came by again, she waved. He stopped and opened his window.

"If you spotted me this quickly, I guess I'm not as good at surveillance as I'd hoped."

"I don't want you to have wasted your effort. Come in and have dinner with Isaac and me. I'm about to warm up leftover chicken."

"I'll park my car and be right there."

Deborah went inside and found Isaac in his room with his math book open and buds in his ears. She motioned to him to take them out.

Since she saw no need to concern her son by telling him why Tom was in their neighborhood, she said, "I spotted Tom Johnson driving by when I got the mail so I invited him to join us for leftovers."

"Is he stalking you?"

"Don't be silly. Go entertain him while I finish in the kitchen."

"You should pay me to babysit him."

Deborah couldn't help smiling. "Enough. Out," she said, pointing at the doorway.

Isaac sighed and got up. "But if he gets depressed when I crush him in some video games, don't be upset."

The front door closed.

"Deborah, can I help you with dinner?"

"No, you need to go to the den where my son will challenge you to a video game."

The three of them arrived there simultaneously. Isaac looked at Tom appraisingly. "I hope you don't mind losing."

"In your dreams," Tom said.

Deborah left and went into the kitchen. As she put a chicken casserole in the oven and made a salad, she heard screechy blip sounds coming from the den along with male voices shouting, "Gotcha."

"Dinner," she called.

No response, just a crescendo of screechy blips.

"Dinner."

Same result.

She went into the den.

"I told you I'd beat you," Isaac crowed.

"Barely," Tom responded. "Best of three. We'll go at it again after dinner."

Isaac grinned. "You don't stand a chance."

Isaac hadn't been this animated since his grandfather's visit. She smiled at Tom.

The man was almost too good to be true.

***

The next evening Deborah was putting the dinner plates into the dishwasher when the phone rang. She hoped it was Tom. She wanted to tell him how much she appreciated the time and attention he'd devoted to Isaac the night before.

"Hello." The only response was Deborah's caller hanging up. Likely someone who, upon hearing her voice, realized they had a wrong number.

An hour later Deborah's phone greeting was answered the same way. She felt uneasy but convinced herself not to make too much of it.

When Deborah finished showering and was leaving the bathroom in her pajamas and robe, Isaac approached her in the hall.

"Some pervert called."

"What do you mean?" she asked.

"I picked up the phone, heard some heavy breathing, and then he hung up."

"It was a man?"

"Guess it was. They're the ones who are usually pervs."

"If it happens again, we'll report it to the phone company. They might have a way of tracing the call."

"Whatever."

Deborah walked into her bedroom, closed the door and sank onto her bed. Could their caller be Jerry Evans or his wife? If they had her home number, they must know where she and Isaac lived.

If she reported the calls to the police, would that be enough to get her and Isaac some protection? She didn't want to go to them and have to deal with Officer Vega if nothing would come of her visit. Tom could advise her. She looked at the clock on her nightstand. After eleven. Too late to phone him.

***

The next morning, being busy with happy meetings – the parents of a baby girl planning to name her at Sabbath services and the parents of a baby boy planning a *bris*, a religious circumcision ceremony, the rabbi had to postpone calling Tom. He phoned her instead.

"I had to give you my good news. My daughter's set a date for me to visit her in Japan."

Deborah remembered Tom's daughter Courtney had been teaching English there when her mother had become critically ill, and that Tom, following his wife's wishes, had kept the news from her. She'd arrived home after her mother had died and blamed Tom for her earlier absence.

"Sounds like this invitation is the start of a healing process," Deborah said.

"My hope exactly."

"When are you leaving?"

"In a week. I hope by then we'll feel confident you and Isaac are safe."

"Of course, we will."

At that moment Deborah got an idea about what she could do if she got another phone call. If she took matters into her own hands, she could protect Isaac and herself and Tom could leave without worrying.

Chapter Fifty-Nine

Deborah heard her phone ringing as she walked into the house. She rushed to answer it and was surprised when the technician from the alarm company was on the line, setting up an installation appointment for the following week. She'd been prepared for the phantom caller.

A little later as she and Isaac were sitting at the kitchen table eating hamburgers and French fries, he asked, "Why do you keep staring at the phone? Are you hoping Tom will call?"

"Of course not."

"Are you worried the heavy breather will?"

"No, I didn't even realize I was looking at it."

Isaac took his plate to the sink and, before leaving the kitchen, told his mother he had to study for a history test.

For once Deborah was grateful her son would have buds in his ears. Listening to music while he worked, he wouldn't hear the phone ring.

Ever since talking to Tom, Deborah had been considering the wisdom of her plan. Likely Roberta had met with Mrs. Evans who, aware her husband would soon be facing a retrial, wanted Roberta's sympathy and assurance she wouldn't be a party to putting him back in jail. She'd received neither.

If Deborah met with her, she could provide both sympathy and assurance that the witness could not identify whoever pushed Roberta in front of Leigh's SUV. Once Mrs. Evans knew that neither Deborah nor Isaac was a threat and that she and her husband were safe, they would leave Isaac and her alone.

An hour later the phone rang.

"Hello."

No answer.

"Don't hang up. I want to meet with you."

Silence.

Deborah was ready to say more, but the line went dead.

Perhaps her request was being viewed as a trick, maybe a way to get someone to say something incriminating. If another call came, she'd have to convince her caller that wouldn't happen.

Though Deborah stayed up until after eleven, the phone didn't ring.

***

The next morning when Deborah passed Margo's desk, she told her assistant she'd answer her phone herself.

Margo chuckled. "You can try, but that won't last long."

Upon hearing the rabbi's voice, most of her congregants made comments such as, "Rabbi, I didn't mean to bother *you* about this."

"This" usually turned out to be a question about what time services were starting that night or whether the synagogue library had a specific book or whether a Passover preparation class was being scheduled.

Deborah was about to request that Margo reclaim her usual duties when the phone rang, and Deborah heard the silence she'd hoped for.

She spoke before her caller could hang up. "You don't have to say anything when we meet. I'll do all the talking. If you have a question, you can write it down and after I've read it, tear up the paper. That way nothing can incriminate you."

The caller hung up with a slam that startled Deborah and made her decide her quest was useless. She walked out of her office and told Margo, "The phones are all yours."

***

As the rabbi entered the sanctuary to conduct Friday night services, her congregants greeted her with, "Shabbat shalom," their wish she would have a peaceful Sabbath.

For as long as she could remember Deborah had always felt the worries and responsibilities of the week fade away as the joy of the day of peace and rest began. This Friday night was no exception. She wiped out thoughts of Jerry Evans and his wife and hang-up phone calls and her disappointment that her plan to end the threat to Isaac and her hadn't worked.

She walked up the steps to the *bima,* and once on that raised platform, lit the Sabbath candles, the congregation joining her in the prayer that thanked God for sanctifying them by His commandments and commanding them to kindle the Sabbath lights.

The rabbi particularly loved what came next – the songs welcoming the Sabbath by comparing it to a beloved bride.

When the evening prayer service ended, Deborah and Isaac went to the home of Gary and Mimi Teller whose son Josh was in Isaac's class. The rabbi almost never had to cook Friday night dinners since one congregational family after another extended invitations to her.

After the rabbi gave her hosts assurances that she'd gotten over the rock thrown through her office window and that the police were still looking into the incident, the five of them sat down at the dining room table which was covered by a white tablecloth embroidered with roses.

Deborah's sense of calm continued as they sang "*Shalom Aleichem,*" Peace Be Upon You. When it ended, the parents put their hands on their children's heads and blessed them.

The Sabbath typified what Deborah prayed Isaac would always have – peace, joy and blessings.

***

Saturday morning, in between readings from the Torah, the five books of Moses, Deborah took part in a naming ceremony in which a baby girl received her Hebrew name that forever linked her to the Jewish people.

Deborah's afternoon was filled with study, some with congregants who wanted to discuss that morning's reading and some on her own.

She and Isaac ate dinner and returned to the synagogue for *Havdalah,* meaning separation, as it's the service which separates the Sabbath from the rest of the week. The rabbi explained to those gathered that they were drinking wine to welcome the new week together; they were enjoying the aroma of spices so the sweetness of the Sabbath would stay with them; and they were lighting the special twisted braid candle with its several wicks to light the way from the Sabbath to the rest of the week.

With the peaceful feeling of the Sabbath still accompanying her, Deborah returned home renewed.

Everything changed a few minutes later when her phone rang.

"Hello," Deborah said.

"When?" her caller asked in a muffled voice.

Deborah was about to say, "When what?" but stopped herself as understanding and anxiety infused her. "Tomorrow, at a public place, like a restaurant."

A pause.

Deborah feared another hang up, but instead she heard, "Skyler's at three thirty."

Chapter Sixty

"You're acting even weirder than usual."

"What?" Deborah asked Isaac. She was curled up in the corner of the den couch with a closed book on her lap.

"Every time I walk through here, I see you spaced out." He sat down next to her. "Then you agreed I could go to the movies with Kyle without even asking the rating of the film."

Deborah sat up. "What is the rating?"

Isaac shook his head. "PG-13. His mother won't let him go to anything else."

Deborah smiled. "Smart woman."

A horn honked. "That's them. See you later."

All day Deborah had been debating whether she should show up at Skyler's at three thirty, just ninety minutes from now. She went over her plan again. She'd picked a public place so she didn't have to worry about her visitor attacking her. She'd arrive early and not leave until well after her guest had. She would show sympathy to Mrs. Evans and convince her that she and Isaac could cause her and her husband no harm. That should insure Isaac's and her future safety. Deborah was assuming it would be the wife who came as she was the one who'd visited her at the synagogue, but it could be the husband or both.

They understood she knew enough to want this meeting, so if she didn't show up, she'd put Isaac and herself in more danger.

If she could convince them she was the witness, at least Isaac would be safe.

***

Skyler's was large enough to seat over a hundred patrons, but when Deborah arrived, she saw about a dozen. They were sitting at dark wood square tables, which contrasted with the neon colored walls surrounding them. Deborah asked for a table in the corner and told the waitress she'd like a cup of coffee while she waited for her guest. The server was in the midst of pouring a second cup when the woman who'd come to Deborah's office the week before walked in.

The rabbi stood so Mrs. Evans would see her. She shuffled over and sat down. Her blonde wig was askew. Her eyes darted from Deborah to the waitress to the few other patrons. Her hands revealed a slight tremor.

Deborah felt a mixture of fear and pity.

"Coffee?" the waitress asked.

Mrs. Evans nodded, and the waitress poured some into her cup.

"I'll let you know when we're ready to order. It may be a bit," Deborah said.

"Sure." The server walked away.

"Thank you for meeting me," Deborah said.

Mrs. Evans' eyes flashed from Deborah's face to her chest and back again.

"I wanted to clear up some misunderstandings," Deborah added.

Mrs. Evans tapped her foot.

Though Deborah had offered to have Mrs. Evans stay silent, she found having a one person conversation disconcerting.

The rabbi rushed on. "I'm sorry for what you and your husband have gone through, but you're both safe now."

Her guest gazed at Deborah who continued. "I'm sure your husband's attorney has told you that without Roberta Krause's testimony, he'll be free for good. I know the witness who saw her being pushed can't identify who did it…because I'm that witness."

Mrs. Evans moved her jaw from left to right and back again a few times.

"I only saw the back of the person so I could give no identification to the police. Their prime suspect is a member of my synagogue who was feuding with Roberta. Since I couldn't identify her, they haven't been able to arrest her yet."

Mrs. Evans looked all around the restaurant before bringing her attention back to Deborah.

"The point is you don't have to try to scare me into keeping silent since I have nothing to tell."

Mrs. Evans stared at Deborah, stood and left.

Deborah's heart raced and her hands shook. Had she made things worse? No, she couldn't think that way. She had to get a grip.

The waitress's voice startled her. "Is your friend gone for good?"

"I hope so. I mean I think so." Deborah took a ten dollar bill from her wallet. "This is to cover the coffee and the tip."

"Thanks. Sit here as long as you like."

"Where's the ladies' room?"

"Behind you."

Deborah walked to the alcove the waitress pointed to. Women's room on the right, men's on the left and in the middle a cart filled with toilet paper, paper towels, cleaning liquids and toilet brushes.

Deborah went into the ladies room and splashed cold water on her face.

The door opened. A large woman about her age dressed in black pants and a black blouse came in with the cart and immediately retreated with it.

Deborah dried her face with a paper towel, exited and found the woman standing behind the cart with it pointing towards the dining room.

"I'm sorry." Deborah said. "I didn't mean to stop you from doing your job. You keep the restroom looking so good that I didn't realize you were coming to clean it. Thank you for your excellent work."

The custodian's eyes filled with tears. She spoke softly with a slight Spanish accent. "I clean the bathrooms in the restaurants and stores in this shopping center for more than a year. No one before ever thanked me."

"I wish they did. You deserve their gratitude."

At first what Deborah noticed didn't fully register. Mrs. Evans rushing towards her, a glint of metal, the custodian pushing her cart into Evans, the wheel catching Deborah's foot so that she slammed her head against the wall.

Just before she lost consciousness, Deborah saw the cart knock down Mrs. Evans and the knife she was holding.

Chapter Sixty-One

Isaac gripped the telephone receiver. Three rings before he heard Tom's voice.

"Tom, can you drive me to the hospital?"

"What's wrong, Isaac? Where's your mother?"

"She's the one in the hospital." The tears Isaac had fought spilled out.

"What happened to her?"

"I'm not exactly sure."

"I'll be right there."

Twelve minutes later Isaac sprang from the house and into Tom's car.

"Which hospital?"

"Memorial Southwest"

Tom sped away.

He tried to sound calm as he asked, "Do you know anything about your mother's condition?"

"Someone from the emergency room called and said she banged her head and they have to check how bad it is."

Tom pulled a handkerchief from his pants pocket and handed it to Isaac.

"Where was she when this happened?"

"I don't know. When I left for the movies she didn't say she was going anywhere." Isaac patted his wet cheeks with Tom's handkerchief. "I should have asked the hospital more questions. I was too scared."

"Anyone would have been."

"It's just Mom and me."

"Your mom's going to be okay."

"Before I left her, I told her she was weirder than usual." Isaac's shoulders heaved as he cried.

"Moms always forgive us for the dumb things we say."

"I have to tell her I'm sorry."

"You will."

With light Sunday afternoon traffic and Tom's tearing through yellow lights, they arrived at the hospital in under fifteen minutes.

Isaac jumped from the car before it fully stopped. Out of breath, he was at the emergency room in a few minutes.

"My mother. Rabbi Deborah Stein. Is she all right?"

The clerk adjusted her glasses. "Whoa. I need to speak to an adult next of kin."

"But I'm next of kin." Isaac pounded his fists on the counter.

Tom rushed to the teen and put his arm around his shoulder.

"Is that your dad?" the clerk asked.

Isaac hesitated for a moment. "Yes."

"He can hear anything you have to tell me," Tom said.

The clerk pulled Deborah's chart from a pile. "Likely concussion. Doctor ordered a ct scan to assess the extent of her injury."

"How did she get hurt?" Tom asked.

The clerk studied the chart. "Someone was coming at her with a knife. As her rescuer was jamming a cart into the assailant, the patient's foot got caught in the wheel of the cart. She hit her head against the wall as she fell."

Isaac gasped.

Tom gripped Isaac's shoulder more tightly and asked, "Any knife wounds?"

"No," was the matter-of fact reply.

"Can we see her now?" Tom asked.

"She's getting the scan now. It'll be a while."

Tom and Isaac sat down next to each other in the waiting room. Tom heard the teen's stomach rumble.

"Have you had any dinner?" Tom asked.

"No, but I'm not hungry."

"Your growling stomach tells me otherwise. You know your mom would want you to eat." Tom pulled out his wallet. "Get us some snacks and bring them back. It won't take you long. And the clerk said it'll be a while."

Isaac stood up slowly and took the money Tom proffered. "I'll be right back."

Shortly after Isaac left, a woman wearing a white coat walked into the waiting room and went to the desk. The clerk pointed to Tom, and the physician called him over.

"I'm Dr. Woodruff. Everything looked good on your wife's ct scan, but in an abundance of caution, we plan to keep her overnight. Concussions can be tricky."

"May I see her now?"

"Down the hall, the third room on the left. I'll be in as soon as I check on one other patient."

Tom found the room, walked in and saw Deborah lying in a bed with her eyes closed.

He went to her and kissed her gently on the forehead.

Deborah opened her eyes and smiled. "I'm so glad you're here."

"And I brought Isaac."

"Tom, I…"

He brushed her lips with his.

Isaac burst into the room. He went to the other side of his mother's bed and bent over her. "Mom, are you all right? I'm sorry."

Deborah sat up and hugged her son.

"I'm the one who's sorry. I need to tell you both about the stupid thing I did."

Chapter Sixty-Two

After a night in the hospital, Deborah was home surrounded by flowers.

Though Margo had emailed the synagogue's members telling them the rabbi was not ready for visitors, the doorbell rang.

Isaac, who'd refused to go to school so he could take care of his mother, answered the door. "No one is supposed to bother my mom."

"But I must," Leigh Goldsmith said and pushed her way into the house and then into the den where Deborah was sitting on the couch. She plopped down next to her and spoke to Isaac who'd followed her into the room. "Please leave. I must speak to your mother privately."

Deborah nodded to Isaac who sauntered out of the room.

"You must forgive me."

"For what?" Deborah asked.

"I did it to get the police involved. I didn't want to be blamed for Roberta's death when I was sure someone had pushed her."

"So you took the air out of my tire and painted a swastika on my door."

"You knew?"

"I suspected."

"I never thought it would lead to your almost being killed. Do you forgive me?"

"What you did was selfish and illegal."

"I was desperate to protect myself."

"You put your needs above those of the people you were endangering."

Leigh opened her mouth, but didn't speak.

"You wasted police time and made the community think they

were dealing with an anti-Semitic incident. You thought all the pain you caused others was worth it to protect yourself."

"I was sure you'd forgive me. You're a rabbi."

"Repentance is part of seeking forgiveness. Let's talk again after you can assure me you regret hurting others to benefit yourself."

Before Leigh could respond, Deborah said, "I'm going to rest now."

Her visitor glared at the rabbi, stood and walked to the door.

Deborah heard it slam as Isaac came into the den.

"Tom called. I told him to come over. I figured if Mrs. Goldsmith was still here, he could chase her away."

Deborah dreaded Tom's visit. He'd listened at the hospital when she told him and Isaac about her encounter with Mrs. Evans and hadn't criticized her, probably because he was concerned he'd upset her. Now that she was home she feared he'd berate her, even more than she'd berated herself, for the risk she'd taken.

And she'd have to act as though she'd never felt his kiss on her forehead or on her lips although she kept thinking about them. She must not give herself false hope that they could have a romantic relationship.

Tom arrived with a box of Godiva chocolates which she opened and shared with him and Isaac, who took the box with him to his room.

"I'm not going to ask you why you did something so foolhardy since there's no acceptable answer."

"I know that now, but at the time I thought I could convince Mrs. Evans to leave Isaac and me alone."

"We were remarkably fortunate the custodian you were talking to acted so quickly."

"Her name is Elia. Synagogue members are collecting money for a thank you gift."

"I'll be happy to contribute. I'm eternally grateful to her."

"What will happen to Mrs. Evans when she gets out of the hospital?"

"I suspect the prosecutor will cut a deal with her husband. He'll plead guilty to the embezzlement in return for her getting a lighter sentence for the assault."

"What about Roberta's murder?"

"There's no evidence connecting her to the scene and no one who can identify her. Mrs. Evans would have to confess, and her attorney won't let that happen."

"If she did, despite him?"

"There'd be an insanity plea."

"No one will be punished for Roberta's death. I hope Dr. Krause can handle that."

"He'll be quite angry at first. But as a psychologist, he'll eventually recognize how mentally ill Mrs. Evans is." Tom paused. "But don't change the subject."

"What do you mean?"

"Promise me. No more risk taking." Tom moved to the couch and sat down next to Deborah. "I don't know what I would have done if I'd lost you."

Deborah's eyes filled with tears.

Tom took her hand and entwined his fingers with hers, brought her hand up to his lips and kissed it.

The doorbell rang.

Isaac came into the room. "It's Rabbi Moses."

"I'm sorry. I have to leave." Tom stood and was hurrying from the room as the rabbi from Beth Shalom entered.

"Tom, nice to see you," Rabbi Moses said. "I didn't realize you knew my fellow rabbi."

"We've met." Tom gazed at Deborah and left.

"How do you know Tom?" Deborah asked.

"He's been studying with me. Brilliant scholar. Said he got interested in conversion after a friend gave him the first volume of Rabbi Telushkin's book on Jewish ethics."

Deborah shook her head. "Amazing. And I never guessed."

"When the time comes, you can be on the *beit din* that judges the sincerity of his desire to convert."

"That won't work."

"Why?"

Deborah smiled. "I can't be objective about Tom."

***

"Don't go to work." Isaac stood at the entrance of the kitchen with his hands on his hips.

Deborah stopped pouring Cheerios into her son's bowl, turned and faced him. "The doctor said I could after three days, so today's fine. I'll drive you to school."

Isaac muttered something under his breath, sat down and started eating.

Deborah kissed the top of his head. "It's because you took such good care of me that I feel ready to go back to the synagogue."

Isaac grunted and added more milk to his cereal.

Deborah was proud of Isaac for another reason. While she was in the hospital, he'd thought to call her father and tell him what happened and that she'd be all right.

Twenty minutes later mother and son were silent as they drove through the street where Roberta had been killed. Deborah bit her lower lip. Would the aftermath have been different if Isaac hadn't skipped school and seen the murder? Had she set everything in motion when she'd confronted Jerry Evans' attorney with the information there'd been a witness, without her knowing it was Isaac. She still felt Roberta's loss deeply. Recognizing how fortunate she was that she hadn't met the same fate, she resolved that during Saturday's Torah reading she'd recite the traditional prayer of gratitude to God for coming through a dangerous situation safely.

After dropping Isaac off, the rabbi arrived at the synagogue to find the hallway, the reception area in front of her office and her office adorned with welcome back balloons. She didn't spot Margo, who was surrounded by them, until her assistant got up from her desk and hugged her.

"You've got to take it easy today," was her greeting.

Pointing to the balloons, Deborah said, "I can't get over this."

"About half from your congregants and the other half from Tom. He's the only person I've agreed to let visit you."

Deborah smiled. "You are one tough gatekeeper."

So ten minutes later when she heard the knock on her door, Deborah knew it was Tom. He came in and sat down in a chair in front of her desk.

"I have some explaining to do," he said.

"Only if you want to."

He leaned forward. "I told you the first time we met that, having been raised with no religion, I wanted to study different ones. As I read the books you guided me to, I felt I'd come home – that I was reading what I'd believed in all my life."

Deborah nodded.

"By the time I decided I wanted to study Judaism with the aim of converting, the way I felt about you…I knew studying with you couldn't work."

Deborah struggled to continue maintaining Tom's gaze.

"I understand that once I'm Jewish, you may have no interest in taking our relationship to another level. I'll be disappointed, but still fulfilled that I've chosen Judaism."

Deborah got up and sat down next to Tom. She put her arms around him and kissed him.

Deborah had always believed Dov to be her *bashert*, her divinely foreordained soul mate. Could a woman have two *basherts*?

It was a question she looked forward to exploring.

The End

About the Author

Photo: By Katherine Poeppel

Judith Groudine Finkel is the author of *The Stooge Gene*, *Where Danger Lurks* and the award-winning legal thriller *Texas Justice*. Her shorter works have appeared in newspapers, journals and magazines, and have garnered national and international prizes. She lives in Houston, Texas.